CLOSE YOUR EYES

There are more than 10,000,000,000,000,000,000 insects on the planet, comprised of more than one hundred thousand species.

New species are being discovered every day.

Some of them are harmful to man.

Duncan VanCamp and his friends are about to find out how harmful...

CLOSE YOUR EYES by J.A. Konrath
What's bugging you?

CLOSE YOUR EYES

A NOVEL OF TERROR

J.A. KONRATH

This book is dedicated to Dr. Francis Paul Wilson, who sold his first stories to Analog *magazine in 1970, the year I was born. If the reader notices any similarities between my writing and Paul's, that is purely intentional. If you're going to imitate someone, imitate the best. You are the best there ever was, brother.*

!!!WARNING!!!

I've added a reader warning in novels a few times. While my books can get pretty horrifying, I try not to go overboard with the violence. Terrible things happen to my characters, but I leave much of the description off the page and let the imagination of the reader fill in the blanks.

I'm a firm believer that less is more.

I've used this same technique with CLOSE YOUR EYES. This story doesn't revel in graphic details. I don't linger on gross-out passages, or fetishize the violence and gore. Mostly.

However…

The events of this book, even though I understate them, are still pretty horrible. This sub- genre is called *body horror* for a reason. Yucky things happen.

So if you're overly sensitive, or you have a vivid imagination, or you're easily repulsed, or if you can make yourself nauseous by thinking of disgusting things, then perhaps this isn't the book for you. I suggest you stop reading right now. I promise I won't tell anyone you chickened out.

Especially if bugs make you squeamish. This book has bugs. Lots of bugs. Stinging, biting, burrowing, egg-laying bugs.

I thought about bringing back the "trigger warning for violence" gimmick I used a few times in previous novels, but I quickly abandoned that idea. Not because it's gimmicky. But because half this book would be a trigger warning. If you're triggered by blood, self- harm, mutilation, gore, bodily functions, or bad puns, this isn't for you.

You should stop reading right now. Really.

If you think you can handle it, I wish you the best of luck. Remember: Some things you can't unread.

You might want to keep some antacids nearby. And some insect repellent.

Also, even though this book is a stand-alone, it features characters from some of my other work, including AFRAID, ORIGIN, HAUNTED HOUSE, THE NINE, and SECOND COMING. You don't have to be familiar with my previous books to enjoy this one, but if you've read any of those you'll see some familiar faces.

Good luck with the icky biological horror to come, and thanks for reading.

Joe Konrath

All human actions are equivalent, and all are on principle doomed to failure.
   —JEAN-PAUL SARTRE

Do it or do not do it—you will regret both.
   —SÖREN KIERKEGAARD

Life is always a rough ride, and it always ends tragically.
   —HARRISON HAROLD McGLADE

If you come to a fight thinking it will be a fair one, you didn't come prepared.
   —F. PAUL WILSON

JAKE

SOME TIME AGO, SOME DISTANCE AWAY...

Jake opened his eyes.

He could not see.

But I'm alive.

Alive, and teeming with life.

So many bites and stings.

So many eggs in my body.

I have to get well enough to travel.

I am burdened with a great responsibility.

To preserve His legacy.

To exact His vengeance.

Jake touched his eyeballs, feeling the maggots squirming and wiggling inside them.

Soon, my lovelies.

Soon...

KATIE

Katie Geers had seen a lot of odd behavior in her three years as a flight attendant. A drunk man bazooka-vomiting over three rows of people. A couple who tried to join the mile-high club but the woman got her foot stuck in the toilet which necessitated an emergency landing. A passenger who tried to hijack the plane to Cuba but was only armed with a banana that he claimed could talk. An elderly woman who fell in the aisle and broke her arm so badly the bone jutted out of her skin almost six inches.

But the guy in 30F was likely the strangest thing she'd ever seen.

Jake McKendrick. His entire face swathed in white bandages like a mummy, or those old black and white invisible man movies. He wore baggy sweatpants and a sweatshirt, boots, gloves, and sunglasses. Not a single sliver of bare skin visible anywhere.

Katie didn't pay him much attention at first, figuring he just had surgery, or an accident, or an illness like porphyria where skin reacted to UV light. Or maybe he was disfigured, and wrapped his face so he didn't attract stares.

But her interest piqued when the guy sitting in the same row, Jim Jorgensen in 30D, flagged Katie down.

"I need to change seats."

She stared up at him. The guy had a posture and tone that Katie pegged as military.

"Is there a problem?" she asked.

Jim's eye twitched. "Look, I'm an RN. I work in a VA hospital. There's something up with that guy. Something off."

"Off? How?"

"His bandages. I don't know how to say this without sounding crazy. They're… moving."

Katie smiled, because it did sound crazy. "How do you mean?"

"They're… pulsating. Changing shape."

"His nose is covered up. Maybe he's breathing inside the bandages."

Jim shook his head. "That isn't it. It's like something is wiggling around underneath."

Katie lowered her voice. "He's just some poor man with a medical condition."

"Also, there's an… odor. Something rotten. Like fish gone bad, decomposing on the beach."

"We have a full flight. The only empty seat is in your aisle. And technically, that isn't empty."

"Did the guy with the bandages buy it?"

Katie didn't answer.

"He did!" Jim was raising his voice. "He did because he didn't want anyone sitting right next to him!"

"Please keep your voice down."

Jim's face pinched. "Look, I'm not a guy who complains. Twelve years as a Navy corpsman tending to Marines. Attended to injuries that would make a civilian faint, and I didn't even flinch. But this guy… there is something going on with him that's making my stomach roll."

"I can tell you now, Mr. Jorgensen, that there aren't any extra seats available."

"How about business class? I'll pay for the upgrade. I don't care about the extra cost."

"We have a full flight."

"How about the flight crew seat? We can switch and you can sit next to him."

"That's against regulations, Mr. Jorgensen. It's probably against the law as well."

The passenger balled up his fists. "I need to change seats."

"Please keep your voice down."

Jim leaned in to whisper. "There is something wrong with that guy. Something very wrong. It's more than a medical issue, and you aren't listening. It's like he's got a snake wiggling on his face under that bandage, and he reeks like gangrene. And he's not there mentally. I tried some small talk. He ignored me. And he's humming something to himself. Humming... or..."

"Or what?" Katie asked in spite of herself.

"Or... buzzing. Like a hornet or a fly."

"There's nothing I can do. I'm going to have to ask you to return to your seat."

Jim didn't reply. He stayed right where he was, staring.

"If anything happens, come and talk to me," Katie said.

He still didn't move.

Katie wasn't sure what to do. She'd had to deal with crazy people before. On the job, and in her personal life. Jim didn't seem mentally unhinged.

He's scared. Really scared.

Katie decided to break a rule. She leaned in close and whispered, "Look, I'm not supposed to say this, but there is an air marshal on this flight. If anything happens, you tell me, and we can take care of it. But right now I need you to keep cool and return to your seat. Can you do that?"

Jim finally nodded. But he didn't rush to sit back down, even though he eventually did.

Over the next fifteen minutes, Katie kept a watchful eye on Jim, and the bandaged Jake.

They sat in silence.

Good. Just keep calm and play nice until the plane lands.

Katie walked the aisle, picked up an empty plastic cup and bev nap from a woman in 3B, and thought about her boyfriend, Duncan, and how she'd be able to see him after the flight. They'd been apart for eight days. Though she lived in Spoonward, Wisconsin, Katie's home base, and the nearest airline hub, was Minneapolis-St. Paul. When bidding for flights, Katie often traveled to odd places at odd times to make sure she landed back in MSP without being totally wiped out, so she could immediately drive the two hours back home.

Back to Duncan.

She smiled, thinking of him. Of his broad shoulders, and kind face. They'd been dating six months. Katie met him during his first bartending shift at Cooper's. A creep had been hitting on her nonstop, and she'd asked Duncan for an angel shot; restaurant code for call the police.

Duncan hadn't needed the police. The creep had been taller and stockier, but Duncan had the guy on the ground and in a choke hold seconds after slipping a punch. He'd dragged the fibber out by his Bears jacket, slapped him awake, and told him not to come back.

Katie gave Duncan her number. They went out the next day, and most of the days since.

She heard the ding of the call button, and put on her practiced smile and went to passenger 29D.

"There's a real bad smell."

The stench hit Katie almost immediately. Rot and death with the pungent reek of ammonia. She immediately checked the next row, caught eyes with Jim Jorgensen who gave her an *I told you so* look, and then glanced at the bandaged Jake McKendrick in 30F.

Jake must have felt her stare, because he turned his wrapped head and stared at Katie, raising his hand and lowering his sunglasses. His eyes peered out through slits in the fabric.

Katie wanted to turn away, but a jolt of fear kept her rooted in place and frozen.

His eyes appeared milky. Ancient. As if they've seen unimaginable horrors.

Then the bandage above Jake's nose undulated, like a mouse was burrowing out of his nostril.

Katie squealed, clapped her hands over her mouth, and then forced her legs to move to the rear of the plane.

She was about to share the details with the air marshal when she heard a shout. Jim had leapt from his seat, pushed her aside, then hurried down the aisle, running into the bathroom and locking the door.

She glanced at the marshal, a burly man in his thirties.

He shrugged as if there was nothing he could do.

Katie couldn't argue. Marshals needed to keep their identity secret unless there was an emergency, and a man running to the john didn't qualify.

Still, I should check on him.

Katie composed herself, put on the pleasant smile that was as much a part of her uniform as her flight loafers, and knocked on the lavatory door.

Jim didn't respond.

She knocked harder.

"Mr. Jorgensen? Are you okay in there?"

Katie didn't get a reply. She discreetly cupped her ear and put it to the door and heard—

Moaning. And something else.

A squishing sound. Like slurping up Jell-O through a straw.

She assumed it was diarrhea and gave Jim some privacy.

When she checked on Jake, he had his head turned away. One hand in his lap, the other tucked inside his shirt, in between the buttons and touching his belly. He seemed to be asleep.

But his facial bandages had a dark smudge on the cheek. A smudge that wasn't there before.

Blood?

Katie held her breath, trying to hear the buzzing sound Jim had mentioned.

She didn't hear that. But she did hear something else.

The suckling of a nursing baby.

The captain announced their final approach and put on the fasten seatbelt light. Katie returned to the lavatory and again knocked on the door.

"Mr. Jorgensen? We're landing. You have to take your seat."

He didn't answer. But Katie heard something high-pitched from behind the door. Something kind of like a pig squeal.

"Mr. Jorgensen? Are you okay?"

Katie knocked again, then used the hidden slide behind the metal LAVATORY tag to unlock the door. When she tried to open it, the door immediately slammed closed again.

"DON'T COME IN HERE!"

Katie recoiled, both in surprise and fear.

He's hysterical.

Is he yelling at me because he's embarrassed?

Or... is he warning me for my safety?

She knocked again. "Mr. Jorgensen, do you need help?"

Then the pounding began. Like he was punching the bathroom wall. Over and over.

The captain came over the sound system, announcing the final approach and telling the flight crew to take their seats.

What do I do? Inform the captain there is someone still in the bathroom? Involve the air marshal? Take my seat and let security handle it after we land?

She decided to give it one more try, and after leaning back, Katie shoved her shoulder into the lavatory door, the accordion hinge suddenly bending inward and snapping open, the flight attendant bumping into the man standing at the sink, driving his fist again and again into the stainless-steel basin.

Katie noticed two things at once.

First; Jim's frantic, maniacal face, punctuated by the bleeding gap where his right eye used to be, the goo and gore slick on his cheek, running down his chin and soaking his chest.

Second; the mashed, gnarled object in the sink that Jim was smashing into sinew with his scarlet fist.

He was popping his own eyeball.

JAKE

Not too close, but close enough.

The body of water had a brown tinge from decaying plant matter and muck. It stretched out for a kilometer before him, and the shoreline on either side formed a gradual curve, dotted with fir trees and an occasional birch popping up among the waving, grassy bulrush.

Jake stepped into the shallows among the cattail and pickerelweed and knelt into the muck.

His sight was blurry and wavy. But his vision was clear.

The primary goal is to infect indigenous biomass.

The secondary goal is to eliminate longtime enemies.

Then...

Resurrection.

The myriad of arthropod life inside Jake sensed the water, and began to burrow out of his body, bursting through his skin and wiggling free into the lake to spread infection.

A long, pale orange worm snaked its way through his intestines and slurped out of his ass, a glistening, writhing tail coated in white mucus.

Pus-colored maggots wiggled out of his tear ducts, bouncing onto the water's surface like drops of rain.

Black flies were born out of his nostrils, spreading blood-painted wings and buzzing into the cool dawn air.

Some of the smaller creatures needed to be manually squeezed out of Jake's pores like pimples, and he pinched and dug at sections of his skin, freeing the buried, squirming nematodes. After making their appearance, they whirled and flapped like translucent scarves before slipping off his wet skin and going on their way.

Jake didn't fully divest his body of all foreign creatures. The larger ones required more time to incubate, and wouldn't be finished for a few more days.

And the main one, the parasite savior that would consume Jake from within, would take weeks to mature.

Which is fine.

There is plenty of time.

A few weeks isn't even a speck on the surface of eternity.

There is plenty of time for Him to rise again.

Jake sat, and then laid onto his back, staring east at the pinkish, bloated, rising sun.

Then he excreted a pheromone to attract frogs.

He began to croak, a perfect mimicry that sounded like dragging a thumb across a wet balloon.

Leopard frogs swam up en masse, swarming Jake, hoping to mate.

Jake scooped them up by the handful and ate them so quickly he barely even chewed.

Disgusting. I know. But I need the calories.

And their struggling spasms, as he crunched on their bones, made them taste a bit sweeter.

LEO

The scars wouldn't heal.

Leo's skin was a road map of gnarled, jagged keloids, crisscrossing most of his body.

Once upon a time he posed in swimsuits for magazine covers. Body, perfect. Face, perfect. The genetics of a Greek god. Or, more specifically, the king of Sparta.

But not these days.

Lately he always wore pants and long sleeves, even in blistering hot weather, to avoid the stares and gawkers. He retained the thick cords of bodybuilder muscle, and his strength and endurance were at the peak of human conditioning.

But he wasn't human. Not quite.

After the evil had been expelled from Leo's body, traces remained. Pain, mostly. Blinding cluster headaches. Cramps that doubled him over. Flare-ups of old, healed injuries that had likely never fully healed.

But the deepest scar, the deepest pain, was emotional.

Memories of the atrocities he'd committed, though his will hadn't been his own.

Nightmares of having power, and losing power.

Suicidal thoughts that tortured him with their clarity.

Visions of ending my life are constant. Every hour, day and night, awake and asleep.

But I haven't done it.

Not because I lack the guts.

But because I haven't figured out a way to die as painfully as I deserve to.

He had money in the bank, linked to an account he no longer had access to. But even if he did get another debit card and reestablish his identity, Leo chose to remain homeless, living outdoors and letting nature have her way with him. He could shiver and get cold, but he didn't freeze, never got frostbite. He could walk through a heatwave and get sunburn the color of a stop light, but he didn't succumb to dehydration. If he cut himself, it healed almost immediately, adding to his growing collection of scars.

Leo tried to lose himself in drugs, but they didn't work for him.

He stopped eating for a month, and then woke up in an alley surrounded by the bloody pelts and pointy bones of dead rats he'd devoured. Sleep-eating. His body forcing him to live even after his mind had given up.

So he wandered. He reflected. He suffered. Aimless. Living in a hell he hadn't fought hard enough to reject.

Until, one day, purpose found him.

His travels had taken him across the United States, wearing out a dozen pairs of hiking boots, heading no direction in particular until he found himself in Madison, Wisconsin, on a warm summer night, sitting on the sidewalk behind a vintage clothing store and crunching on an uncooked square of dry ramen noodles.

That's when Leo felt it.

The Tug.

He looked around, trying to understand what tugged at him. All the nearby pedestrians—skaters and pink hairs and college stoners—gave him a wide berth, but this wasn't the same as someone pulling on his arm or grabbing him by the shirt.

This was akin to standing in a fast-flowing stream, feeling the water relentlessly push in a direction. Or like the force behind two magnets when their polarities were reversed.

Something is summoning me.

Leo had an idea who it was. His cells could almost sense it.

The loss.

The longing.

The disgust, and the sick pleasure that was even more disgusting.

He could feel his DNA being plucked like microscopic guitar strings, playing a rancid, evil tune older than the earth.

Leo did his best to ignore it. He got up and began walking in the opposite direction of the flow.

The effect was instantaneous.

His skin itched. His mouth went dry. His crisscross network of scar tissue burned.

He turned a corner, walking parallel to the Tug, and his discomfort lessened.

Curious, Leo turned again, walking into the invisible force.

All pain ceased.

Leo halted, and the itching returned.

Can't get more obvious than that.

It wants me.

Living so long without any direction, suddenly having one, Leo considered his options. He realized there were three.

Ignore the Tug.

Head in the opposite direction and embrace the pain.

Go to it and see what happens.

He glanced down at his hands, the knuckles scarred.

I don't deserve to still be alive.

The things I've done. Things I can't undo. Things I can't make up for.

I have no redemption arc.

The Universe will never forgive me.

I will never forgive myself.

I need to suffer.

The Tug picked at him, at his cells, at his soul.

Succumb?

Resist?

Fight?

Leo chose to fight.

I will find out what is beckoning me.

And I will destroy it.

Or it will destroy me.
If I'm lucky, it will be both.
Leo lifted his chin and followed the Tug.

DUNCAN

NOW, AND HERE...

The noonday Northern Wisconsin sun cut through the reddish haze in the air and continued its brutal assault, and there wasn't a sliver of shade to hide from it on the forty-year-old pontoon. Duncan VanCamp had removed the folded bimini top—the canvas cover used to protect boaters from the UV rays—and left it on the shore to make it easier for everyone to fish. But a breezeless lake, coupled with a temperature hovering around ninety degrees, conspired to make him rethink his decision.

We're sitting on a rectangular, floating broiler. The bimini sure would be nice right now.

Good thing we brought water.

"Can you toss me a water, Stu?"

His friend leaned over the cooler and took out a bottle. "Last one," he said, throwing it over.

Duncan caught it. "We've gone through six bottles of water?"

Stu shrugged. "I only brought six bottles. Didn't expect the sun to be so bad with all the smoke."

The sky's dim hue, pretty but unhealthy, was due to ongoing and widespread Canadian wildfires. The smoke had drifted over most of the Northern US and hung there, stinging the eyes and irritating the lungs.

Earlier the trio had awoken to simultaneous automatic text messages.

The Wisconsin Department of Natural Resources (DNR) is recommending Wisconsinites to reduce their time outdoors due to ongoing air quality alerts.

They recommended wearing an N-95 mask if staying outdoors for extended periods of time. They weren't fooling, either. An AQI over 200 was declared unhealthy, even for healthy people. That morning it had hit 315.

But they weren't going to let that stop them.

They'd been working the lake since eight am, thrown at least five hundred casts among the three of them, and hadn't hooked a thing. The plan had been to wake up at dawn and start fishing early, but beering past midnight kept them in bed later than expected, which meant a late morning, with high noon approaching fast.

No worries.

It's the first morning of a three-day brocation. Me and Stu and Chuck.

No families. No girlfriends.

Just the boys, clowning around, maxing and relaxing.

We have plenty of time to catch those elusive bass.

But it was really bugging Duncan that nothing was biting. He opened the water bottle and took a long pull, draining half of it.

Hot as it was, and smokey as it was, Big Lake Niboowin still radiated peace and tranquility. It boasted good fishing, with weed beds aplenty for the lunkers to hide. Part of a chain of seven connected lakes that stretched across Safe Haven, where Duncan's parents owned a lakefront home, to the sister town of Spoonward, where Duncan lived. Over ten thousand acres of sporting paradise, water as far as you could see in every direction.

Duncan hadn't noticed any other boats, and they seemed to have the lake all to themselves.

Odd. Niboowin is renowned for fishing. The previous state record Northern Pike had been caught here back in the 1960s, nearly thirty-nine pounds.

A combination of heat and air quality must be keeping people off the water.

It wasn't going to stop Duncan. He was used to heat. For a few years he lived with his family in Hawaii, where heat was omnipresent and omnivorous.

But tropical heat and Midwest heat are two different things.

On an island, surrounded by saltwater, the weather is energizing.

In Wisconsin, the sun beat on you like you owed it money.

He put the water bottle in the cup holder next to the steering column and tossed out his lure once again, his baitcast reel whirring as the line played out, his crankbait landing exactly where he'd intended. Then he began a jerky, erratic retrieve, working the lure hard, trying to imitate a baitfish in distress, cutting it back and forth over the nearly waveless mirror of lake surface.

Perfect spot. Perfect cast. Perfect bait action.

No hits.

Not a single bite all morning.

And not normal for Niboowin.

After the move, Duncan had briefly lived with his parents at their lakeside home, where he was currently staying with his buddies while Mom and Dad went to a craft beer festival in Madison.

They'd chosen to move back to Safe Haven and live on the lake chain because it had been a weekend getaway spot for the family, years ago.

Duncan couldn't reside in Safe Haven. While the fishing had been great memories, other memories that weren't so great often overrode them. He moved to nearby Spoonward to be close to his parents, and would visit often, even keeping his pontoon on their property.

Earlier that summer, fishing had been good.

But this was the opposite of good fishing.

It's like a giant net came and scooped up all the fish…

His cell buzzed, and Duncan winced. He put his hands on the lumps in his pockets—his EDC of multitool and flashlight and a lockpick kit for later—hoping his friends thought he was reaching for one of those instead of his phone. They hadn't glanced at him, so he quickly slid the phone out of his shorts and peeked at the text.

Katie.

LOVE U, GOOD MORNING! FLIGHT GOT CANCELLED. CREW SKED HAS ME ON CALL. FINGERS CROSSED THEY SEND ME SOMEWHERE WITH A BEACH. HOW'S THE AQI?

"No phones." Stu used an accusatory, parental tone and pointed a stubby finger.

"I thought it was off," Duncan lied.

"You know the rules." Stu held out his palm. "Captain's rules, Captain."

Duncan looked to Chuck for support. Chuck shrugged. "I left my phone back at your parent's house. Captain's rules."

"And mine's off," Stu said. "Captain's rules. When we're on the boat, no phones. Or does the captain have rules for everyone else but not himself?"

"That's not it. I need to keep it on in case—"

Chuck laughed. "In case your girlfriend needs to sext you from California after her flight lands?"

Duncan didn't want to discuss the real reason, the scary reason, so he went with a weaker excuse.

"She's gone half the month."

"Sounds like the perfect partner." Chuck laughed at his own joke.

"You guys don't know what it's like to be in a serious, committed relationship."

"Serious and committed?" Stu asked. "You put a ring on it without telling your buds?"

Duncan shook his head. "Come on, man. I woulda told you guys."

"Moving in together?" Stu pressed.

Duncan looked away, across the endless expanse of water, feeling his neck get even redder under the blazing sun.

Stu pointed again. He was a pointer. "You're asking her to move in!"

Duncan went sheepish. "Maybe."

"When?" Chuck demanded.

"I'm thinking after this trip, when I get back to Spoonward."

"Is she gonna say yes?"

Duncan predicted she would. It made no sense to have two apartments, especially when Katie was gone so often. They'd discussed it, casually, but neither had pressed the issue. They were in their mid-twenties and enjoying the current chapter of their lives. But a few weeks ago Katie had a really bad flight. Some guy went bonkers and pulled out his own eye. Since then, she'd been pretty freaked out and basically stayed at Duncan's place the entire time.

And it has been… nice. Really nice.

She's practically living with me anyway. She has half my bedroom drawers and most of my closet, and had taken over almost all of the bathroom.

We should make it official.

Hopefully, Katie will agree.

Hopefully.

"She'll say yes," Duncan said.

"You are so whipped," Chuck told him.

Duncan rolled his eyes. "Whipped? How old are we? Sixteen?"

Then he quickly texted back:

AQI SMOKEY, LUV U 2, GOT 2 DO GUY STUFF, KEEP ME POSTED

"Shut the front door, you're whipped as hell," Stu said, laughing. "Gimme the damn cell."

Duncan handed his phone to Stu. Rules were rules.

"I promise not to send her dick pics and steal her away from you," Stu said.

Duncan smiled. "If you do, the camera has a macro zoom."

Chuck snorted. Stu tucked Duncan's phone into his backpack. Fishing resumed.

I'm not whipped.

I'm in love. And protective.

And I want Katie to be happy.

Shit. That does sound like I'm whipped.

Duncan shifted his wiry frame in the hot, vinyl captain's chair, adjusted his sunglasses, then made another cast. When he was eleven years old, Duncan caught his first keeper on this lake; a bass that tipped the scales at nearly five pounds. He'd landed much bigger fish since, but that was still his favorite angling memory. The surprise of the strike. That epic tug of war. His stepfather, Josh, urging him on, ready with the net. That swell of pride when he was holding his trophy and Mom took a picture. A picture that—over a decade later—was still tacked to the wall in his old bedroom.

Duncan had caught more than just a fish that day. He'd also caught the fishing bug; a lifelong obsession that consumed his free time and much of his recreational income in the form of reels and poles and lures and the latest purchase; his vintage boat. The pontoon they were currently fishing on—essentially a three meter by seven-meter flat platform covered with green plastic carpet and sitting atop two large, cylindrical floats with a 25 horsepower Mercury outboard attached to the back—was a Facebook Marketplace find. Even though the vinyl bench seats were faded and cracked, and the aluminum railing held together in spots with plastic zip ties, and the dashboard instruments semi-functional, and the motor not fast enough to tow a kneeboarder, and the plastic carpet looking like worn out 1970s Astroturf, it was worth every penny.

Some feelings you just can't put a price tag on.

The cherry on top; Katie loves to fish. If we move in together, maybe we could rent a place on a lake, and I won't have to keep my pontoon at my parent's house.

After a tough childhood, and a few near-death experiences, life is finally coming together for me.

The future has never been brighter.

It's as bright as this unrelenting sun in my face.

Duncan finished his retrieve, considered changing lures again, considered changing locations again, and decided to give the area a few more casts. He threw out his bait, reeling in slowly along the top of the water, making a zig-zag pattern known as *walking the dog.*

It was a more laborious, and time-consuming, way to fish, but the method sometimes worked when the bass were being picky.

This time, it didn't work.

Duncan sighed, though he wasn't sure if it was from frustration or contentment. Along with learned skills, angling required luck, patience, and perseverance. Some never discovered the appeal of fishing. They found it boring, or stupid, or inhumane.

For Duncan, it was an addiction.

He made another cast.

There was a slapping sound, accompanied by a muttered obscenity. Duncan glanced at Chuck, who'd stood up and gone to the bow. He had the lanky frame of a varsity basketball player, his sleeveless Johnny Cash tee boasting a dark strip of damp sweat down the spine, all the way to his swim trunks. Chuck made a Mr. Yuck face as he stared at the black smear on his palm.

"Frickin' flies." Chuck wiped the dead bug onto the Man in Black.

Stu adjusted the bill of his *Science Pimp* ball cap and asked, "Was it *Chrysops callidus* or *Hybomitra micans*?"

Not as wiry as Chuck or Duncan, Stu had outgrown most of his teenage pudge but retained most of the social awkwardness. Like his friends he wore a swimsuit and a tee, his sporting the classic photo of Einstein sticking out his tongue.

"Captain's rules. No phones on the boat, no work on the boat." Chuck threw his Bloody Eye Minnow lure next to the weed line, and began a slow retrieve. "I don't talk cars, Duncan doesn't go on and on about cutting off drunk townies—"

"Last week I got sucker punched by a seventy-seven-year-old woman who thought her Old-Fashioned pour was too light," Duncan offered.

"—and you don't break into bugspeak."

"It's Latin."

"It's annoying."

"It bugs him," Duncan laughed.

Stu shrugged. "Just wondering if it was a deerfly or a horsefly."

"It didn't look like a deer or a horse."

"How big was it?" Stu asked.

"The size of a freakin' toaster. Maybe it was a toasterfly."

Stu pushed the bridge of his slipping eyeglasses. "The bigger ones are *Hybomitra micans*. Horseflies. The females have six chitinous stylets with serrated edges that slice side-to-side to cut through skin. Like scissors, or wire snips. They don't have a proboscis like a mosquito. A proboscis penetrates to suck blood. Horseflies just slice a big hole in the skin, then feast on it when your blood seeps out."

Chuck snorted, then scratched at his hipster beard. "Honest question, Stu; when was the last time you got any? Because when you talk like that, I picture chicks just peeling off their panties and launching themselves at you."

Stu shrugged. "I've got a doctorate in entomology, and you work at the Quickie Lube. Just sayin'."

"And I make as much as you and don't have to pay back a billion dollars in student loans."

"It's only half a billion. And my fingernails are clean, while yours are that lovely shade of black. I bet that's a real panty peeler. Is smelling like 10W-30 a turn-on these days?"

"Is smelling like butterfly shit a turn-on?"

"Do me next," Duncan interrupted. "What do small town bartenders smell like?"

Chuck: "Like stale beer and unfulfilled dreams."

Stu: "Like drunk losers and bad decisions."

Duncan: "Tough, but fair. What do EMTs smell like?"

He'd been seriously considering training to be an emergency medical technician, even though he had a big problem with the sight of blood, and had discussed the plan with his buddies more than once.

Chuck: "Like wannabe nurses."

Stu: "Like wannabe firefighters."

Duncan: "Ouch. Keep 'em coming."

Chuck: "Like small town bartenders with delusions of grandeur."

Stu: "Like a college dropout who suddenly realizes the value of education."

Duncan laughed. "You guys are brutal."

"I'll tell you what they don't smell like," Chuck added. "They don't smell like fish. Who's got the bug spray?"

Duncan reached for the aerosol can of repellent resting on the instrument panel above the steering column. He tossed it to Chuck, who missed the catch. The spray thumped on the flat bottom of the pontoon with a hollow clang, then rolled across the rough plastic carpet to rest next to Duncan's oversized Umco tackle box. Duncan picked up the can and sprayed a thick cloud around himself.

"All you're doing is accelerating mutation." Stu cast again, frowning. "Female horseflies can lay a thousand eggs in a few days. Because insects have such fast reproduction cycles, they can evolve faster than the pesticide industry can keep up. You kill the susceptible, the survivors pass on their genes. Same thing is happening with antibiotics."

"Make Stu shut up, Duncan."

"Stu, shut up."

"Insects rule the planet, guys. They were here before we were, and they'll be here after we're gone."

"He's not shutting up, Captain."

"Captain's rules, Stu," Duncan said. "No more bugs."

Stu coughed, then spat. "What else is there to talk about? We're not catching anything, and we've already discussed the Brewers, the upcoming season of *Chainsaw Man*, and that new mole that's growing on Chuck's neck."

"I've always had that mole." Chuck frowned. "Right?"

"I'm just saying that the *don't discuss work while on vacation* rule shouldn't include situations that are relevant. Duncan slings beers, and we still talk about beer. I'm not going on and on about my *Lepidoptera* research. But Chuck was bitten by an insect, I know about insects, so I'm keeping the conversation rolling."

"My mole isn't really getting bigger." Chuck was touching his neck. "You guys are shitting me. Right?"

Duncan squinted up at the sun, wondering if he should call it a morning. They'd worked the lily pads with topwater buzzers, tried out old-school Terminator spinners on several weed beds, jigged artificial worms at the drop-offs, and were now drifting on the east side of the lake throwing crankbaits. An hour ago, Stu claimed to have missed a topwater hit, and two hours before that Chuck insisted he had a strike, which looked more like a weed to Duncan for the half a second he had it on.

The lake is playing hard to get. And I don't know how to turn things around.

Sometimes the fish don't bite no matter what you threw at them. Like they all decided, en masse, to go on a hunger strike.

Maybe it was feeding cycles. Or moon phases. Or just playing coy.

Or maybe the fish are staying in their lairs, like all the vacationers staying in their houses because of the shitty air quality.

Seriously, Canada, don't you have firefighters?

Duncan looked out across the great expanse of water, searching for other boats. Sometimes other fishermen found the hotspots, and moving closer to them resulted in a few strikes. But the lake was uncharacteristically empty.

He eyed the east shoreline, which wasn't as lush as the rest of the lake. A big forest fire, a homegrown one years back, had burned away all the old growth, and nature hadn't quite recovered yet. Rather than tall trees, the presiding feature was an eighty-foot-tall steel fire tower, erected after the blaze as an early warning system.

Soon after its construction the DNR abandoned their 100+ statewide lookout posts for modern technology. The tower's metal siren still glinted from the peaked roof, never used.

Earlier, Duncan had discussed climbing the tower with Stu and Chuck and drinking a few beers on the observation deck. He knew how to get through the gate.

Maybe at night we could even see the fires in Ontario. I have no idea how far you can see from that height.

But that's for later. For now, we're fishing.

Duncan scanned the shore for watercraft, turning north, then west. Lots of boats tied to piers, but none on open water.

Except for…

The marsh. A hundred meters into the marsh, Duncan spotted a bass boat half-hidden by reeds.

The only other boat on the lake. He must be catching some fish.

But do I really want to go into the marsh?

Do I even have the balls to go there? After last time?

Duncan had lived through some bad things. Some scary things.

But the marsh was a different kind of scary.

Because what happened in the marsh, fifteen years ago, had been my fault…

LEO

THREE DAYS AGO, GETTING CLOSER...

Leo arrived in Eau Claire on foot, the soles of both shoes detached and flapping with each step like baby alligator mouths. He hadn't eaten in a few days, and hadn't really thought about it.

All he thought about was the Tug.

He'd walked the hundred and seventy something miles up I-94, drinking out of ditches and ponds and occasional bottles of trash tossed alongside the road by motorists, even if those bottles were full of piss.

Leo didn't care about the taste. He just needed the hydration.

He made no attempts to hitch a ride, and no one offered. Twice, police pulled up to question him. The first time, they left him undisturbed alongside the road, unwilling to contaminate their squad cars with his stench.

The second time, they demanded ID and got grabby.

Did they deserve four broken arms for abusing their authority and violating his civil rights?

Probably not. But Leo didn't care about that.

All he cared about was the Tug, pulling at every cell in his body, drawing him north.

Wausau was one ninth the size of Madison, but still large enough to boast dozens of restaurants. Leo was hunting through the dumpster of a chain burger store, stuffing half-eaten food in his mouth, when a car pulled up and honked.

He expected another cop car—they were definitely looking for him—and wondered if he'd have to fight his way out of the situation. While searching the garbage for a weapon, a calm, steady voice asked, "Are you hungry?"

Leo peered over the edge of the dumpster and saw an elderly woman leaning out of her car window. Her face didn't appear hostile.

In fact, it seemed kind.

He was very hungry. He was always very hungry.

And his cells hurt. All of them. Especially, for whatever reason, his right wrist.

"What do you want?" Leo asked, his voice low and scratchy from disuse.

"I can buy you lunch."

"Why?"

"Because human beings aren't meant to eat out of dumpsters."

Maybe some are.

Maybe some don't even deserve that luxury.

"I'm not judging your lifestyle choices," the woman continued. "But if this is desperation, not choice, we could go inside and I can buy you a fresh meal, rather than one someone discarded."

Leo wasn't sure how to handle the offer. Since he'd been purged, he'd run into some charitable people among the losers and cops and desperates. Some had offered him money. Some had offered him food.

Since Leo burned through calories like a high schooler on the wrestling team, he usually accepted food when offered.

He nodded, then vaulted over the side of the dumpster and landed like a cat next to the woman's car.

"You're a spry one," the woman said. Her nose crinkled. "And ripe. How about before we have a burger we get you cleaned up and into some new clothes?"

What's her end game here? Just charity?

Does she want sex?

Not likely. Not with how I look.

One of those religious types, looking to save my soul?

Lady, you're too late for that…

"There's a thrift store a block south of here. If you don't trust me to get in, I can meet you there."

Don't trust you?

You're the one who shouldn't trust me.

He leaned closer to the vehicle and studied her. Late seventies. Gray and wrinkled. With a hard edge behind the kindness.

"I'm Mary," she said.

"Leo."

"You smell awful, Leo."

Nothing to say to that. She's right.

I'm no doubt gross.

But life is gross, isn't it?

"I'll meet you at the thrift store. Go into the bathroom there and clean up. Don't be stingy with the soap. I'm thinking you're about six three, size twelve boot?"

He nodded, rubbing his aching wrist.

She smiled and pulled away, turning south out of the parking lot.

Leo stood for a moment, pondering what to do.

The Tug tells me to keep going north.

But I'm dehydrated and hungry and I stink. My clothes are trashed, my shoes are falling off.

I've spent months living among people, looking at their faces as they look at me. I've seen revulsion. Pity. Contempt. Suspicion. Fear. Hate.

But this woman is the first one to treat me like a normal person.

Interesting.

Was I ever a normal person?

No. I went from being one of the lucky ones. Good genes. Handsome and healthy. I had money. Power. I was lusted after and feared.

Then I became… this. A reject. An outcast.

The highest highs, then the lowest lows.

But never average. Never normal.

Maybe this is a chance to find out what normal feels like.

Leo headed south, the Tug making his skin tingle and his insides cramp up.

"I'm obeying you," Leo said. "But you don't control me."

It felt like walking into a sandstorm with his eyes open, but Leo managed to make it the block to the secondhand store. He saw the woman's parked car, empty, and he went inside the building and got the usual stares. Thankfully, no one prohibited him from entering, and Leo found the bathroom and walked to the sink, wincing at the reflection in the mirror. He was filthy, his scarred face looking like a patchwork quilt with scraggly discolored beard poking through the seams, his eyes bloodshot and droopy, his clothes tattered.

I've never looked worse.

Maybe nobody has ever looked worse.

Leo cleaned up at the sink as best he could, using almost the entire contents of the liquid soap dispenser, washing his hair, his arms, his chest and groin. The sensation of his own hands on his body was muted by the Tug, pulling at him on a cellular level, the nerves responding to that magnetic sensation more than his own skin-on-skin contact.

Leo took a moment to examine his wrist. Besides being swollen, the skin around it sort of…

Wiggled. Like an invisible hand is squeezing and pulling the flesh.

He made a fist, then gave his hand a shake to see if it was still firmly attached.

Hurts, but seems okay. For the moment.

When he finished washing himself, his tattered shirt in the garbage and his remaining clothes wet, he stepped out of the bathroom and faced the woman, standing there with several plastic bags.

Her eyes widened slightly at the sight of his disfigured, gnarled chest.

"What happened to you, Leo?"

"I was… possessed. By a demon."

She maintained steady eye contact. "Is the demon gone?"

"I'm not sure."

"Do you feel as if you're a danger to yourself or others?"

"Not right now."

"Are you carrying a weapon, Leo?"

"Not right now. You a cop?"

"Ex-cop. Get dressed and we can talk over lunch."

She handed him the bags and Leo returned to the bathroom. Mary had sized him up pretty good. He put on boxer shorts, khakis, an old Panama Jack T-shirt, thick wool socks, some well-worn Colorado boots, and a Cubs baseball hat. There were also extra pairs of socks and underwear, and an old, beige trench coat, 44 long, with a high collar.

For future bad weather. This woman has actually thought of everything.

He tucked the extra clothes in the oversized coat pocket and stepped back out of the bathroom. Mary gave him a once-over but didn't say anything. Then she led him out of the store.

They didn't go to her car. Instead she marched him across the parking lot, back to the fast-food place, and they went inside.

She ordered a cheeseburger, fries, and a pop, and bid Leo to get whatever he wanted. He repeated her order, and she added four more burgers. They filled their cups at the self-service dispenser, Mary with diet and Leo with something bright yellow, and took a seat in an adjacent booth.

"How did you know I was a cop?" Mary asked.

"Your questions by the bathroom. And you're carrying a gun behind your right hip."

"You're perceptive."

"I didn't notice things, before. Now I seem to notice everything."

"Have you done time?"

Leo shook his head. "When I had my looks, I worked for a bad woman, did some bad things. Then the demon came, and I did more bad things."

"Do you still want to do bad things?"

"No."

"What is it you want, Leo?"

"I want to die."

Or more specifically, I want everything to be over and done with.

Mary stared at him, hard. "You want to kill yourself?"

"No."

"But you want to die?"

"I want to get to the ending."

"What ending?" Mary asked.

"Everything ends. I want to reach my end."

"So why keep going?"

"There's something I have to do first."

"What's that?"

"I'm not sure."

"You're looking for your calling?"

Leo looked away. "No. I have a calling. I just don't know what it is."

The cashier announced their number, and Leo got up and grabbed the food tray.

He ate joylessly, not really tasting anything, but knowing he needed the calories. The yellow soda tasted no better than the piss he had consumed alongside the interstate.

They were silent while he began to eat, but Mary spoke up halfway into her cheeseburger.

"I'm in town for my ex-husband. He left me and our daughter, Jacqueline, more than forty years ago."

She seemed to be waiting for Leo to say something, so he asked, "Why did he leave?"

"He realized he was gay. Back then, it wasn't like it is now. There was a stigma to it. I hated him because I thought he chose that lifestyle over his family. I hated myself because I didn't do enough to make him love me." Mary shrugged, and her face sagged. "Different times. Rather than explain it to our child, we agreed to tell her he was dead."

"So she grew up thinking she didn't have a father."

Mary nodded, "Sometimes, when we think we're making things better, we make them worse."

"But you're here for him now. Your ex-husband."

Mary's face brightened up. "He wrote a book. Had a signing at a local store. So I flew in from Colorado to support him."

"Because you didn't support him years ago."

Mary smiled, which had a sadness to it. "Isn't that strange? Blame is a toxic thing. We all feel like victims, because we hurt. That victimization gives us permission to hurt others. And when we do that, we hurt ourselves even more. Sometimes, with so much hurt, we can't recognize what's really important."

"What's that?"

"Kindness," Mary said. "We can solve every problem in the world with kindness."

Leo didn't believe that.

We can't solve disease. We can't solve natural disasters. We can't solve bad luck.

"You don't believe me," Mary said.

"Bad things… happen. Kindness won't solve them."

Mary winked at him, in a way Leo imagined his grandmother would have, if he'd had one. "Try it sometime, see if it works."

"Is that why you helped me?"

"Now that's interesting."

"What is?"

"You think I helped you… for you?"

I'll have to let that sink in and reflect on it later.

"What's his book about?" Leo asked.

She reached down and pulled a book out of her purse and set it on the table.

FORGIVENESS – LIFE LESSONS BY WILBUR STRENG

"A self-help book?"

"More like a book of thoughts and advice. It can be read in less than an hour; I doubt it's more than a few thousand words. He did that self-publishing thing, so he isn't going to make any money at it. But wrote it. And he's proud of it."

Again Leo felt like she wanted him to ask a question. "And how do you feel about it?"

"I don't know. Six people came to the signing. But Wilbur was happy. He read some of his book. He answered a few questions from the book-store owner."

"Did your daughter come?"

"She's with him now. Having drinks somewhere."

"Why aren't you with them?"

Mary smiled sadly, then tapped the word FORGIVENESS on the book cover. "I'm still working on that. Do you want to hear some of his advice?"

Leo nodded. He had three more burgers to eat.

Mary opened the book to the first page and began to read. "Forgive others. Forgive yourself. You can't change the past, so don't let it ruin your present."

She flipped to another page.

"Have faith in something bigger than you."

She flipped a few more.

"Don't offer advice unless asked." Mary chuckled. "Seems like I'm breaking that rule right now, aren't I?"

"No. You're being kind."

Mary sniffled, nodded, wiped away a quick tear, and turned to another page, one she'd dog-eared.

"We can solve everything with kindness," she read. "Even tragedy. Once we accept that everything happens for a reason, kindness is the only way to get through it."

Leo found it odd that he was just thinking that kindness can't solve everything, but the quote showed that it did.

He also found it odd that this stranger found him at this precise moment, to show kindness, and to tell him that everything happens for a reason.

That hit Leo in a strong way.

"You told me there's something you have to do," Mary said.

Leo nodded.

"Do you think, after you do what you need to do, you'll still want it all to end?"

Leo rubbed his wrist. "I'm not sure. But…"

"But?"

"If everything happens for a reason, if I have some destiny I'm supposed to fulfill, then maybe we were both meant to be here right now. And maybe what your ex-husband wrote about forgiveness is what both of us need to hear."

Mary focused on folding up her hamburger wrapper.

"Did he sign your book?" Leo asked.

"He did."

"Did he inscribe anything?"

"He wrote, 'You'll Always Be The One.'"

"That's nice."

"He wrote that in our daughter's book, too. He wrote that in everyone's book."

"That doesn't mean it isn't true."

Mary sniffled again, then smiled.

"I need to go meet Wilbur and Jack for drinks, don't I?"

"You know what you have to do, Mary."

She reached for Leo's hand and gave it a squeeze. "Thanks, Leo."

"Thank you, Mary."

They finished eating, and Mary asked Leo if he needed a ride anywhere.

"I appreciate the offer, but I'd rather walk. I've got a new pair of boots and I'd like to break them in."

"Do me a favor. Promise me you won't hurt yourself."

"I promise."

Leo was sincere in that reply.

I won't hurt myself.

But I feel, deep down, that something is waiting to hurt me.

Something very, very bad.

Mary stood, nodded, placed a twenty-dollar bill on the table, and walked out of the restaurant.

A fat, black horsefly buzzed past, quick and darting, and without thinking Leo held open his hand. The fly immediately landed on his palm—

—and bit, causing a small shock of pain.

Leo's hand closed like a trap, crushing the fly. When he opened his fingers, the insect had been smashed, its blood mingling with the blood it had drawn.

Leo felt the Tug ripple through his body, beckoning him to head north.

He got up, took Mary's money, and headed north.

DUNCAN

BIG LAKE NIBOOWIN, FIFTEEN YEARS AGO...

"Woof and I are going fishing," Duncan declared, his preteen mind judging the overcast conditions to be perfectly suited for big bass.

His mother looked up from her newspaper and raised an eyebrow. "Can you handle the boat yourself?"

"Of course I can, Mom. Tell her, Josh."

When Duncan's mom, Fran Stauffer, married Josh VanCamp, Josh legally adopted Duncan. Duncan took his last name, but he hadn't begun calling him Dad yet.

Josh forked the last pancake from the platter onto his syrup-soaked plate. "He can handle it. If anything goes wrong, Woof will save him. Right, Woof?"

Woof, the beagle who was so fat he was often mistaken for a basset hound, said, "Woof!"

The dog was less interested in being part of the conversation and more interested in the half a strip of bacon Duncan hadn't eaten yet.

Mom frowned. "Woof is too fat to swim. He sinks like a dog-shaped rock."

"Woof!"

"We'll be fine, Mom."

Duncan set his plate on the floor, letting the hound lick it clean, and then went to the hat rack to grab his Bass Pro Shops cap.

"Wear your life jacket," Mom told him.

"It's hard to fish wearing a life jacket," Duncan complained.

"It's harder to fish when you're drowned," his mother replied. "And stay in line of sight."

"I've got the walkie-talkie."

"There are dead spots on the lake," Mom said.

"I've got a cell phone, too."

"Dead spots," Mom repeated.

"Josh?" Duncan looked to the stepfather for help.

"There are dead spots," Josh said. "And stay out of the marsh. If there's a problem with the boat, I can come and get you with the pontoon. But that beast would have a tough time making it through the marsh."

"Got it."

"Got your EDC?"

Duncan patted both pockets of his jeans shorts, confirming his every-day carry was on him. Josh, a firefighter, taught him that a man should always have a flashlight and a knife, and had gifted him with both on his last birthday. The flashlight was a 3.6V rechargeable, waterproof Olight, and the knife a Victorinox Swiss Army Cyber Tool, which had several blades, a screwdriver and bit set, and various other stainless-steel tools.

Duncan called Woof, and the pair walked out of the rental house and into the yard. Mathison, the capuchin monkey who lived with him (he was really smart so he wasn't so much a pet as a brother), squeaked a greeting at boy and dog as they walked under the tree he was in. When they arrived at their vacation rental, Mathison has discovered a nest of squirrels and had made friends, and they spent most of the day chasing each other through the canopy.

"Want to go fishing, Mathison?"

Mathison gave them a squawk that signaled no. He then issued a stern bark that was an obvious warning to be careful.

Seriously? Doesn't anyone in this family trust me?

Duncan and Woof went to the pier and walked down the short dock, past the pontoon they'd rented in town for the whole family to use, up to the moored fourteen-foot aluminum rowboat that came with the cabin rental. Duncan and Josh had spent an hour on the first day of vacation learning the intricacies of the 9.9 HP Johnson outboard motor, in preparation for Duncan taking it out on his own. The engine had a hard pull start and a rough idle, but seemed reliable enough, and Duncan had proven himself yesterday, fishing alone for almost ninety minutes.

One small bass caught, which brought my total to six for the week.

If I get lucky, I could double that right now.

Duncan told Woof to stay, then he carefully climbed into the wobbly boat at the stern, keeping his balance and placing his knee on the seat float and his free foot on the V-shaped bottom of the boat. He pulled out the engine choke knob, gave the gas bulb a firm squeeze to make sure it was full, and then gave the starter cord a tug.

The engine sputtered, but didn't start.

He did it again.

Same result.

C'mon. Josh is probably watching.

I can do this.

He pulled once more, hard as he could—

—and the engine caught and roared to life.

Duncan slowly pushed the choke back in and turned the tiller grip to rev it, making sure it was getting gas while warming up.

Then he unhooked the stern line from the dock, helped Woof into the boat, unhooked the bow line, put on a life jacket, eased back on the gas and switched from neutral into forward, and off they went.

There weren't many things for an eleven year old that offered the sense of freedom, power, and satisfaction as piloting your own boat. Duncan got to decide the destination and the speed. Duncan chose the length of the trip, and how long to stay in each fishing spot. Duncan got to taste what it felt like, for a brief amount of time, to be an adult, and he took the responsibility seriously.

I can do this. I'm not a little kid anymore.

Now I just need to catch some fish.

He headed out to a spot where the weeds poked up through the water, gauged which direction the waves would take his boat, and killed the engine. Duncan moved the net resting on the seats to the side, and picked up his Shimano baitcast pole and reel outfit. It already had a spinner bait clipped to the steel leader.

This should be weedless enough.

He cast.

He retrieved.

He felt good.

Like an adult.

After twelve casts and no hits, coupled with dying wind so there wasn't a drift to carry the boat to a new area, Duncan posed a question to Woof.

"Think we should move, boy?"

Woof went, "Woof!" which was not a surprise. He was at the bottom of the boat on his side, his tail thumping against the bench seat as he wagged it. Sometimes Woof got up on the seat and looked out at the water and barked at various things. But mostly the lazy dog napped, sometimes on his belly, sometimes on his side, sometimes on his back with all four paws in the air.

After answering Duncan he immediately put his head down and began to snore.

Duncan started the boat in a single pull, smiled smugly, and headed north up the lake, to another spot, further from the rental house but still in a direct line of sight.

Twelve more casts in all directions.

Twelve more retrieves without a bite.

He stared up into the overcast clouds, contemplating where to go next. Catching fish was a tricky relationship between right time and right place. Duncan and Josh had fished enough parts of the lake that they knew the weed beds, knew the best spots for bass, and knew the best times of day; early morning around sunrise, an hour before and after sunset, and overcast with a slight wind.

It was around noon, so not a good time. No waves at all, so the boat wasn't moving on its own.

But a sun obscured by clouds meant the fish would be more active.

There should be something biting.

Duncan moved fifty meters north, made twelve more casts—

—and got nothing.

He worked the area once more, casting in all directions around the boat, working it like he was at the center of an analog clock face.

Fish are always moving. Maybe something just swam up.

Twelve more casts.

Not. A. Single. Bite.

Forty-eight casts. I should have had a nibble by now. Or even a follow.

"Woof!"

Duncan glanced at his dog, and saw Woof with his paws on the gunwale, staring across the vast expanse of water…

At the marsh.

"We're not supposed to go into the marsh," Duncan said, partly to Woof but mostly to himself.

But there's nothing wrong with fishing next to it.

Right?

Duncan yanked the starter cord. The boat sputtered, but didn't turn over.

He made sure it was in neutral and tried again.

No start.

He checked the fuel line, gave the gas bulb a squeeze, and tugged it again.

Sputter, stop.

Do I need to call Josh for help?

No. I can do this.

Duncan took off his life jacket, which was restricting his movement, and set it on the bottom of the boat. Then he pulled again, both hands on the grip, putting his shoulders and back into it.

The motor started, and Duncan headed for the marsh. He stopped two meters away from the reeds, changed his lure to a red head/white body Arbogast Jitterbug, aimed his cast for the reed line, and just when the bait hit the water a gigantic bass hit from underneath, its whole body breaching the surface.

A six pounder! Maybe bigger!

Duncan set the hook while the fish was still jumping, giving the pole a firm yank, feeling the weight bend the rod tip and—

—gaping wide-eyed as the lure came flying free, arcing through the air, plopping into the water near the boat.

The bass side-flopped, its big tail swished, and it darted straight into the marsh, its dorsal fin making a wiggly line as it blended into the reeds.

Woof began to bark, and Duncan sat there, shocked and trembling with excitement.

That was the biggest fish I've ever seen.

What a pure rush.

And I almost had it.

He did what everyone did after losing a trophy fish, staring at the spot where it got away, thinking about what could have been.

Then Duncan snapped out of his reverie and cast again. And again. And again and again and again, working the reed line, working the surface lure, working his butt off.

The big bass didn't strike again.

Because it went into the marsh.

I bet it found a new hiding spot, and is just sitting there. Waiting for its next meal.

Duncan eyed the off-limits area. According to Josh, the water was less than two feet deep, full of weeds, dead trees, and sunken logs, with a thick muck bottom. The motor propeller and intake would likely get clogged, causing a stall, and all of the living and dead plants would make rowing difficult. Swimming was probably impossible. So was wading.

But does that really make sense?

Boats float. And if the engine stalled, I could row. Or, worst case, I'm comfortable in the water. It's just a lake. How can swimming be impossible?

"I should go in," Duncan said. "Just a little ways."

Woof, uncharacteristically, didn't reply.

Duncan started up the motor, which caught on the first pull, which he took to be a good sign. Searching for an entry point, he buried the growing disappointment that he couldn't find one.

The weeds are so thick. Reeds and cattails and dead trees and—

An opening!

A small one, barely the width of the boat. But it's a path through all the plants.

Duncan headed for it and entered the reeds slowly, and the plant life immediately surrounded the boat, closing in and swallowing it up, rubbing against the aluminum hull and giving off an echoey drumming/scraping sound that made Duncan uneasy.

How can I even throw a lure in this slop?

Bad idea. I need to turn around and—

The engine sputtered, sputtered, sputtered… and then stopped.

Duncan put it in neutral and tugged the cord.

And tugged.

And tugged.

And tugged and tugged and tugged until his shoulders burned and his arms felt ready to fall off.

The motor refused to start.

He unlocked the tilt and pulled the lower end up out of the water, seeing a propeller caked with muck and weeds, the water intake slots fully clogged.

Exactly what Josh said would happen.

He picked off the slop, cleared the grilles, eased the motor back into the water, and gave the cord another heroic pull.

This time the motor did start, and immediately a shrill whistle blared from under the cowl.

This irritated Woof, who began to howl in protest.

Engine alarm. It's overheating.

If it runs while overheating, it could seize the motor.

That's unfixable. And even a cheap, old outboard cost several hundred bucks.

Duncan hit the stop button. Woof also stopped howling, and cocked his head at Duncan.

"Okay. I row out."

He picked up a wooden oar resting on the slat seats, which was heavier than he anticipated, and as he tried to get the metal pivot into the oarlock it slipped from his hands and fell into the water, slowly gliding away from the boat.

Duncan reached over the edge, stretching for the oar before it floated away, and then the world's fattest beagle got up on the gunwale to see what was happening and that was enough to tip both Duncan, and Woof, overboard.

Duncan went into the water head-first, immediately getting a mouthful of filthy water, and came up, choking, as his feet sank into the muck.

Woof didn't come up.

Duncan couldn't see anything in the blackness he'd stirred up, and he knew Woof was too fat to swim, so he held his breath and ducked down into the darkness and tried to sweep his hands around to find his dog.

Please, oh please, oh please oh please oh—

Duncan's hand brushed something solid, and he leaned into it, pulling it close to him, taking it to the surface, and the boy and his dog spent a moment gasping for air.

Woof didn't even try to doggy paddle. He clung to Duncan with all four paws, holding on for his life.

Duncan wrapped his arms around the dog, trying to maintain his balance with his feet stuck almost up to his knees.

"It's okay, it's okay," he repeated over and over.

In the meantime, the boat floated silently away, getting caught in the reeds two meters from Duncan's position.

It might as well have been two kilometers away. Because Duncan couldn't get his feet free.

Exactly what Josh said would happen.

Josh was right about everything.

Duncan let the scenario play out in his head.

I can't swim because I'm holding Woof.

Even if I drop the dog, I don't think I can get my feet out of the muck.

The boat is too far away. It has the walkie-talkie.

But I have my phone!

Duncan used one hand to carefully pull his cell out of his pocket, hoping against hope that it still worked even though it had been in the water.

His phone did not work.

He looked around, but all he could see were reeds.

I'm in trouble.

I'm in big, big trouble.

Duncan clutched his trembling dog, and began to cry.

JAKE

My body is a vessel.

A vessel for Him.

He will spread His seed throughout this lake.

And He shall grow inside me and be born again.

Jake sat in the muck among the reeds on the north side of Big Lake Niboowin. Occasionally, something would wiggle out of one of his orifices and swim into the water.

Before Jake had been infused with His genetic material, he'd been a scientist. He'd always wondered, in his self-absorbed, borderline-obsessive way, how many orifices the human body had.

Twelve?

Counting pairs as individual openings, I believe it's twelve.

The mouth, of course. The largest hole in the body. Jake had birthed many leeches through his mouth.

Thousands of eggs had dribbled from both nostrils, though Jake wasn't sure what the eggs would become.

Mosquito larvae grew in both his ears, buzzing free after pupating, often returning to Jake to suck some blood before going off into the world to explore.

He cried worms of some kind, thin and long and wiggling out of his tear ducts. Some were several centimeters long. Perhaps nematodes. Or flukes.

Maggots, squirming in his swollen breasts, pushed out through his nipples, slick with Jake's blood.

He pissed out black flies—though pissing might be too strong a word since they crawled out in a slow, steady parade—and every few hours had to turn over so his ass breached the surface of the water so he could release wasps, by the hundreds.

Jake didn't like the wasps very much. Eager to escape his body, they stung multiple times as they made their way through his colon, and he had to bite his own arm to keep from screaming whenever a brood emerged. He'd bitten all the way to the bone.

The outer, thicker bone. The radius.

It's like chewing electric rawhide, the pain white hot.

If I wasn't already nuts, this would drive me there.

Jake had one final orifice, sealed since birth, but now open and gaping with something growing deep inside. He stared down at his distended stomach, half submerged in blackish water, and his red belly button opened and closed like a small mouth.

He stuck a finger inside, and let Him suckle, His needle-teeth tearing at Jake's skin and gnawing at his bone.

"Soon," Jake cooed. "Soon You will be born again."

DUNCAN

"I guess we could try the marsh," Duncan suggested.

Chuck made a face. "You said there's nothing in the marsh but weeds and muck and flies."

"I haven't fished it since I was a kid."

And that memory is among my worst, which is saying a lot.

"Did you catch anything?"

I remember clinging to Woof, the foul water clogging our noses and mouths, fearing we'd die there...

But even though that terror, fifteen years later, still felt fresh in Duncan's mind, the marsh still called to him in a forbidden, primeval way.

Maybe the fish are in the bullrush, bellied down in the mud and milfoil, hiding from the blazing sun which the dirty air seems to be magnifying.

"I lost the biggest bass I ever had on, by the marsh."

"Gotta risk it for the biscuit." Chuck wiped his forearm over his brow.

"Marsh is tough fishing," Duncan admitted. "Topwater only, buzz baits and scum frogs. Lots of places for a lure to get snagged. And a big fish in there could get tangled up in the weeds, be hard to pull out."

Stu waved away a black fly. "That sounds like a quality problem."

"Boat could stall, too. Happened when I was a kid."

"You call for help?"

Not exactly.

"Sort of," was all that Duncan would admit to. "Long story."

"You lived, obviously."

A memory of Duncan's dog, Woof, came into his head. "Yeah. But it was a shit show."

"I don't want to have to swim for help if we get stuck," Stu said.

"Swimming would be… problematic." Duncan shrugged. "But I got a walkie-talkie in the tackle box."

"Who are we supposed to call? Your parents aren't home."

"We have neighbors. Andy and Sun Dennison-Jones. They're preppers, and have all sorts of radio equipment that they monitor. They're flaky, but if they're home, they'd help."

"Before I came up I read all the back issues of the Lake Niboowin e-newsletter," Stu said.

Chuck shook his head. "Of course you did."

"This spring, some residents got DNR permits to use aquatic herbicide to kill water milfoil."

Chuck scratched his head. "In English?"

"Weeds," Stu said.

Duncan followed the thought train. "So maybe the marsh won't be as marshy."

Stu nodded. "That's what I'm saying. The herbicide they use can be pretty strong."

Chuck squinted at Duncan. "How'd you get stuck when you were a kid?"

"Intake clogged," Duncan said. "If that happens again, I can fix it in two minutes. I've taken this outboard apart three times. Muck plugs up the thermostat coil, and engine warning siren trips. Four bolts, easy access, you can clean the spring with your fingers."

Chuck nodded, then cleared his throat and spat in the lake. "I know motors. Compared to a modern F-150, this is cake."

"So we doing this?" Duncan asked. "We all need to agree. All in."

"All in," Stu said. "Even if we don't catch anything, I bet there are dragonflies. Dragonflies are apex predators, man. Those things are badass. After they hatch, they're called nymphs and live underwater for a few years. They have this hinged jaw called a labium that shoots out like praying mantis arms and grabs water bugs. Some of the bigger ones can even eat tadpoles and fish. They don't attack humans, but if they did, ooh boy that would be a one-sided fight."

Stu stopped talking, his face creasing in a frown. "I'm talking like a bug lord again, aren't I?"

"Yes you are, Bug Lord." Duncan turned to Chuck. "How about you, man? Marsh?"

"I'm for giving it a shot," Chuck said. "We came here to catch some bass, right?"

Duncan nodded. "Bass, perch, walleye, pike. The cast-iron skillet had no prejudice. But first we have to catch them."

"And you can't catch a fish unless you fish," Chuck said.

Stu pointed at each of them. "So let's fish."

"Okay. Reel 'em in."

The guys finished retrieving their baits, and Duncan twisted the ignition key. The engine caught on the second turn, and he pushed forward on the side mount control.

Stall.

He shifted back into neutral, pressed in the key to engage the choke and give it more gas, then fired it up again. The motor sputtered, sputtered, sputtered, and finally started, and Duncan eased the boat forward, slowly accelerating until the 25hp Mercury roared. Full speed wasn't very fast on this old boat, but it was enough to blow Chuck's cap off. It danced around the floor of the pontoon on the worn green carpeting, Chuck grasping for it, and eventually blew toward the stern where Stu stomped on the bill, preventing it from exiting the boat.

Around them, the lake appeared quiet and empty and endless, a bright mirror reflecting the murky sky and unyielding sun.

Brutal UV. I hope the SPF-50 is enough.

Duncan closed in on the marsh, throttling down, squinting for a good place to enter.

No good place existed. Whatever herbicide the DNR used must not have worked, because the weeds and muck seemed impenetrable. Duncan looked for the bass boat he'd spotted, judging it to be fifty meters away. But it was deep into the bullrush, and he couldn't find the path it had taken to get there.

I lost that huge bass around here. I remember an opening, in the marsh. If it still exists, we'll be able to get a few casts in.

Duncan scanned the thick overgrowth until he saw it; a tiny path, half the width of the pontoon. He leaned over the starboard side, gazing into the murky lake. The electronic depth finder wasn't working, and he judged they were at about three feet deep.

But things get shallow, fast.

Duncan pressed the electric motor tilt switch, slowly raising the plane so the propeller wouldn't hit bottom, and then steered for the narrow path. As he approached, Duncan almost turned the watercraft away. The marsh was thicker than he'd expected. Florida everglades-slash-Amazon jungle-slash-New Orleans bayou thick. With so many tall reeds and dead sapling trunks and floating clumps of vegetation and mud, navigation would be difficult, and fishing would be almost impossible.

This is a bad idea.

But there's another boat nearby.

They must be here to fish.

Duncan headed into the thick of the overgrowth, heading toward the boat. Reeds scraped along the two pontoon floats and under the raised hull, the dragging sounds amplified by the hollow aluminum. Duncan slowed their speed to a crawl, squinting at the biomass surrounding them, trying to spot the clearing while the brutal overhead sun seared his eyes.

It was near a submerged tree, which stuck out of the water at an angle. Like a Tommy Bartlett waterski ramp.

He put the boat in neutral, scanning the port-side horizon, looking for a clearing to make a few casts.

And then, like an oasis in the desert, it appeared.

Open water. Enough for all of us to throw a few.

Maybe one of us can pull a monster bass out of this slop.

Shifting the motor back into forward, Duncan weaved through the thickening weeds, keeping the spot in sight while remaining alert for obstacles. The pathway he'd entered had disappeared, and he'd begun to worry that the prop would get bound up with plant matter, but the reeds parted and they coasted into the clearing.

Perfect. This is perfect.

Every so often, Duncan would get what he called his *fish feeling*. It wasn't any sort of psychic stuff—he didn't believe in that—but maybe one in a thousand casts he would set eyes on a spot and know, for sure, that something hungry was there, watching, waiting for him to cast. He had that tingle as he cut off the motor and the pontoon glided to a slow stop.

"There's something here," he softly spoke, as if raising his voice would scare the fish away. "Top water lures, work the reed line, slow retrieve, make it look like your bait is injured."

Opening his tackle box carefully so it didn't make noise, Duncan switched lures, taking the Heddon Lucky 13 from his leader clip and replacing it with a Dying Flutter. The Flutter looked like a fluorescent green blunt, pinched at either end, with two metal propellers to churn up the water.

Not that bass's natural prey had propellers, but the action mimicked a wounded baitfish.

If a lunker is nearby, this should entice it to strike.

Just as Duncan put on the bait and lifted it overhead to cast, Chuck pointed at the water and said, "Is that a bass?"

Duncan followed his friend's finger, and saw something floating in the water two meters away from the boat.

Something big.

"Too large for a bass," Stu said. "Right, Duncan?"

The floating, greenish white mass was over two feet long, and definitely a dead fish of some sort.

"Could be a pike. Or a sturgeon."

"Musky?" Chuck asked.

"No musky in the lake."

"Let's net it and find out," Stu said.

Duncan shook his head. "Leave it alone. Let's fish."

"It's really big. I want to see what it is," Stu said.

"It will stink up the boat."

Duncan considered the debate over, and cast to the west. The Dying Flutter plopped next to a skinny, dead fir sapling sticking out of the water.

Fish like cover; weeds, logs, rocks, sunken watercraft. They're ambush predators.

You have to lure them out.

Duncan let his bait rest for a few seconds, then gave it a twitch.

He paid scant attention to Stu and Chuck, making their casts, and then Duncan began a slow-and-stop retrieve, jerking the lure for maximum noise, then letting it rest like it was too wounded to continue.

Fish, like all predators, obey natural selection. When it comes down to survival of the fittest, the sick and the weak are picked off first.

I just need to keep tension on the line, to set the hook when I get a strike.
"Got it!"

Duncan turned to Stu, saw his pole bending. When someone hooked a fish, boat rule was everyone else reeled in to assist in landing it and to make sure lines didn't get tangled. Duncan hesitated for half a second, because he'd really had a feeling about his cast, and then did a quick retrieve, ruining the dying baitfish illusion and scaring off any bass that could have been watching.

Setting down his rod, Duncan located the net by the port tailing and snatched it up, one eye on the bend in Stu's pole.

But something wasn't right. Whatever Stu had on wasn't fighting back.
Like he's reeling in dead weight.
Wait a sec…
Duncan scowled. "Stu, you jackass."

"I was casting next to it and got snagged."

"Snagged my ass."

Stu had aimed for the dead fish and hooked it on one of the trebles.

"It's a big one, Duncan. I'm gonna win biggest of the trip with this."

"Bullshit," Chuck said. "It has to be alive to win."

"Then if this is still twitching, I win. Fifty bucks each."

"Snags don't count."

"Rules don't say that."

Duncan sided with Chuck. "Hooking a floating fish in the side isn't fishing, Stu. And if you get rotten fish guts all over the boat, you're cleaning it."

"Look! It *is* a bass!"

Duncan didn't want to encourage this kind of behavior, but he couldn't help but take a peek. Seeing a large bass, even a dead one, gave him hope that there were others of equal size in the area.

Stu dragged the corpse up to the edge of the starboard float, his line still tight, and the trio leaned over the aluminum guardrail for closer inspection.

It was the biggest bass Duncan had ever seen. As big as the one he missed when he was younger. Maybe even bigger.

Chuck whistled. "Eight pounds, at least."

"Probably closer to ten."

"What killed it?" Stu asked.

The bass didn't have any apparent injuries on the side that was facing upward. Its eye was cloudy and protruding, but Duncan had seen many dead floating fish, and that was probably due to decomposition, or the searing summer sun, or both.

"Let's bring it in." Stu reached for the net.

Duncan vetoed that. "You ever smell rotting meat? It's the worst stink ever."

That was an understatement. Decomposing garbage was bad. Getting skunked was bad. The Porta-Potties at Coachella were bad. But decay…

Decay is the Mother of All Stenches.

If hell is real, it won't be burning in flames or medieval tortures. It will be a billion people forced to smell each other as they rot.

"My hook is caught." Stu gave a few feeble tugs on his pole to prove his point.

"Hand it over."

Duncan took the rod and gave it several vicious yanks, causing the dead bass to bob up and down.

The hooks stayed hooked.

Duncan considered cutting the line. That was how much he hated the rancid odor of decay. Decay reminded Duncan of death, and he didn't do well when being reminded of death.

But Stu was using one of Duncan's lures; a vintage Creek Chub Injured Minnow that he'd paid fifteen bucks for on eBay. Replacing it would be expensive, if he could even find that same color.

"Get the net," ordered Duncan. "You're taking the hooks out."

Net in hand, Stu leaned over the gunwale and scooped up the dead fish. As he brought it up, Duncan noticed the entire underside of the creature was covered in thick, black muck, and the stench was otherworldly. He dropped the net and turned away, retreating to the stern of the boat and putting a hand over his mouth and nose.

He heard Chuck swear, "Jesus, man! What the hell!"

"*Hirudo medicinalis*," Stu said. Duncan heard something like awe in his friend's voice. "They aren't supposed to grow that big."

"That's disgusting! Those things are over a foot long?"

Those things? What the hell were they talking about?

Curiosity overtook revulsion, and Duncan chanced a look.

Revulsion instantly returned.

That isn't lake mud on the underside of the bass.

It's leeches.

A wriggling, slimy tangle of leeches, undulating like octopus tentacles.

And Stu, the moron, brought them onto my boat, gazing at them like he's got a junior high crush.

"They're hematophagous," Stu said. "Blood drinkers. Their saliva has anesthetic and anticoagulant chemicals in it. You can't feel it when they're sucking on you, because they numb your skin while they feed. And your blood won't clot. They keep sucking until they get their fill."

Duncan could feel his stomach begin to cramp.

"Get them off the boat, Stu."

"They shouldn't be this size," Stu said, reverently. "*Haementeria ghilianii*—the giant Amazon leech—can grow to eighteen inches. But these are even larger. This could be a new species."

"I don't give a shit about your new species. Toss the fish overboard."

But Stu didn't toss the fish overboard. Instead, he bent down—

—and touched the squirming mass.

Chuck slapped his thigh, grinning. "Man, there is something seriously wrong with you!"

Duncan couldn't turn away, disgust churning inside of him as his entomologist friend pinched a leech between his thumb and forefinger. The leech responded by detaching from the bass and curling itself around Stu's hand. When the worm contracted, it was the width of a hot dog.

A slimy, black, undulating hot dog that feasts on blood.

"These look like overgrown medicinal leeches. *Hirudo medicinalis*. They have a sucker on each end to secure themselves to their host, but only the anterior is used for feeding." Stu stroked it with his other hand, like it was a pet. "Three sets of jaws, over a hundred teeth. Ten eyes. They can consume fifteen times their body weight in blood."

Chuck appeared as creeped out as Duncan felt. "Don't let it bite you, bro. I heard they lay eggs inside your body."

"That's a myth. Very few species lay eggs inside humans. Leeches are still used in medicine for reconstructive surgery. Look… it's feeding on me."

Duncan purposely didn't look. But as he glanced away, he saw the leeches that had piggybacked onto the boat via the bass were beginning to crawl around the floor of the pontoon, one of them slinking up Stu's rubber soled flip-flop and over his bare toes.

A moment later, Chuck was stomping on the creature, blood squirting out like a squashed ketchup packet. One that had a thick line of spoiled yellow custard running through it.

Duncan had to turn away. He suffered with vasovagal syncope; getting light-headed by the sight of blood. He hated gore the same way he hated rot.

From that tragic childhood event in Safe Haven.

I don't handle death in a healthy way.

He managed to avoid vomiting by taking some deep, slow breaths, which tasted faintly of soot. "Dude. You're getting worm guts everywhere. You gotta clean that up, man."

Chuck, being Chuck, seemed unconcerned about his friends' opinions. He was frowning at the bottom of his Nike. "You think we could fish with these things? You can fish with leeches, right?"

Stu had his camera out and was photographing the bloodsucker feasting on his arm, its black body pulsating as it gulped.

Duncan turned away, his stomach wrenching like it was filled with leeches, wiggling and gnawing and squirming to get out.

I'm starting to lose it. I need to take a few deep breaths and calm down.

But how am I supposed to take a deep breath with the stink of death in my nose and mouth?

"Get it out of the boat, Stu. Now."

"Gross, dude," Chuck said. "There's a baby leech coming out of its eye."

Against his better judgment, Duncan looked. Protruding from the bass's eye socket, wiggling like a finger, was a white worm.

"That's not a leech." Stu squatted down for a closer look.

"So what is it?" Chuck asked.

"I'm not sure. Too big for a *Loa loa*."

Duncan didn't want to know what *Loa loa* were, but sure enough, Stu explained.

"*Loa loa* are parasitic roundworms that live in the conjunctiva of the eye. They're spread by deerflies. They eat eye tissue and cause blindness."

"Deerflies?" Duncan could see several deerflies buzzing around the boat.

"They live in rainforests, not Wisconsin. And these don't look like nematodes. They're more like…" Stu made a face. "Maggots. That's weird."

"No shit it's weird," Chuck said. "Think we can fish with it?"

Stu took a pic of the maggot. "That's a big one. Maggots don't have teeth. They have these mouth hooks that tear out flesh."

Stu pinched the maggot and it came out of the fish eye with a slurping sound.

"Big sucker." He placed it next to himself on the vinyl pontoon seat. "It can move, too. Look at the little sucker go."

"Get the fish off the boat," Duncan repeated. "Now."

"I need to get your lure."

"Fuck the lure. I'll cut the line. Get it out of the boat. Chuck?"

"I ain't touching that thing."

Stu rolled his eyes. "Jesus, Duncan. It's just nature being nature. Death is part of life. No need to act like a baby."

"He's not being a baby, Stu. Remember that incident? When he was a kid?"

"It wasn't an incident," Duncan clarified. "Some psychopaths massacred everyone in my entire town. The whole town, Stu. Over a thousand people. That's more than a goddamn incident."

"Easy, brother. I'm not trying to get you upset."

But it's too late for that.

Duncan leaned down and opened his Umco tackle box. After pulling out the expanding trays, he felt around in the bottom for the gaff. It was a large metal hook with a rubber grip, used for landing big fish. Duncan had never used it for that purpose; he practiced catch and release, and gaffs could cause serious injury to the fish. But he'd inherited it from his grandpa, and it was a good luck charm of sorts.

He handed it to Chuck. "Can you…?"

"Sure, man."

Chuck speared the large hook into the dead bass with a wet *THUNK!* He lifted the fish and its leech and maggot passengers out of the net and over the side of the boat and shook it off, letting everything plop into the water.

When it hit, the fish's belly popped open, exploding with a wiggling knot of worms.

Duncan came over to cut Stu's line, using some nail clippers he had hanging around his neck on a lanyard. Thankfully, the smell of rot went away, which made his stomach settle a bit and his stress ease up.

But Stu was still fondling the gigantic leech sucking on his hand.

"Get rid of it," Duncan told him.

"I study this kind of stuff, Duncan. I'm telling you, nothing like this is supposed to live in this area."

"I want it off the boat."

"I can put it in a water bottle."

There were five empty plastic bottles they'd finished earlier that morning.

"I'm not playing, Stu. Throw it overboard."

Stu seemed annoyed, but Duncan didn't care. With his free hand, Stu pinched the end of the worm and pulled. The leech stretched out like a rubber band, so long that Stu appeared to be shooting an arrow from an invisible bow. Then it snapped off, flicking a line of blood across Duncan's face.

Duncan fell to his knees, his world going dizzy, and as he blacked out he didn't notice Stu putting the maggot in an empty water bottle.

SUNSHINE

Sunshine Dennison-Jones stared, wide-eyed, at the creature on her window screen.

That hornet is enormous.

Sun's veterinary skills encompassed domesticated animals and pets, including arthropods. In her previous jobs she'd helped the owner of a tarantula get rid of mites. She'd saved an ant farm from fungus. She'd even worked with a boy to set up a habitat for his giant Madagascar hissing cockroach. And on Lake Niboowin she'd helped a local beekeeper remove an infestation of *Galleria mellonella*; wax moths.

But her animal-loving heart had no affection for hornets. Not with all the animals she had in the house and around the property. Not with Francis, a child who was fearless around all creatures no matter how creepy or dangerous. And especially not around her husband, Andy, who was stung by a yellow jacket a few months ago and had an allergic reaction. Anaphylactic shock. His throat closed up, and he could barely breathe.

Luckily, Sun had a few EpiPens on hand; epinephrine injector devices which she'd stockpiled before their costs went up to almost a thousand bucks a shot.

Well… if three extra pens can be considered a stockpile.

Andy quickly recovered, the yellow jacket nest was located and destroyed with the help of the bee suits they'd purchased to deal with the wax moths, and life on the lake went on for all (except for those stinging pests).

But this hornet wasn't anything like the paper wasp that had gotten Andy.

This is something different. Something strange. Something worse.

Fighting a twinge of dread, Sun took out her cell phone to take a picture of the insect clinging to the outside living room window screen, carefully putting her thumb, which wasn't as long or wide as the bug, alongside it for scale.

She snapped the pic—

—and the hornet pounced, clutching at her finger, sticking its abdomen through the screen holes. Sun jerked her hand away just as the stinger poked through the mesh, the centimeter-long tip glistening with venom.

That's uncommonly aggressive.

Sun's expertise didn't extend to *Hymenoptera*, but she knew that hive insects became more likely to attack as winter neared. However, this was the height of summer. Sun hadn't touched the wasp, hadn't threatened it.

So it's not defending itself.

Why is it attacking?

I'm much too big to be food.

Sun stared, curious, as the stinger retracted and the wasp began to chew at the screen. It wings beat frantically, quickly getting up to a speedy blur and giving off a deep, frightening buzz, while the creature shook against the metal scrim like a crazed prisoner trying to escape a jail cell.

It's trying to get in.

Interesting. Very—

Sun gasped, taking a step back as its mandibles cut through the screen and its bulbous head poked through.

"Nope!" she said, and then scraped her cell phone against the screen and cleanly decapitated the flying insect at its thorax.

The headless body continued to buzz, and the severed head that had fallen to the floor—next to Sun's pinky toe and almost as large—continued to open and close its mandibles, seeking something to bite.

"What's up, babe?"

Andy had come up behind Sun without her noticing, and she let out an uncharacteristic squeal, causing her empathetic husband to yelp in response. That caused Bertram, their miniature silky fainting goat who had tagged along with her husband, to immediately keel over and faint, stiff legs sticking up into the air.

"You okay, hon?" Andy asked.

They both ignored the goat, and Sun focused on the insect. The wasp's body continued to twitch and buzz, its feet hooked to the screen.

"Holy hell," Andy said after following her gaze. "Where did that thing come from? Outer space?"

"It looks like a *Vespa mandarinia*," she told her husband.

"An Asian Murder Hornet?"

Andy didn't know animals, but he was an expert at languages. Latin was a favorite.

"Yeah. But the coloring is off."

"I didn't think they'd come to North America," Andy said.

"They haven't. And this one doesn't look right."

"No shit. It's the size of a mouse."

"Yeah, it's big. But there's something about the eyes."

Andy squinted at the bug. "What eyes? I don't see a head."

Sun squatted, and Andy squatted next to her. Sun reached into her pocket for her vet kit; an essential assortment of medical tools in a canvas wrap. She opened up the pack and selected a pair of forceps, then moved to pick up the severed head.

She didn't have to. The mandibles opened and clamped onto the tip of the tweezers, holding them tight.

Sun raised it up to eye level for a closer look.

"See it?" she asked Andy.

"See what? That it's trying to eat your tweezers?"

"Wasps and flies have compound eyes called ommatidia. Each little multifacet is its own lens. But what do you notice here?"

"Pupils," Andy said. "Elongated pupils."

Sun nodded, a lump growing in her throat. "Horizontal. Like Bertram's."

Their goat had recovered from the faint and jumped on the couch to sleep next to their snoring bulldog, and Sun completed her disturbing observation.

"This wasp has the eyes of a goat."

LEO

He was walking west on I-94 when the burning in his right wrist became unbearable. Leo squatted alongside the highway, wincing while he gripped his undulating, wiggling skin.

It feels like my hand is going to—

Then his hand fell off.

He blinked, unsure it wasn't a hallucination.

Leo stared at his wrist, watching as the puckering flesh continued to pulse, staring at the cross section of his bones, his veins and arteries, his tendons and ligaments, his muscles and viscera, which, oddly enough, looked like a hunk of bloodless, raw ham hock. As he watched, the reddish-pink flesh color darkened, scabbing over at an accelerated rate and forming a hard crust.

It reminded Leo of a badly skinned knee two days after falling off a bike.

This isn't a promising development.

It didn't hurt, much. But the tingling sensation in his stump wasn't pleasant.

He reached for his severed hand, realized a moment too late that he was trying to grab it with his stump, and then picked it up with his remaining hand. It felt like picking up a dead animal.

Unsure of what to do, he stuck it in his trench coat pocket and continued to walk up the highway.

So... a hospital?

I have this crazy accelerated healing power. Maybe they could just stick it back on.

Or...

Testing the insane idea, Leo stretched out his bare wrist. Just below the stump he used a fingernail to scratch the skin, deep enough to draw blood.

The wound knitted itself, almost instantly.

Okay. So maybe I don't need a doctor.

Maybe I can do this myself.

Setting his jaw, Leo picked and scratched and tore at the stub on his arm, clawing off the scab, then pinching and twisting the sealed ends of his arteries to get them to start bleeding again.

The pain got real bad real fast.

He drew some blood, but not much. After an unpleasant thirty seconds of trying to reopen the wound, he stuck his severed hand back on the stump and held it there, as if waiting for glue to dry.

After another thirty seconds, his fingers began to tingle, and he was able to wiggle his pinky.

He smiled, for the first time in as long as he could remember, and tried to make a fist.

His hand immediately fell off. Again.

Smile gone, Leo picked up his hand, tucked it away, and hiked three more kilometers to the town of Yonder Bay, where he found a big box store just off the highway. Fighting against the Tug, he walked across the parking lot with a vague idea taking shape in his mind.

Biological glue.

He roamed the aisles, forming a strategy, and used the twenty bucks that Mary Streng had given him to buy four things.

In the hunting section, an upswept skinner knife with a three-inch blade.

In the hardware section, some powdered rat poison.

In the cooking section, a four-sided aluminum cheese grater.

In the pharmacy, the cheapest bottle of aspirin they had.

He had a quarter left, and put it in a gumball machine by the front doors.

The machine ripped him off.

But, bonus, he found a thrown-away fast-food cup in the garbage, still mostly filled with ice.

Back in the parking lot, Leo sat on the waist-high concrete post supporting a giant overhead light. He set the cup next to his hip, thumbed off the plastic lid, and clumsily poured in the rat poison from its cardboard carton.

Leo couldn't get the lid off the aspirin bottle using only one hand, so he pried it off with his teeth and dumped half the tablets into his mouth, the other half into the cup.

The rodent poison contained warfarin, an anti-coagulant. It stopped the blood from clotting.

The aspirin was a vasodilator. It widened the veins and arteries, improving blood pressure and also prolonging bleeding.

And of course, aspirin is also a painkiller.

Hopefully, it will help with some of the pain I'm about to inflict on myself.

He swirled the mixture in the cup until most of the ice melted, then choked down the lumpy slurry in five big gulps.

There's a chance this will kill me.

I can live with that.

The cheap skinner knife, likely made of soft metal that wouldn't sharpen well, happily came razor-sharp out of the package. He gripped it firmly, and held the blade to the top of the scab on his stump, as if ready to slice the butt off a loaf of bread.

So… cut in a sawing motion? Or whittle and carve?

Decisions, decisions…

The straight cut seemed like it would be less damage, so Leo took a deep, full breath and then attacked his scab like he was in a deli cutting some ham for a sandwich, moving hard and fast and only screaming through his clenched jaw a little bit.

I should have bought a better knife. And more aspirin.

And something to bite down on.

The skinner didn't do well with bone, so Leo carved around it, this time imagining a Thanksgiving turkey leg being stripped. The result wasn't pretty, but the blood was coming pretty fast, in little fountains.

Before the bleeding stopped Leo again tried sticking his dead, limp hand back onto the stump.

For a moment it seemed to work better than his earlier attempt at reattachment, and after sixty seconds of sticking he could actually wiggle his fingers.

But once he tried to lift his arm, his hand once again fell off. It fell slowly, a few veins holding on and stretching out like pizza cheese.

Everything is a food metaphor. I think I'm hungry again.

As the stump began to heal, Leo considered his options.

What's the best method for glueing something back together?

Rough the edges, then put the glue on both pieces.

So he held the four-sided cheese grater between his thighs, tight, and then freshened up the wound on the severed hand, scraping the wrist up and down and taking off a few millimeters of skin, flesh, and bone. As he did, a mother pushed a full shopping cart past him. She was preoccupied with her cell phone. But her child, sitting in the cart, stared at Leo with huge eyes and immediately began to wail.

I know how you feel, kid. I'm about to start sobbing any second.

Once his severed hand was prepped, Leo set it on his thigh and gave his stump a serious grating, reopening the wounds, hoping the aspirin and warfarin would work long enough to keep fluids pumping for a proper reattachment, and hoping he didn't pass out.

Leo clenched his jaw so hard he felt a molar crack, which hurt almost as much as filing down his arm bones with a cheese grater.

Grin and bear it.

It's for the grater good.

Ha! Grater good!

I have amusing thoughts when I'm out of my mind with pain!

Half-laughing/half-sobbing, Leo halted the self-torture and then he stuck his gooey hand on the stump and held it there—

—and held it—

—and held it—

—and third time was a charm.

Leo wiggled his fingers.

Good.

He made a fist.

Good.

He even gave his hand a slight tug.

Good. The attachment held firm.

It works.

I lost maybe a half inch of length, but it works.

I'm pretty lucky, all things considered.

Then he noticed his left wrist, and his right ankle, began to tingle and burn.

One crisis at a time. I'll deal with that when I need to.

He tapped the cheese grater on the asphalt, shaking out all the little fleshy and boney bits. Then Leo hung the handle on his trench coat belt and once again obeyed the Tug, letting himself be drawn in a northwestern path.

Whatever I'm heading for, it can't be worse than what I've just gone through.

If I can handle that, I can handle anything.

It was an optimistic thought.

It was also completely wrong.

DUNCAN

On his hands and knees, the blood returning to his head, Duncan regained his focus and got his erratic heartbeat and shallow breathing under control.

That's it. Fishing is over.

"You okay, bro?" Chuck patted his back.

"We're going in."

After dragging the back of his hand across his cheek to wipe away the streak of leech blood—or maybe it was Stu blood—Duncan got to his feet and took his seat behind the steering wheel.

"Seriously?" Stu said. "I got rid of it. Didn't mean to make you freak out, man. Let's fish."

"We're done. I'm the captain. Captain's rules."

"C'mon, Duncan." Chuck took off his ball cap and rubbed his hand through his hair. "We should at least take a few more casts. This spot looks perfect. Stu was acting like an idiot. Stu, apologize."

Stu shrugged. "Sorry. I'm interested in that sort of stuff. Life cycles of bugs are my thing. I didn't know it would be that gross for you."

Duncan considered staying, then reconsidered his consideration.

I can get over the dead fish. And the leeches. And the maggots. And the blood.

But there's still the hot sun. The lack of wind. The air quality. The mounting thirst. The utter failure at not even getting a single bite.

And the marsh. The marsh was freaking cursed. I never should have come back to this part of the lake.

I'm done. We're done.

He tried to hide his frustration by being positive. "Let's go in, grab some food. And beer."

"Beer sounds good," Chuck agreed.

"I've beaten my hangover just enough to be up for a beer," Stu agreed. "We still climbing up the fire tower?"

"I'm up for that," Chuck said.

Duncan hid his sense of relief. "All in. A brew with a view. Let's do it."

He turned the ignition key.

Once.

Twice.

Three times.

The motor didn't start.

He made sure the boat was in neutral, pushed in the key to activate the choke, and tried again.

Nope.

Again.

No dice.

Once more, Duncan turning the key hard, silently willing the Mechanical Gods to show mercy.

The motor sputtered—

—caught—

—and died.

The Mechanical Gods are assholes.

A large, black fly buzzed angrily past Duncan's ear, and he swatted at it with his palm, his irritation level rising.

There are plenty of reasons why a motor wouldn't start. I need to go down the checklist.

He stood up and went to work.

Safety lanyard in place; it hadn't tripped the kill switch.

Wires to the control box looked good.

Battery cables tight, no corrosion.

Gas in the tank. Bulb firm. Cap vented.

Hoses good, no leaks, firmly attached at the tank and the motor.

He trimmed up, and the lower end of the Mercury rose out of the water, proving the battery worked and was fully charged.

Some weeds tangling the propeller, but not enough to seize it.

Intake ports appear clear.

Duncan went into a lure box and took out a ½" crescent wrench. Then he removed the motor cowl, set it aside, and carefully took off the four bolts holding the thermostat housing.

And there's the problem.

"Thermostat is totally blocked." Duncan chuckled in relief as he dug the mud and weeds off of the spring. He also checked the exit tube, leading to the telltale, aka the *pee hole*. Outboard motors drew in lake water with an impeller to cool the engine, then shot a stream of hot water out the back, hence the rude nickname. The pee hole was clogged with muck, which Duncan unclogged using a piece of weed wacker plastic wire that he kept on board for that purpose.

Then he put the cleaned thermostat in place, bolted the housing back on, and tilted the lower end back into the water.

Fingers crossed…

Duncan went back to the start key, pressed it in, and turned—

—and the motor kicked on—

—and died again.

He cranked it five more times, but it didn't catch.

If I keep trying to start without it starting I'll drain the battery.

So what the hell can be wrong?

"All engines need three things," Chuck said. "Fuel, air, and fire."

"Could it be the smoggy air?" Stu asked.

Chuck shook his head. "If we can breathe, the motor can breathe."

"Spark plugs?" Duncan asked. "Flooded?"

"Worth checking. If they're wet or gunked up they won't spark. They need to keep lighting to combust the fuel. No fire, no combustion."

It was a good suggestion. Duncan popped off the cowl again and followed the black wires to locate the plugs. He tugged off the rubber-shrouded wire clips and peered in the mounts on the cylinder head. They were deep-seated, like in a car engine. He tried turning one with his fingers.

Too tight. And I don't have a spark plug socket on board.

"Hand me the fishing pliers," he told Chuck.

Chuck winced. "Wrong tool for the job."

"Only tool we got. The needle-nose should be able to fit."

"I work on cars all day. Wrong tool always leads to more problems."

"Do we have a choice?" Duncan asked.

"We could just wait it out," Chuck said. "If they're flooded, they'll dry."

A good point.

"And we can get a few more casts in," Stu said.

Duncan sighed, resigning himself to the situation. "Okay. I guess we get to keep fishing."

Stu didn't have to be told twice. He picked up his rod and cast out.

Chuck did as well.

Duncan reached for his half bottle of water in the cup holder, and killed half of it, wincing because it had gotten warm. He squinted up through sunglasses at the hazy angry sun in the reddish sky, then found his tube of sunscreen on the floor and slathered more on his face, arms, and neck.

While he protected himself against UV rays, nature took advantage and attacked him a different way. He yelped and slapped his thigh with a loud *CRACK!* as something stung him, or bit him, just above the knee, causing an electric jolt of pain.

"What gotcha?" Stu asked.

Duncan lifted his hand, and whatever he'd whacked—hard enough to get his friends' attention—shook off the blow and flew into the air.

It was big, and black, and buzzed away before Duncan got a good look.

Then he checked his leg. A welt was already forming, with a bloody dot in the center oozing a drop of murky fluid. He carefully ran his fingertip over the bump, tender and hot to the touch.

"Damn. That freaking hurts. Like I got a cigarette pressed to my leg."

"I missed it," Stu said, getting up to take a look. "Was it a horsefly? A bee?"

"No idea."

"Bees leave the stinger behind." Stu bent down and squinted. "No stinger there. How much does it hurt on the Schmidt scale?"

"Schmidt? Like Schmidt beer?" Chuck laughed. "That stuff really hurts."

Stu adjusted the brim of his *Science Pimp* cap. "Justin O. Schmidt. Creator of the Schmidt Sting Pain Index. He rated insect stings on a scale from 1 to 4. A fire ant is a 1, a honey bee is a 2, paper wasp is a 3, and so on."

"What's a 4?" Chuck asked.

"Schmidt had a few. The bullet ant. The warrior wasp. The tarantula hawk. Others have gone on to make their own ratings, to find which sting hurts the worst. There's a general consensus of the worst. The executioner wasp. The Japanese murder hornet. The velvet ant."

"What's with all the ants?" Chuck asked. "Everyone knows a wasp hurts worse than an ant."

"A velvet ant is technically a wasp without wings. But ants are badass. Did you know that if you took all the ants in the world they'd weigh more than all the humans? More total biomass. We're talking over 20 quadrillion ants. That's the number twenty, with fifteen zeroes after it. A thousand billion. It's an unimaginable number."

"You've got to do something with your life, man," Chuck told him.

Stu was nonplussed. "Ants are going to take over the world someday. They use a hive-mind mentality. The leader, the queen, controls the colony, and the entire population communicates with pheromones. It's like airborne telepathy. Each ant functions like the cell of a larger animal. It's known as a super organism."

"A super orgasm?" Chuck said. "I'm all for that."

"Funny." Stu didn't seem like he found it funny. He continued, "They can link together like a rope and climb over each other. Some ants can lift fifty to a hundred times their own body weight. During the rainy season, some ants build a raft out of their bodies so they can float on the flood waters. We're talking millions of ants, all linked together, several meters wide."

"Don't they drown?" Chuck asked.

"They take turns being underwater so none of them drown," Stu explained.

"They should make that a ride at the waterpark," Chuck said. "Call it a *bite barge*."

"Ants can bite, but the stings are what really hurts. Spiders and centipedes are like snakes; the bite contains venom. With ants and wasps, the venom is in the stinger on the end of the abdomen. And ants have some of the most toxic venom in the world. The bullet ant is called the bullet ant because getting stung hurts worse than getting shot."

"I'm pretty sure getting shot is worse," Chuck said.

"You get shot, you're in pain, and it immediately starts to heal. A bullet ant sting is agony for over twenty-four straight hours. And that's if you're lucky and only one bites you. You get attacked by the colony, and there are stories of people killing themselves to stop the pain."

Duncan, who was watching his leg swell up and was only half-paying attention, finally chimed in. "I'd call this a 3 out of 4 on your Schmidt scale," he said.

Maybe even a 3.5. This hurts like hell.

Stu raised an eyebrow. "Seriously? There's nothing in Wisconsin that should reach a 3. Most of the heavy hitters are from Central and South America."

Duncan shivered, then rubbed his hands on his face. "Ever smash your thumb with a hammer? That's what this feels like."

"I wish you saw what it was," Stu lamented.

"I wish I never see another one." Duncan squinted at his thigh, which continued to puff up, and then remembered he had one of those insect pain relief pen sticks in his tackle box. He hunted for it and gave it a shake before uncapping it and bathing his thigh in benzocaine and menthol.

It helped, but his whole leg still burned.

On a whim, Duncan turned the ignition key and tried to start the engine.

The engine didn't start.

So what now?

Duncan picked up his pole.

While waiting for the spark plugs to dry, we might as well fish.

When in Rome, right?

Duncan eyed the clearing and cast out his lure, and for some reason couldn't stop thinking about the fall of the Roman Empire.

KATIE

SAME TIME, MILES AWAY...

Katie loved being part of the flight crew.

She loved the travel, loved the pay, and for the most part loved the up-in-the-air nature of the job (literally), where schedules, destinations, and layovers could change at a moment's notice.

But cancellations are the worst. And my first flight was cancelled due to Canadian wildfires.

This meant waiting, which Katie didn't mind. There always seemed to be old friends to catch up with, or new friends to meet. Every airport had its quirks and secrets that were fun to explore. Her home base, MSP, wasn't very big compared to other airports, but it was a quick and free shuttle to the nearby Mall of America—her current destination—and that place was massive and never got boring.

Which was fine for delays. But a cancelled flight was a completely different animal. Katie was on call for a three-day pairing, MSP to Seattle, overnight layover, Seattle to San Diego, overnight layover, back to Minneapolis-St. Paul, then the drive back home to Spoonward. She liked this run, and bid a lot to get it. But miss the first on-board and the whole trip evaporated. The personnel at scheduling were usually good at reassigning crews, but if everything was full there really wasn't much to do except hope.

It was going on six hours since she'd checked in, and nothing had opened up. Looking out the shuttle window going west on I-494, Katie's mind wandered.

Worst case scenario, they can't find anything, and I get sent back home tomorrow.

That would suck. She needed the money and only got paid for block time, which began on the plane once the door closed. Ground time didn't pay, except for meal stipends.

And rent is coming…

While Katie made a decent living, constant travel meant constant temptation to spend. New restaurants. New tourist traps. New shops. While working, Katie treated herself well.

Sometimes too well. And bills are due and I need a big paycheck. The money came from being on crew, not from being grounded. Losing this run meant losing three good flights.

She thought about her boyfriend, Duncan. Currently on vacation with his buddies, at his parent's house on Lake Niboowin.

It would save us both a lot of money if we moved in together.

But that's a big step. A big commitment.

They were already a couple. Katie's hesitation wasn't due to monogamy aversion. While being an FA offered her almost unlimited opportunity to meet attractive guys, and she'd had a few flings since starting the job, after dating Duncan for a while they'd decided to become exclusive, and Katie hadn't regretted it.

But moving in represented a much higher level of commitment.

I'm not sure I'm ready for it. And I have a feeling he's going to ask me after his trip.

And I don't know what my answer will be.

On one hand, I love him and practically already live with him when I'm home.

On the other hand, having my own apartment is more than just a place for my stuff and for occasional needed privacy. It's symbolic. I'm a young, self-sufficient woman in the prime of my life. It wasn't too long ago that I was dependent on my parents.

Do I want to be dependent on a guy?

The shuttle reached its destination and Katie got off, turning her face to the summer sun while walking across the parking lot, past the giant multicolored star-sculpture, to the massive red, white, and blue marquee above the Mall of America entrance.

The largest mall in the Western hemisphere. Five hundred shops and restaurants, an indoor theme park, an aquarium, movie theaters, a flight simulator, and pretty much everything a person needed to waste time and money while waiting for a scheduling call.

Katie wandered the mall with a vague notion of finding something caffeinated, and perhaps a snack. When her cell phone buzzed, she had it in hand fast, hoping it was crew sked or Duncan.

It was neither.

And it was bad. Very bad.

HOW'S THE MALL, BITCH?

Katie's heart rate kicked up, but she fought her emotional response and instead went on practiced autopilot, taking a screenshot and blocking the caller.

I thought this was over.

I hoped this was over.

But it's happening again.

Katie tried to shake off the fear and focus on the plan.

I need to stay calm. Stay calm and focus.

Keep all evidence.

Don't respond.

This isn't my fault.

I can't dwell on it.

I won't dwell on it.

This person doesn't deserve to be spending time in my head.

But even though she knew the best course of action, the scary thoughts came anyway.

How did this psychopath get my new number?

Or know where I am?

And why the continued obsession, after so much time has passed?

How nuts was this nut?

Her phone buzzed again. A different number. Katie winced at the texts.

YOU CAN'T BLOCK ME.

YOU'LL NEVER GET RID OF ME

YOU

FUCKING

WHORE

Another screenshot, another block. Katie considered turning her phone off. But she couldn't, because she was on call for work.

I either deal with the wacko, or lose my job.

Katie walked to a nearby bench and sat down, focusing on her breathing, on getting her heartbeat under control.

She considered the pills in her purse.

Xanax. Prescribed for panic attacks.

They take the edge off, but they also make me lethargic. And being on a flight crew didn't mesh well with lethargy. It's about being high energy. Being happy and helpful and busy and attentive.

Xanax isn't an option. I can hold it together. I'll just do some shopping and—

Yet another buzz. Yet another text from yet another new number.
YOU LOOK SCARED.

Alarmed, Katie immediately stopped and turned in a full circle, searching for anyone staring at her. The mall was busy enough, easily fifty people within the line of sight, plus more above her on different floors.

No one stood out. Katie screenshotted the text and blocked the new number and wondered how this could still be going on, after all this time.

I'm not being watched.

It's a bluff. It's got to be a bluff.

How is this still happening?

I've changed numbers twice. I've bought privacy apps. I've called the police.

Involving the police worked for Duncan.

Why can't they do anything to keep this crazy asshole out of my life?

Convincing herself that the stalker couldn't possibly be in the mall with her, Katie blocked the latest number and briskly walked to the escalators. As she ascended her eyes were constantly scanning the area.

I don't see anyone watching. Just shoppers. Couples. Mothers pushing strollers. A group of older women doing a mall walk.

Nobody looking at me. Nobody I recognize.

A new bad thought rose up among all the other bad thoughts.

Should I be looking for a disguise? A hat and sunglasses? A fake beard?

If someone's spying on me, it could be anyone.

Katie went up another level, her paranoia rising. She considered going to mall security, but dismissed it.

If no one is actually following me, what can they do?

Then she considered her personal defense items. In Spoonward, Katie carried pepper spray. But TSA didn't allow it on flights, so all she had was her personal keychain alarm—kind of an electronic rape whistle Duncan had given her—which let out a piercing electronic shriek when pressed.

It is super loud and can draw attention. But it likely wouldn't scare away this stalker.

Nothing will scare away this stalker.

Katie shook her head quickly, as if trying to fling away the fear.

It's just gaslighting. Trying to scare me.

No one is watching.

No one is stalking.

It's just some harassing texts.

There's no threat.

I'm not in danger.

I'm not in—

YOU THINK YOU CAN GET AWAY BY GOING UP?

Katie almost dropped her phone.

She raised it to take a screenshot and block, and another text came on her screen.

IF YOU BLOCK ANOTHER NUMBER I'M GOING TO FUCKING KILL DUNCAN

Then a picture popped onto the screen.

A picture of Duncan. Fishing on his pontoon, with his buddies Chuck and Stu.

DUNCAN

SAME TIME...

"How's the sting?" Stu asked.

Duncan, whose eyes had been closed, stared up at his friend, and then he glanced down at his leg.

Still swollen and red, but the pain had receded.

"Better."

"Could have been some kind of wasp. Did you know there are over one hundred thousand species of wasp?"

"Why would I know that?" Duncan asked.

Why would anyone know that was the better question.

"Stu is the Bug Lord," Chuck said, throwing out another cast. "Oh mighty Bug Lord, please tell us how many insects there are in the world."

Stu bit. "All insects combined? That's over 10 quintillion. Ten with eighteen zeroes. It's an unimaginable number. Over a billion metric tons. They weigh more than all people and all livestock, combined. Think human beings are masters of this planet? We're not even close. It's arthropods for the win."

Chuck did a mock bow. "Thank you, Bug Lord. We are but your humble pupils."

"You mean my humble pupas," Stu said, then laughed at his own pun.

They'd fished the clearing in the marsh for a solid half an hour, without a single bite. Duncan had tried two more times to start the boat, and had failed both times. The day had gotten hotter, the bottled water was gone, and there weren't any signs of another boat anywhere on the lake except for that one deeper in the marsh that hadn't moved.

At least the bugs have stayed away.

"I am parched, guys." Chuck mopped some sweat off his brow with his forearm. "Want to try it again, Duncan?"

Duncan once again tried to start the boat.

And once again it failed to start.

After a moment of frustrated silence, Stu said, "Your boat sucks."

"It's better than your boat."

"If I had a boat, I'd have one that starts," Stu countered. Then he gave the rickety gunwale aluminum railing a shake. "And one that wasn't held together with zip ties."

"Zip ties are like duct tape," Duncan said. "A million uses."

"So why didn't you use duct tape on the railings?" Stu asked.

"I didn't have any."

Duncan rubbed his sore leg, wondering what to do next.

"Fire," Chuck said. "Gotta be the plugs. No combustion."

"We've been waiting for the spark plugs to dry out. How long do we have to wait?"

"If they're gunked they won't dry. They need to be wiped off."

"All I have are the needle-nose pliers," Duncan reminded him. "You said they're the wrong tool."

"They are. Break a plug, we're screwed."

"We're already screwed," Stu chimed in. "Unless we finally get some sort of breeze, we're dead in the water. And I am thirsty. Really, really thirsty. Beer sounds so good right now."

So what are the options?

Try to clean the spark plugs after taking them out with pliers?

Or wade into the leech-infested marsh and try to make it to shore without getting stuck in the muck?

Duncan remembered the muck. He remembered it all too well. Him and Woof, slowly sinking, scared out of their minds.

So he reached for the pliers and went back to the outboard, unplugged the wire, and gazed at the first spark plug. The tips were just long enough to reach the hex shell where a socket would fit. Duncan clamped down tight, twisting... twisting...

The tips slipped.

He tried again, putting his shoulders into it, and the plug began to turn.

After getting it started Duncan used his fingers to finish twisting it free. Sure enough the threads were dirty and the electrodes black and fuzzy, with oil and carbon completely filling the gap.

"You were right, Chuck. It's fouled."

"Give it here."

Duncan handed it to Chuck to clean off, then tried to loosen the second plug.

It was really stuck in there. Duncan grunted with effort, his back tightening, his hands clenched white, the cords in his neck stretched out like steel cables.

"Don't crack the ceramic, bro," Chuck warned.

Duncan squeezed his eyes shut, seeing stars, his ears ringing, putting all his strength into it—

—and then giving up.

"I can't get it." Duncan wiped the sweat off his forehead with his forearm, then scratched the bump on his sore thigh.

Why did I have to go into the goddamn marsh?

Again?

Didn't I learn my lesson from last time?

"Maybe only one was bad," Chuck suggested. He handed over the plug he'd polished. "Put this back and try."

Duncan took the spark plug and carefully placed it back in the socket. He tightened, first with his fingers, then with the pliers. After replacing the wire, Duncan sat back in the captain's chair and gave the ignition key a desperate twist—

—and the engine caught.

Not prepared to celebrate until they were back on his dock and heading for beer, Duncan shifted into gear and the boat lurched forward. He eyed the bare spot in the reeds where they'd entered, keeping the speed low, checking behind him to make sure the trim was high enough so he didn't get the lower end foul with muck and weeds again because he didn't want to risk another stall.

Maybe it's time to overhaul this old motor, clean it top to bottom. Too hot to fish today anyway. With Chuck helping, a few beers, and some online videos, we can strip it down to the bolts and make sure everything works perfect.

Chuck gave him a pat on the shoulder. "Teamwork makes the dream—"

The motor coughed, then died.

Undeterred, Duncan pulled the shifter back into neutral and tried to start it again.

It chugged, but didn't catch.

Again… same thing.

Again… same thing.

Again… same goddamn thing.

Duncan smacked the steering wheel with his palm in frustration as the pontoon slowed down and eventually came to a stop in the reeds.

There was a slapping sound, and Chuck swore, "Goddamn flies."

"Goddamn flies?" Stu snorted. "Goddamn boat."

Duncan scratched his thigh. "Gotta be the other plug. We just need to get it loose."

"Lemme try." Chuck held his palm out for the pliers, and Duncan tossed them over.

Chuck pulled off the wire and spent a minute grunting and straining, unable to get the plug out.

"Any chance you got some WD-40 on this boat?"

"Naw." Duncan scratched his thigh. "Got some reel oil in the tackle box."

"We can try it."

Duncan opened his Umco and fished around the bottom to find the tiny vial of oil that came with a reel he'd bought years ago. He found it under the first-aid kit, and gripped the clear plastic bottle between his thumb and index finger and gave it a shake.

A few drops left.

He passed it to Chuck, who squeezed the contents onto the spark plug.

Duncan scratched his thigh again, then took a closer look. A serious bump had formed, with a yellowish top, like a boil. Duncan pressed it, and winced at the instant pain that rivaled the original sting.

"Stu, got a bug question."

"As the Bug Lord, I shall answer appropriately. Speak, minion."

"Can bugs kill a person?" Duncan asked.

Stu scratched his chubby cheek. "That's complicated. They have, throughout history. Half of the people who have ever lived have died of malaria, spread by mosquitos. That's 52 billion people, going back to the dawn of humanity."

"An unimaginable number," Chuck teased.

"Plus they carry other viruses, hemorrhagic fever, encephalitis, parasitic worms. Bubonic plague, the black death, was spread by flea bites. That's two hundred million. Ticks and flies can spread bacteria, viruses, parasites, protozoa. Want to gross yourself out? Google images of *Leishmaniasis*. A sandfly bite spreads protozoa that breed in the skin and cause these gaping ulcers—"

"How about insects killing people without any diseases?" Duncan interrupted, purposely.

"You mean by themselves? Just venom?"

Duncan nodded.

Stu scratched his arm. "Only about a hundred people die a year from insect stings in the US. And that is usually a result of anaphylactic shock; an allergic reaction. Insect venom by itself is delivered in such small amounts, and it takes a lot of venom to kill a person. There have been a few cases of babies being stung to death, like a parent leaving a stroller next to a wasp nest."

"Jesus," Chuck coughed and spat, "that's awful."

"But an adult? Even with multiple stings? I don't know any cases where that happened."

"How about killer bees?" Chuck asked.

Stu shrugged. "The Africanized honey bee isn't more venomous than indigenous bees. It's just more aggressive. There have been stories of ants in South America that take over towns and eat everything that can't run away. Like a colony of a few billion marching ants swarming over a hospital, the people evacuate but leave a patient behind. Can you imagine? You're a burn victim, or recovering from surgery, stuck in a bed, unable to move, and then you're slowly covered with biting, stinging ants."

"That's horrible," Duncan said. "On the big island, in Hawaii, we had a problem with Little Fire Ants."

"Electric ants." Stu nodded rapidly. "*Wasmannia auropunctata*. They're so tiny you can barely see them unless you're really close up."

"You can sure feel them, though."

"They stung you?" Chuck asked.

"I was barefoot, and I stepped in some dead leaves. They swarmed up my ankle like I was wearing a red sock. It felt like I was being electrocuted. Hurt even more than that time I broke my finger. Whole foot swelled up, had welts for a week."

"Insects have been used as forms of execution by torture." Stu was obviously relishing the conversation. "There have been stories of Native American tribes smearing a victim with honey and staking them to an ant hill. Sometimes with the eyelids cut off, or skewers in the mouth forcing it open. Insects would sting the mucus membranes, and inflammation would close the airways. Suffocating in agony."

"Nice," Chuck said.

"Worse was scaphism. Do you want to hear about it?"

"Not really," Duncan said.

Stu glanced at Chuck, who shook his head. "Nope."

"Scaphism involved taking a person—"

"He's telling us anyway," Duncan said.

"—and tying them up, naked, in a boat. You force-feed them milk and honey, which causes diarrhea—"

"Gross," Chuck said.

"—which fills up the boat, attracting bugs. So then the victim is floated out into a bog or swamp—"

"Or marsh," Duncan interrupted.

"—and the bugs begin to feast. They can't be slapped or waved away because you're tied up. So they bite and they sting. But they do more than bite and sting. They also wallow in your shit… and lay eggs… *everywhere*."

Chuck began to laugh. "Jesus, man, there really is something wrong with you."

Stu laughed along. "Persian form of execution. Happened to a soldier named Mithridates. Supposedly took him seventeen days to die."

"I call bullshit," Duncan said. "Would have died of thirst before that."

"They kept feeding him more milk and honey."

"Guy wouldn't have drank it."

"They pricked his eyes until he swallowed."

"Jesus." Duncan rubbed his eyes. "I'm sorry I asked. Chuck, can you give the plug another try?"

Chuck approached the outboard, rolled his head on his neck in an apparent attempt to loosen up, and went at the spark plug again.

He grunted.

He strained.

He failed.

"Did you freakin' glue it in?" he asked.

Shit.

"Maybe if we both try?" Duncan suggested.

Chuck agreed, and Duncan put his hands on the handles of the pliers, and Chuck put his hands on Duncan's. They both twisted until Duncan felt like his fingers were cracking and his skin was rubbing off.

"Stop. Stop!" Chuck let go and Duncan dropped the pliers onto the floor of the boat and shook his hands, trying to get the pain to fade. "Shit, that sucker won't budge."

"Maybe it requires a more scientific touch," Stu said, picking up the pliers and coming over to the stern.

They gave him a wide berth, and Stu placed the pliers on the spark plug and began to strain with effort.

"Careful," Chuck warned. "Don't break the plug."

Stu heaved, his face turning stop-sign red.

He gave up after less than five seconds.

"I think I loosened it," he declared, in the lamest way possible.

"Lemme try again." Chuck raised his hand.

Stu tossed the pliers, a poor toss, and Duncan watched in horror as Chuck tried to make the catch and the tool bounced off of his fingers—

—and went right over the edge of the boat, plopping into the water.

"Shit," Stu said. "Sorry, Duncan."

"Yeah," Chuck concurred. "Sorry, man."

Duncan rubbed his eyes. "Oh man, guys. Just… man."

"Seriously?" Stu said. "They were an old set of pliers. You can get them for fifty cents at a thrift store."

"I got a dozen pairs of pliers," Chuck said. "Decent brands. I'll give you one."

"It's not the money," Duncan lamented. "I've got five pairs of pliers."

"So why the sad face?" Chuck asked.

"Those were the only needle-nose pliers I had on the boat, guys."

The three men exchanged glances.

"How about other pliers?" Chuck asked.

"I've got my Swiss Army knife." The one Josh had given him so many years ago. "It has pliers. Good for taking out fish hooks, but too small for a spark plug."

Stu uttered a nervous laugh. "So, what now? We have to row back?"

That would have been possible if Duncan had bought a bass boat. Bass boats had an emergency oar. Most bass boats also had a trolling motor along with a gas motor.

But Duncan had gone for the pontoon. The party barge.

You can't row a party barge.

"No oar locks on a pontoon," Duncan said, "and no place on board to paddle from. But we can check. Maybe the previous owners left something."

On the off chance that there was an oar stashed somewhere on board, Duncan told his friends to open the padded seats. Beneath the cushions was storage space, usually used to hold life jackets and floats.

They found four jackets, a rusty old air horn, some extra nylon rope attached to an anchor, and a fire extinguisher.

But no oars.

"I have zero signal," Stu said, holding up his cell.

"Try mine," Duncan told him.

Stu reached into the bag and checked Duncan's phone. After fiddling with it for a few seconds, he handed it over.

Black screen.

"Stu, did you turn this off when I gave it to you?"

"I just threw it in the bag."

"Dead battery," Duncan said.

"Is there a charger on the boat?" Stu asked.

"It's a 1984 Palm Beach," Duncan said. "The radio has a cassette deck. USB wasn't invented."

"You could have hooked up a port to the battery," Stu said.

"I could have. I could have also kept a spark plug wrench on board. And extra pliers. And oars. And I could have hooked up a goddamn trolling motor in case the engine ever died. But I didn't. I didn't do any of that shit, because I never could have predicted I'd be in this situation. So let's move on. Chuck? Phone?"

"Left my cell at the cabin," Chuck said without prompting. "Captain's rules, right?"

Shit. Shit shit shit.

What the hell are we supposed to do?

Being stranded on a lake, even a big lake like Niboowin, was usually nothing more than an inconvenience. All boats eventually floated to shore. Before that happened, there was the option to swim. And cell phones weren't even needed to call for help; in the tourist season, there were usually plenty of other watercraft within earshot.

So there was no reason to panic yet. The wind would eventually come back and carry them out of the reeds. Or another boat would come by. Or Stu would get reception on his phone. Or, absolute worst case, they could put on the life jackets and doggy paddle out of the marsh.

"Hey!"

Chuck's shout startled Duncan out of his thoughts. He stared at his buddy, saw Chuck had his hands cupped around his mouth.

"We're stuck!"

Duncan followed Chuck's gaze, saw he was yelling at the bass boat, floating a hundred or so meters away. The same one that lured Duncan into the marsh because it was the only other boat on the lake. There was a guy sitting on the bow seat, but it was too far away, with too many tall reeds between them, to make out any detail.

"Hey! We need some help over here!" Chuck waved his arms in the universal *look at me* gesture.

"I don't feel so…"

Stu staggered and began to pitch forward. Duncan managed to reach out and grab his elbow, steadying him before he face-planted. He helped Stu onto one of the seats, gripping him by the shoulders and staring into his face.

Stu appeared pale. Zombie-pale.

"Dude, your hand…"

Chuck pointed, and Duncan saw the blood dripping down Stu's fingers.

"I'm okay. Just a little dizzy." Stu held up his palm. A small circle, no bigger than a match head, was oozing blood. "Leeches secrete hirudin. It's a peptide… prevents the blood from clotting."

"I think I got some bandages in the tackle box."

"That won't help."

Duncan eyed the Rorschach splotches of blood on Stu's bare toes. "Dude, you're bleeding a lot."

"It should stop on its own. If it keeps up, I'll make some kind of tourniquet."

"HEY!" Chuck scowled to Duncan. "That asshole isn't answering."

"Might not hear us." But Duncan didn't believe his own words. Sounds tended to carry over open stretches of water. Especially when there wasn't any wind, like now.

Chuck threw up his arms. "Well this is fucking ridiculous. What the hell are we supposed to do?"

Duncan opened his tackle box and gave Stu the first-aid kit. He also grabbed the walkie-talkie at the bottom, switching the knob to turn it on.

It crackled to life.

Twenty-four channels.

Duncan started with Channel 1. The most common channel, used by his family, and the neighbors, Sun and Andy.

"Hello? This is Duncan VanCamp. My friends and I are stuck in a boat in the marsh on Big Lake Niboowin. Can anyone hear me? Repeat, we are stuck on the lake and need help. Can anyone hear me?"

SUN

A BIT EARLIER...

"This isn't right," Sun said, peering into the microscope.

She was in her home veterinary office and had the hornet head on a slide, magnification via a 4x scanning objective lens and a 10x eyepiece.

"Have you seen this stinger?" Andy asked. He was prodding the hornet's body, which was in a petri dish, using a wooden tongue depressor. "It's longer than my dick."

Sun normally would have laughed at that, but the head was freaking her out a bit.

"Look at this." She moved over and let Andy squint into the scope. "What do you see?"

"A gross bug head."

"A gross bug head with what looks like a mammalian eye. And what does that eye remind you of?"

Andy stared at her, his face going pale. "You're not saying..."

"I don't know what to say. I'm going to do a quick dissection, see if I can confirm."

"Should we call Frank?"

They'd named their child Francis after their close friend, Dr. Frank Belgium.

"If my suspicions are confirmed, Frank needs to know." Sun checked her Citizen watch. "Our son gets out of summer school in two hours. Let me dissect this, figure out if it's *Vespidae* or something else. You can check the windows and isolate the animals."

"On it."

While Andy left to secure their many pets, Sun located a book on *Hymenoptera* anatomy from her shelf and then unwrapped a fresh scalpel. She checked the shelves for her dissection tools, which consisted of a small aluminum drip pan filled with two centimeters of white wax, a pack of pins, and a plastic squeeze bottle containing lightly tinted distilled water. She tugged on some nitrile gloves, pulled her vet kit from her back pocket, and began the task of pulling the wings and legs from the insect's body.

After setting the appendages aside she gently gripped the wasp in her fingers and began to cut the underside of the exoskeleton, starting at the thorax, through the connective petiole, then continuing on through the abdomen. As she did the stinger wiggled, and Sun dropped the bug in surprise. It fell onto the wax and lay there, motionless.

Reflex action. It's dead.

But she made no move to pick it up again, instead continuing to stare.

Dead. Totally dead.

I'm probably exaggerating the threat.

This is probably something entirely mundane, and I'm overreacting.

She steeled herself, then used forceps and a scalpel to pry open the shell and pin each half to the wax, opening the insect up to view its anatomy.

The anatomy was… off.

Sun added a few drops of water, tinting the opaque organs light blue to make them easier to see, then referred to the *Vespidae* section of her book for comparison.

This thing has no midgut. Or hindgut.

It doesn't even have a rectum.

Instead it seems to be filled with tiny, round parasites.

Sun wanted to get it under the microscope, but first she checked the stinger.

It has no venom sac.

Wait… are these…?

She used tweezers to tug out the internals and the parasites in the abdomen, carefully placed them on a slide, teased them apart so nothing overlapped, and then gave it a look.

Uh-oh.

The stinger isn't for defense. It's a true ovipositor.

And those tiny parasites…

Sun switched to a low power objective lens, 10x. With the eyepiece, she was viewing at 100x magnification.

Wow. Just... wow.

Shivering from something other than cold, Sun located the severed wasp head, secured that to a slide using the surface tension of a water droplet, and took a peek through the scope.

Definitely not a compound eye.

Sun plugged her phone into the microscope and snapped a pic. Browsing the web, she went to her favorite search engine and dragged the pic into the search box.

It did not match with photos of wasps.

It matched with photos of *Caprinae*.

Goats. Those really are goat eyes.

There's only one reason I know that insects would have goat eyes.

"Pets are safe."

Sun yelped in surprise at Andy coming up behind her. He went sheepish.

"Sorry. Didn't mean to scare you."

The family had a set policy about not scaring one another. Their lives had been scary enough.

"Stingers evolved from ovipositors," Sun told him.

"Of course they did. Everyone knows that."

Her husband, for sure, did not know that. She continued.

"In early arthropod history, ovipositors developed to deposit eggs in specific locations. Female insects needed to be able to lay them in plants, or directly in the male brood pouch, or under some sort of protective cover. As species diversified, some ovipositors evolved to be used as defense. Stingers, with venom sacs."

"Things just evolve like that?" Andy asked.

"Just because science points to evolution doesn't mean it fully understands evolution."

"So the pointy egg thing became a pointy poison thing."

"A pointy venom thing. Poison is consumed, venom is injected."

"I like it when you sciencesplain to me," Andy said. "It's hot."

Sun had zero desire to flirt at that moment. She pressed on.

"Parasitic wasps are the best of both worlds. They use the stinger to lay eggs, but they lay them inside of other animals. Sometimes this includes a paralyzing venom, so the host is immobilized as the eggs hatch and mature inside of it."

"This is the best of both worlds? Sounds like the worst."

"For the host, yes. It gets eaten alive from the inside out. But for the wasp larvae, the host provides shelter and sustenance."

"You're about to tell me something awful about this wasp, aren't you?"

Sun swallowed, then continued. "Certain insects, like moths and may-flies, never eat. When they mature into their final adult forms, their only purpose is to mate. This wasp I found has no digestive system. No mouth, no rectum, nothing in between. Its only purpose is to sting things and lay eggs inside of them. So when it tried to sting me, it wasn't for food or defense."

"It wanted you to be a baby wasp home," Andy said. "Yuck."

Sun nodded. "We need to put on our bee suits, grab our propane weed burner, and look for wasp nests."

"Sunshine… is this thing natural? Or…?"

Andy didn't need to finish the question.

They'd moved to Big Lake Niboowin to get away from the craziness of the world. But in the recent past, the craziness had caught up with them.

I thought that was finally over.

But what if it isn't?

"I don't know, Andy. Do you… um…"

"Do I feel anything?" Andy asked.

Sun winced, then nodded. The unspoken thing on both of their minds had once possessed Andy.

"No. I don't feel any pull or attachment or link or anything. I feel like myself. Though a lot more nauseous than usual."

"If he was back, do you think you'd sense it?"

"I have no idea. My body was invaded, we can call it a possession, by something we still don't fully understand. Could it have left traces on some cellular or molecular level? Imprints on my DNA? Or on my soul? Maybe. But it doesn't feel like it. I feel like myself."

Sun wasn't sure if she could go through seeing her husband like *that* again. When she didn't reply, Andy pressed.

"I mean it. I think I'm okay. And if it's him… I'll make sure he's dead this time."

"Let's see if there's a hornet's nest on the property," she finally said. "We'll start there."

They went to get their bee suits in their basement walk-in gun safe, so they didn't hear the plaintive voice coming from Channel 1 on their walkie-talkie plugged into the charger in Sun's office.

STU

When Stu was a kid, his fears revolved around social awkwardness. His thick, geek glasses. His zits. His obesity, which was centered in his core so he had skinny arms and legs but a pot belly and earned him the mean nickname *big momma* because they claimed he looked pregnant. His appearance led to insecurity, which led to more insecurity, and he disappeared in his studies and books and solo videogames and both ignored and was ignored by his peers of both sexes.

In college, his face cleared up, he began to eat better and work out, and his geek glasses somehow became en vogue. He made friends, finally got laid, and pursued a career in science with a fearlessness no one expected.

Stu hunted and captured desert scorpions at night using nothing more than a UV light and a shoe box. He milked tarantulas for their venom. He went swimming with Portuguese man o' war jellyfish. He respected Mother Nature, but didn't fear her. Venomous creatures that freaked most people out, like centipedes and wasps and snakes, were fascinating to Stu. His childhood love of insects blossomed into a lucrative entomology career. He exercised caution when dealing with dangerous specimens, but he was never afraid.

This leech bite, however, made him more than a bit concerned.

Leeches had sucked on Stu before. As a rite of passage, in college, all the students in his taxonomy class put their hand in a leech jar for as long as they could stand it, and the one with the most sticking to them won a hundred-dollar pot. Stu had emerged with twenty-six, one Benjamin richer.

But after removing those *Hirudo medicinalis*, the wounds had only oozed for a few minutes before clotting. Bleeding had been minimal, pain negligible.

The leech bite currently on his hand dripped like he'd yanked a nail out of his palm. Plus, it ached.

It might have been because the leech vomited. The correct way to remove a bloodsucker was to quickly break the suction by scraping it off using a fingernail or credit card edge. Pulling tended to make the worm regurgitate the contents of its stomach into the open wound.

Stu had stretched out the leech to show off; he found it funny to gross people out. In hindsight, a stupid move. He had no idea how much blood he'd lost, but the growing puddle between his feet had to be a few ounces. Maybe more than half a pint. And it didn't seem to be slowing down.

Which made him think that his offhand comment to Duncan—that it could have been a new species—had some merit. All entomologists secretly longed to discover some new bug. The one who discovered it got to name it. That looked great on a Wikipedia page. And a resume. When Stu finished the research aspect of his career, he wanted to teach. A peer-reviewed, published paper about the species named after him would go a long way to getting him a position at a good university.

He stared at his wound, watching it drip drip drip drip drip, and considered his options. First, he needed to stop the bleeding. But a close second was the remains of the leech-infested bass, which had burst when thrown back into the lake, though large pieces of it still floated next to the boat.

Duncan would throw a hissy fit it I netted a chunk and brought it back on board.

Either I talk him into it, or do it without him noticing.

He decided to try the first option. "Duncan?"

"Celox," Duncan said.

"Huh?"

"It's in a white packet in the first-aid kit. It clots the blood."

Stu unzipped the red plastic pouch and hunted for something called Celox. He found three of them in pouches, each individually packaged and stuck together like condoms. Squinting at the instructions he read that it contained hemostatic granules meant to be poured onto a wound.

Says it clots blood containing anticoagulants, like leech enzymes.

Doesn't list ingredients.

What sort of medicine doesn't list the ingredients?

Maybe I'm a skeptic, but hard pass.

I can do more research when I have Internet access, but right now I'm sticking to what I know.

Stu glanced at Duncan, saw he was messing with the walkie-talkie, and put the Celox back in the kit, grabbing a plastic bandage instead. He unwrapped and stretched it over the leech bite.

"So, what's the emergency protocol for being stuck?" he asked.

Duncan looked up from his radio. "There is no protocol. This normally doesn't happen."

Stu didn't understand. "The motor is broken. So how do we get back to shore?"

"There's usually a drift."

"You've gotten stuck before. What did you do?"

"I called for help."

Stu frowned. "On that Toys R Us radio?"

"It's waterproof, shock-resistant, and has a range of twenty miles. When I was a kid and got stuck I called like Chuck just did. Yelling for other boats. This is a popular lake. There are always boats around."

Stu did a quick 360 of the lake. The only other boat he saw was that guy in the reeds who wasn't responding to them.

"So what if there aren't any other boats because no one else is stupid enough to go on the lake when the National Weather Service tells people not to go outside because of the wildfires?"

Duncan shrugged. Stu felt his blood pressure in his ears, his heartbeat thrumming.

"Isn't there some kind of emergency plan?" Stu's voice came out high and squeaky.

"I never needed a plan," Duncan barked. "There were always other boats out there. One will come along. It's the start of the tourist season. I know the AQI is bad, but we've been out here for hours and we're doing okay. We just need to keep an eye out, and get their attention when we see them."

"This is ridiculous. And totally irresponsible, Duncan."

"The pontoon has been running fine, Stu. And there's normally people on the lake. Or a breeze."

"And now there's neither."

"Except for that guy." Chuck pointed to the boat seventy or so meters away, surrounded by bullrush. "HEY!" Chuck yelled again. "Is this asshole deaf? Help me out, guys. Shout *help* on three. One, two, three…"

The trio all called out *HELP!* to the guy in the bass boat.

The guy didn't answer. He didn't even seem to move in his chair.

A fly buzzed past Stu, and he lost focus on the dude in the boat to indulge in his habit of trying to identify whatever insect he just saw.

Green. Green usually means Calliphoridae *or* Muscidae.

That was pretty damn big for either, though. Two centimeters long. The size of Tabandae; *a horsefly.*

Stu got another brief look when it circled back and landed near his feet, on a spatter of blood.

Its attraction to blood could mean Calliphoridae. *A blow fly. Blow flies were so named in medieval times. They laid eggs on dead animals and dung. When meat had maggots—maggots were the larvae that hatched from the eggs—the meat was called* fly blown.

Stu leaned down, peering at the insect.

Feeding on blood means it's a female. They need to consume protein to lay their eggs. A good way to tell is—

In a blur, the fly took flight and zoomed directly at Stu's eye, bouncing off the lens of his glasses with an audible *fffwip.*

Stu flinched, swatted at empty air, and then jerked away as it buzzed past his ear.

"I thought you loved bugs." Chuck, being his usual asshole self.

"You love muscle cars," Stu countered. "Does that mean you want to get hit by a Dodge Charger?"

"I'd prefer the Challenger."

Duncan repeated his plea for help into the walkie-talkie, and Chuck howled at the same moment he slapped himself in the right cheek.

Chuck immediately doubled over and began to rock up and down and shout out a string of swear words, both hands clasped to his face.

"My eye! Freakin' bug bit my eye!"

Stu immediately went to him, and Duncan clipped the radio to the waistband of his shorts and grabbed his friend's shoulder.

"You okay?"

"I'm not okay! Feels like I got an icepick in my damn eye!"

"Let me see." Stu tried to gently tug Chuck's hand away from his face, but Chuck shook himself free.

"Don't touch me! Nobody touch me! God damn this HURTS!"

Chuck stepped away, and his eyes fell to the floor of the boat and began to scan it, foot by foot.

There, next to the tackle box.

Dead bug.

Stu knelt next to it and gently picked up the corpse by its crooked wings. He set it in his palm and scrutinized the insect, its head partially mashed.

Same body and coloring as a blow fly, but much bigger than any he'd heard of. But its size wasn't the only strange thing about it.

The eyes are… wrong. They don't look like fly eyes at all.

And at the end of its abdomen, there was something that shouldn't be there, making Stu question if this was actually a fly or some other type of insect.

Because flies bite. But this one has defied evolution, speciation, and all known science and taxonomy.

Because this fly has a stinger.

LEO

Thirty miles from Yonder Bay on I-94 heading west and nearing the mid-size town of Greenport, Leo's right foot fell off.

He didn't know it happened until he tried to take a step and his body pitched forward too far, causing him to break the fall with his hands and land in a push-up position on the ground.

Leo looked underneath him, seeing the boot still upright, the wool sock hanging over the side like a dog's tongue on a hot day.

He crawled to it, took the cheese grater off of his trench coat belt, and got to work.

There wasn't much to work with on the foot itself. It had come off at the ankle bones, and Leo was worried that shaving off too much would inhibit flexibility and make walking impossible. So he pared down what he could with the boning knife, then frayed the flesh with the small-hole side of the grater, likely used for lemon zesting or nutmeg.

But you wouldn't want this sprinkled on top of your eggnog.

Now on to the fun part...

Peeking out of his tight twist of severed muscles and tendons was the cartilage-wrapped end of a large bone (*the tibia? the fibula?*) which proved extremely sensitive to being rasped. Leo didn't know how many nerve endings were in bones, but this qualified as torture. Especially since the aspirin had long ago worn off.

So he screamed. A lot. So much he damaged his vocal chords, which unfortunately repaired themselves faster than it took him to shave off half an inch of bone and tissue.

When he got the blood flowing pretty good he found the easiest way to reconnect his parts was to pull his sock back on, which pulled his shoe back on, which pulled his foot back on.

As he healed alongside the road, watching the cars on the highway pass, his eyes landed on an eighteen-wheeler with a bright advertisement painted on its trailer for a large farming supply store chain. It had its right turn blinker on, and was slowing down to take the next exit. At the exit stood a large sign for said chain store, proclaiming it open 24 hours a day and less than one mile to the south.

Not the direction the Tug wants me to go.

But those farm and feed stores sell hardware and tools.

And this cheese grater isn't cutting it.

Literally.

My other hand and other foot are really starting to hurt.

I need to find something… more efficient.

He gave his reattached foot a tentative twist, and it seemed to have stuck back together pretty good. After a few careful steps, testing weight and balance, Leo followed the direction of the truck off the exit ramp and headed for the store.

Halfway there his ankle hyper-extended in a very wrong and very painful way, and he fell again.

He stared at his foot, bending outward so far that the sole of his boot was touching his calf. But the dislocated foot wasn't floppy or loose; bone was tight against bone and it seemed to be locked or jammed that way.

Leo spent a bad sixty seconds whacking his foot against the pavement, trying to rebreak the bones to straighten it out. There was bleeding, and a cheeky crow flew down and took a peck at his soaked pants leg, trying to grab the gory fabric and tug off a piece for itself.

He shooed the bird away and banged his foot back in a position that seemed normalish. Tough to gauge, because his ankle had now swelled up to volleyball size, and he had to undo his boot laces to stop the leather from splitting.

The sight of his swollen foot made his vision go all wavy and dark and Leo likely passed out, because the next thing he knew there were three crows pecking at his bloody foot, one trying to fly away with a shoelace and pulling like a hooked fish.

Leo picked up some roadside gravel, scared away the crows, and managed to get upright again, this time walking slower and favoring his good leg.

By the time he got to the farm supply store his hand seemed ready to fall off, and his elbows weren't feeling so good either.

What happens if both arms fall off? Do I reattach them using my teeth?

A store employee approached Leo. Tall, stocky, bald, nametag ROB. "Can I help you, sir?"

"Do you have anything for livestock?" Leo asked.

"We have everything you could possibly need. Can you be more specific?"

"Butchering livestock."

"Do you mean carving knives?"

"Big ones. One that could cut off a cow's leg."

"So, a bone saw?"

"A bone saw might work." Leo rubbed his chin. "Are there automatic bone saws?"

"We have some butcher saws that run on 120 volts and 240 volts."

"How about battery powered?"

The employee blinked. "A battery powered bone saw?"

"Something portable. Let's say I wanted to cut off a cow's leg and there weren't any electric outlets."

"Like you were sneaking up on a cow while it was grazing?"

Leo nodded, then realized how ridiculous that sounded.

"Forget it," Leo said. "How about a Sawzall?"

"Reciprocating saws are in Aisle 37, right side. I don't recommend you trying to sneak up on a cow with one of those. The noise would scare them off."

"Thanks."

"You could try ear protection," Rob said.

"Ear protection?"

"You put noise-dampening earmuffs on the cow, so it doesn't hear you coming."

"I'll keep that in mind," Leo said, limping away. Rob followed behind him.

Leo found the Sawzalls, but they seemed too big to lug around. Especially if he had to walk another fifty miles. The circular saws seemed too heavy. The jigsaws too small. He picked up a multitool with a vibrating sander that also had a small saw blade.

"That won't take off a cow's leg," Rob told him. "If you're looking for something compact, check out the angle grinders over here."

Leo spent a moment staring at angle grinders. They were all about eighteen inches long, with 4.5-inch circular blades. The base grip was held like a flashlight or sword, and then they also had a perpendicular handle to keep it steady.

"Which is the best?" Leo asked.

"You'll want to go with twenty volts." Rob pointed. "Those three brands are all top-of-the-line."

"Which has the longest battery life?"

"I like this one." Rob picked up a boxed grinder. "On a full charge, you could probably cut off the legs of three to four cows. If you're not a math guy, that's sixteen legs."

"Do the batteries come charged?"

Rob raised an eyebrow. "Really eager to get out in that pasture?"

Leo gave him a blank stare.

"These come charged, yes."

"How about blade options?"

Rob pointed out items hanging on the pegboard wall. "Those are cutting blades, and those are grinding blades. Both can get through bones."

"What's that?" Leo indicated one that looked like a chainsaw, but was circular.

"Carving blade. Let's say you wanted to hollow out the cow's skull, carve out the brains. That's your go-to."

I'm not sure if this guy thinks he's funny, or if he's out of his mind.

Either way, Leo grabbed the carving blade, the other two blades Rob mentioned, and a two-pack of extra batteries.

"There are also blades for cutting metal," Rob said. "You know, in case it's a robot cow."

So he's being funny. For some reason, that's somewhat disappointing.

"Backpacks?" Leo asked.

"Camping, Aisle 16. Are you looking for a rucksack, or something larger? Say… to carry some cow legs?"

Leo limped off to the camping section, and Rob continued to tag along, whistling to himself, apparently happy to play the amusing sidekick.

Without asking for advice, Leo selected a small, black backpack. He sat on the floor and used his boning knife to begin unboxing his items.

Rob lost his happy-go-lucky demeanor. "You, uh, can't do that."

"I'm taking everything. I want to make sure it all works, and it fits in the pack."

Leo quickly attached the grinding blade to the grinder, slapped in the rechargeable battery, and pressed the trigger.

It whirred to life, giving off a high-pitched whine.

Leo set it down, then removed the shoe and sock from his newly attached foot, revealing his severely swollen ankle. The skin was stretched so tight, it visibly throbbed with his pulse.

"Holy hell!" Rob took a step back. "You... you really need to get that looked at."

"Can't tie my shoe with this swelling," Leo said.

"No kidding. It looks like someone inflated your ankle. Like a giant flesh balloon. With some toes on the end. How can you walk around on that?"

"I have a pretty good tolerance for pain."

"Do you want me to call an ambulance or something?"

"No. I got it."

Leo picked up the grinder and switched it on, watching Rob laugh nervously.

"You're not actually going to—"

Leo touched the spinning disc to his ankle, the blade slicing a neat line across his skin and instantly releasing the pressure, an eruption of blood squirting all over Rob like it had been shot from a Super Soaker.

Rob backpedaled, his hands pressed over his mouth as vomit spurted through his fingers. Leo massaged his loose flesh then pulled his sock on and pushed the skin folds inside like he was tucking in a shirt. Then he tugged his boot back on, able to tie his laces, and stuck his new tools into his new backpack.

"I was just kidding about the cows," Leo told Rob, who'd fallen onto his ass. "This is a personal grooming appliance."

Rob didn't offer any quips. Instead, his eyelids fluttered and he fainted.

So much for my comic relief.

Leo shouldered the pack and walked out of the store without paying, and no one paid any attention because he'd removed the alarm tags when he'd unboxed the items, and store security was attending to the unconscious employee and bloody clean-up in Aisle 16.

Back outside, Leo followed the Tug down I-94 west, then exited on WI-25 heading north, a newfound spring in his step.

DUNCAN

SAME TIME...

Chuck sat on the vinyl-covered pontoon bench seat, clutching his eye with both hands, while Duncan hovered over him, his face awash with concern.

"Lemme me take a look, man."

"Hurts so bad." Chuck sounded less like Chuck and more like a schoolboy who fell off his bike.

"I know it hurts, Chuck. Lemme see it."

"You're not a med tech, Duncan," Stu reminded him. "You pass out when you see blood, and you haven't even taken an EMT class."

"I took some online courses."

"You think that's enough?"

Duncan shot back, "It's enough to know you need to put some damn Celox on your leech bite, Stu. You're leaking blood down your leg. Those online classes are why I keep Celox in my first-aid kit. It stops bleeding."

Stu stared at his red soaked bandage and Duncan put his hand on Chuck's shoulder. "Show me your eye, brother."

Chuck slowly dragged his hands away from his face. His eyelids were squeezed shut, but the swelling had already begun in earnest.

"Looks like someone punched you," Stu offered. "It's red and turning purple. Some insects are attracted to lacrimal secretions. Tears."

"Stu, shut up," Duncan told him. "And use the Celox."

"I don't trust pouring weird powder into an open sore."

"You're a scientist," Duncan reminded him.

"Scientists are skeptics. I've never heard of coagulating powder. I want to do some research before I stick it into my damn body."

Duncan ignored him. "Can you open your eye, Chuck?"

"It's not open now?"

Chuck's eye looked like a maroon lemon with an eyelash glued to the middle.

"I'm going to take my fingers and gently spread it open. Okay?"

Chuck nodded. Duncan sucked in a breath and steeled his wobbly legs and forced his stomach not to clench as he gingerly touched his friend's puffy face, trying to pry apart the mottled flesh. But when he spread Chuck's eyelids open, all he saw was more red.

A bright red eyeball, with a bumpy yellow pupil.

It doesn't even look human. It looks like some monster or zombie eye, bulging and slathered in mucus.

That's when Duncan realized what he was looking at.

That's not his pupil. It's the lower white of his eye with something stuck in it. Some foreign body that looks like a discolored pupil.

A stinger?

"Stu, do flies have stingers?"

"That one did. Never saw anything like it."

"Do they detach their stingers, like bees?"

"Sting autonomy? No. The fly that got Chuck still has its stinger, if it's even a real stinger. Lemme see." Stu stood behind Duncan, peering over his shoulder. "Holy shit, that's disgusting! What the fuck, man!"

Duncan whirled on his friend. "Stu, you're not helping."

"Sorry. Jesus, Chuck, does it hurt?"

"My whole eyeball is throbbing. It feels like there's something inside."

"Shit." Stu walked away, pacing to the stern of the pontoon. "Shit. Shit. Shit. It's an ovipositor. Shit."

"Ovi—what?" Chuck asked.

Duncan had no idea what that word meant, either. He scratched at his sore thigh and felt something weird.

Something… moving.

He glanced down at his leg. The fly bite he'd gotten earlier had burst like a zit, with a big, moist drop of pus coming out.

Except—

The pus is wiggling.

Because it isn't pus. It's some sort of worm, squirming its way out of my wound.

Duncan tried to brush the creature off, but it pulled itself inward, retreating back inside Duncan's body.

I'm going to be sick.

I'm going to pass out.

"What's happening?" Chuck asked, his voice high-pitched and frantic.

I need to keep my shit together.

I can do this.

I can get over my squeamishness.

Duncan dropped to one knee and pressed his thumbs on either side of the worm and tried to squeeze it out. The pain, and the pressure, made his vision get spinny. Grunting with effort, Duncan pinched hard as he could, and the thing shot out of his leg like a spit watermelon seed and bounced onto the pontoon flooring where it tried to squirm away.

Duncan reflexively stomped on it.

"What was that?" Chuck groaned. "Was that in your leg?"

"Fly larva," Stu said. "That fly laid an egg inside you, it hatched into a pupa."

"Like the movie *Alien*?" Chuck said, at this point fully hysterical. "Do I have some kind of maggot growing in my eye?!?"

"Keep calm, Chuck." Duncan turned to Stu. "We need to get him to a hospital."

"Get it out of my eye, Duncan!"

"Screw-worm flies—*Cochliomyia hominivorax*— they lay eggs in open wounds." Stu took off his glasses and tried cleaning them on his shirt. "Their maggots eat the host's tissue as they grow. Most bugs prefer necrotic—dead—tissue, but the screw-fly likes it alive. Botflies, too. They make a little cave inside a victim's flesh, a little carved out home. They live there for weeks. They poke their heads out to breathe. In old times they used to put raw meat over the bite to lure it out. The maggot would chew its way through it in order to get some air."

Chuck clenched his fists and beat them against his hips. "GET IT OUT OF MY EYE, DUNCAN!!!"

Duncan turned the ignition key and tried to start the boat.

It didn't start.

"DUNCAN!"

"Stop yelling, Chuck," Stu turned away. "You're freaking me out."

"I'm freaking out!"

Duncan kept trying to start, without success, until the motor began to click.

Bad sign. The battery is dying.

"This is your goddamn fault, Stu!" Chuck moaned. "Why'd you throw the pliers!"

"Why didn't you catch the pliers!"

"You guys need to stay calm," Duncan said.

Stu pointed at him. "It's your damn fault, Duncan. Piece of shit boat. You got a full first-aid kit and eight thousand damn lures, but you don't have a second pair of pliers?"

"I think I can feel it moving," Chuck moaned. "I can feel it moving in my eye."

"Why didn't you have more than one pair of pliers on the boat? Or a goddamn socket wrench?"

"Because I didn't think we'd get stuck in the middle of the goddamn lake and get attacked by bugs!" Duncan barked back. "It wasn't on my goddamn bingo card for the day!"

Something buzzed by them, and all three men hunkered down, cowering. Duncan grabbed a can of bug spray, and Stu went for the packets of bug repellent wipes. After they covered their skin, and then Chuck's, Duncan said, "No more fighting. Captain's rules. We're friends. We're best friends. Right?"

No one answered.

"C'mon, guys," Duncan pleaded. "We can do this."

Stu nodded slowly. "You're right. Ride or die. You guys are my brothers. We stick together and figure this out. Chuck?"

Chuck didn't reply. He seemed to be in shock, sitting there with his hands pressed to his face, tears streaking down his good eye.

"Chuck," Duncan soothed. "We need you, buddy."

"Ride or die," Chuck whispered.

"When you were a kid," Stu said to Duncan, "you got stuck in the marsh. How'd you get out of that? Maybe we can do the same thing. Do you remember?"

Duncan looked away, squinting into the haze.

I remember it perfectly.

But that won't help. It won't help at all...

DUNCAN

Calf-deep in the muck, clutching an overweight, terrified beagle, Duncan had no idea what to do.

If I let go of Woof, he'll drown.

But my legs are slowly sinking in. If I fall forward, we'll both drown.

Duncan wept. He wept for a whole lot of reasons.

Regret, for making all the stupid mistakes that led to that point. For taking off his life jacket when he was told to wear it. For going into the marsh when he was warned not to. For getting his phone wet.

But most of all, he hated himself for thinking he was grown up enough to go fishing by himself, when that obviously wasn't the case.

And worst of all, I took Woof with me.

I'm such and idiot.

An idiot, and a loser.

Deep regret comingled with deep fear.

Fear that Woof might die.

That I might die.

That even if we both somehow survive, Mom and Josh will never trust me again.

I'll never trust myself again.

I can't believe we lived through the Safe Haven Massacre, and we're both going to die in a frickin' marsh.

Not knowing what else to do, Duncan began to wail for help.

His voice, sounding weak and pathetic, managed to echo out across the vast surface of Lake Niboowin.

Woof began to howl, his voice joining Duncan's.

All of reality shrank, Duncan's entire existence being reduced to a boy and his dog, stuck in a lake.

No before. No after.

Just a sad, terrifying moment, without end.

Woof began to wiggle, and his howls turned to barking.

Duncan held him tighter, nuzzling his face in the dog's wet fur, and Woof finally stopped freaking out and said, "Woof!" in the same happy, enthusiastic way he always did.

"Need a hand, sport?"

Duncan looked up and saw Josh, in the pontoon, coasting toward him through the reeds.

I hadn't even heard his engine with all the barking.

Duncan's happiness at being rescued was almost immediately replaced by shame. The pontoon glided up, coming to a perfect stop next to him, and Duncan reached for the bow tie on the starboard float, Woof scrambling to climb about.

Josh leaned down and snatched the dog up, bringing him on board. Then he reached out a hand for Duncan.

Duncan reached for it, and Josh pulled, making him feel like he was being stretched like a piece of chewing gum. The lake bottom refused to give up its hold, and Duncan thought his arm was going to be pulled out of its socket, but he came free.

Or rather, his feet came free of his gym shoes, which remained stuck in the muck.

Josh got Duncan onto the pontoon, and Woof immediately began to lick the dirty water off of Duncan's bare legs. Duncan didn't want to meet Josh's eyes, but he forced himself to, even though he was embarrassed and still scared.

Josh was smiling. "Quite an adventure you just had. You okay?"

"You're not mad?"

"Mad?" Josh laughed. "I'm proud of you."

"How can you be proud of me? I messed up. Bad."

Josh tussled Duncan's damp hair. "Bad things happen. We can try to stop them, but we'll never stop them all. You're okay. You saved Woof. I call that a win."

"I lost my phone," Duncan said. "And my shoes."

"Everything has a cost. I'd say you and Woof being safe is well worth that cost."

Duncan went from shameful to slightly confused. "But you told me not to do this."

"Duncan, it's a parent's job to get a child ready for life. But parents can only do so much. The only thing that can prepare you for life… is life. Did you learn something?"

Duncan nodded, enthusiastically.

"That's a better lesson than anything I can teach."

"Is Mom mad?"

"You're mother doesn't know. She was in the shower. I went out on the pier to take a few casts, and I heard Woof howling."

Duncan noticed the binoculars hanging around Josh's neck.

He wasn't fishing.

He was watching out for me.

Duncan had been fond of Josh moments after they'd met.

But the feeling he had now was a lot stronger than fondness.

"Thanks, Dad."

Dad nodded. "Men help and protect. It's what we do. Get the boat hook. Let's grab the motorboat. It wouldn't start?"

"I think it got clogged. Like you said it would."

"That's because I know everything. I'll show you how to clean out the thermostat when we get back."

Duncan picked up the telescopic pole and leaned over the gunwale to snag the boat while Dad started the pontoon's motor. As they passed, Duncan reached out the hook and snagged the bow of the rowboat. Dad shut off the engine, and Duncan tied the bowline to the pontoon's stern float cleat.

A few moments earlier, Duncan was trapped in one of the lowest points of his life.

But now he felt strangely happy.

And best of all, I learned from my mistake.

A mistake I'm sure I'll never make again.

DUNCAN

I swore I'd never make this mistake again.

Yet, here I am.

Now how do we get out of this?

First things first. As Dad told me, men help and protect.

I need to help Chuck.

"Let's get that thing our of your eye, buddy."

"Thanks, man. Thank you thank you thank you."

Duncan took his Swiss Army knife from his pocket. The well-worn Cyber Tool, given to him by his dad, had a hidden pin tucked away behind the corkscrew, next to the plastic toothpick that he'd never picked his teeth with because replacements were a ridiculous six bucks. Duncan removed the pin—also a six-dollar replacement piece—with his thumbnail, and also took out the small tweezers housed in the red plastic casing.

"Stu, there's a Zippo in the top compartment in my tackle box. Bring it and help me out here."

Stu followed his command, and found the Ace of Spades lighter, opening the top and striking the flint wheel. Duncan ran the needle and tweezers through the flame to sterilize them, then gave Chuck a beach towel to bite down on while Stu stretched open his eyelids.

It was the most revolting thing Duncan had ever seen. Chuck's eye, bloodshot so deep it looked like he'd been in a car accident, with a bulge below the pupil where a yellow maggot stuck out like a large, wiggling grain of rice.

"Look up, Chuck, and don't move."

"I can feel it," Chuck mumbled, mouth full of towel. "It hurts."

"It's trying to burrow in deeper," Stu said. "Or maybe it's eating."

"Stu, stop talking. Chuck, stay absolutely still."

Keeping his hands steady, Duncan brought the needle up to the worm's protruding tail, hoping to slowly spear it from the side. The moment the tip touched it, the maggot flinched, then Chuck yelped and flinched, and the needle pricked Chuck's eyelid.

"Keep still."

Chuck spat out the towel. "It didn't like what you just did," he whined. "I think it bit the inside of my eyeball."

"If it eats his optic nerve he'll be blind," Stu said.

"Stu, I told you to stop talking."

"The optic nerve, man," Stu went on. "You got to do this fast, or you might as well just yank his whole eye out."

"Do it fast, Duncan. Please get it out."

Duncan didn't argue and went in fast, snagging the tail and then pinching it with the tweezers, giving the worm a steady pull.

The rice-sized maggot turned out to be much longer than expected as Duncan stretched it from Chuck's eye like a rubber band. But it was a slimy little bastard and escaped the tweezers, slurping back into the tunnel it made, causing Chuck to scream and shove his friends away.

Okay. Plan B.

"Stu, I need the Zippo again."

This time Duncan sterilized the small pliers that folded out of the Cyber Tool. Not big enough to remove a spark plug, but good enough to get a hook out of a fish's mouth.

And hopefully good enough to yank a maggot out of an eyeball.

Again, Duncan picked at the maggot's tail with the needle to tug it out, but the little bastard kept squirming, which made Chuck squirm.

"Stop moving, Chuck."

"There's a maggot in my eye and you're poking it with a fucking needle."

"Kneel down. Stu, put him in a headlock to hold him still."

With Chuck suitably immobilized and biting on the beach towel, Duncan tried once more. Blood had now mixed with all of the tears and mucus, making the maggot even more slippery.

Come on, you little shit. Get out of there.

Duncan prodded and stabbed and finally skewered the tail, quickly locking on the pliers and giving it a fast pull.

It came out with a sucking sound, and there was blood.

"It's out!"

Stu released Chuck, who pressed the towel to his eye. "Thanks, guys."

Duncan squinted at the maggot, dangling at the end like a piece of macaroni. As he watched it, the worm began to ooze a light green, viscous fluid, which smelled like turpentine.

"Pheromones," Stu said. Then he slapped the bug off of the pliers, knocking it into the lake.

"I thought you would want to save it," Duncan said. "Study a new species."

"Hive insects communicate with pheromones. I think it was calling for help."

As if cued the trio watched as a green fog lifted up off of the bullrush.

But, of course, it wasn't a fog.

It's flies. Hundreds of flies.

Coming right at us.

SUN

The summer sun waged a brutal overhead assault, aided by zero breeze, and the bee suits trapped heat like thermal blankets.

They'd been walking their wooded property for the past ninety minutes, and Sun had so much sweat stinging her eyes—sweat she couldn't wipe off because of the netting in the face shield of the hood—that her vision had become compromised by a constant squint.

Andy also kept rubbing the screen with his gloved hand, then swearing in languages that Sun hadn't ever heard before.

They hadn't found any more giant red goat-eyed murder hornets. Though they had discovered, to Sun's delight, a thriving beehive on the edge of the property, boasting a comb with several pounds of honey.

Honey bees are a good indicator of an ecosystem's health.

Also, fresh honey is delicious, and bees don't mind too much if you take a smidge for pancake use.

But aside from the bees and a few random ants, they hadn't located any other *Hymenoptera.*

Francis will be home soon. His bus drops him off in twenty minutes.

I think the bug hunt is over.

"We should have worn headbands," he said, kneeling on the uneven forest floor and inspecting a dead tree. "Do they even sell headbands anymore? Or did history retire them with Björn Borg?"

"A bandana would have worked. Or a hat."

"And make this suit even hotter? I could steam a potato under my balls."

That line would have made their son cry with laughter. But Sun was too distracted to be entertained by her husband's inner sixth grader.

Something nagged at her.

"We should check the eaves."

"Again? We walked around the house, the chicken coop, the pole barn, and the garage. No nests."

Sun chewed her lower lip. "They could be inside the eaves. Wasps like attics."

"Then we'd see them in the house. The one you found was outside. If they were inside, we'd find them inside."

That sparked a bad thought. "I drove to town last week, that's the last time we used the car. When was the last time you went in the garage?" she asked Andy.

"I dunno. When did I fix the sink?"

"Three days ago."

"Then three days ago, to get my plumbing gear." He looked up at her, grinning lasciviously. "You want me to put on my toolbelt before the kid gets home?"

Some time ago, after a bottle of wine, Sun had admitted to a home repairman sexual fantasy, and Andy was always happy to put on his toolbelt and strut around like a peacock, which she adored.

Not the right time for it, though.

"Let's check the garage."

Andy stood up and hefted the propane weed burner; a two-handed flamethrowing device attached to a gas tank backpack that made him look like a Ghostbuster.

Also a turn-on. Maybe we put Francis to bed early tonight.

Sun led the way back to the unattached garage, taking a narrow dirt trail through the trees that had been there before they'd purchased the ten acres. She got to their paved driveway and walked to the keypad remote next to the automatic door. As she was punching in the code, Andy tapped her shoulder.

"If there is a nest in there, the big door will let them all out. We should go in the side door."

I should have thought of that.

Andy walked from the car entrance to the human entrance, turned the knob, and flipped on the wall switch after walking in. Sun followed him inside, closing the door behind her, and they looked around the cramped enclosure. Besides their SUV, their snowmobiles, and their ATVs, the space was crammed with shelves of tools, a wall of garden tools, some beer making equipment, and a spare refrigerator. In the upper right corner, a propane gas heater, currently turned off for the season, was attached to the ceiling beams.

Also attached to the ceiling beams—

"Holy shit," Andy said. He reached into his pocket for the magnesium striker as Sun stared, slack-jawed, at a paper hornet's nest the size of a beanbag chair.

How did they build that in just three days?

Almost immediately the faint humming sound amped up to a loud buzz, the insects surrounding Sun and her husband. Sun felt her suit get dive-bombed by wasps, hitting like hard rain, bouncing off of her bee suit. Her mesh hood was soon covered with crawling bugs, each of them upwards of three inches, red and angry and unnaturally fast, their long stingers prodding and poking through the netting and coming very close to her face.

"They can sting through the suits!" Andy yelled.

Sun didn't think that was possible. But then she remembered some species of wasps with ovipositors could drill over an inch straight into tree bark to lay their eggs.

That's what they're trying to do.

To lay their eggs in us.

The thought of being injected with wasp larvae caused Sun to freak out for a moment, and then she felt the electric spark of a sting on her right shoulder, followed by another on her chin. She shook her whole body like a wet dog and reflexively swatted at the mesh, smashing a dozen insects directly onto her face. Feeling them squirm and crunch and wiggle against the netting, getting stung multiple more times, each one feeling like a lit cigarette being ground into her skin.

She switched from smashing to wiping away the bugs, then whipped around to see her husband, who was waving his hands around like a crippled bird, his brush burner dropped on the garage floor, the nozzle unlit.

Sun frantically searched for the striker he'd also dropped, feeling her face swell and burn and watching Andy fall to his knees gasping for breath.

Allergic reaction. He's going into anaphylactic shock. His airway is closing up.

And that's when she heard someone yell, "Mom! Dad!"

Francis's bus had just dropped him off in front of their house.

KATIE

After calling crew scheduling and letting them know she was headed home, a very frightened and very paranoid Katie drove her SUV out of employee parking and burned down I-94 heading east, back to Spoonward.

Duncan didn't answer her half dozen calls and texts to his cell phone, or the two she left on his parent's answering machine.

That psycho is watching him.

Watching him and planning something.

But planning what?

What was the end game here?

Katie had only met Duncan's former stalker—her current stalker—one time. In the ladies room at Cooper's while Duncan had been bartending. She had been squatting over the toilet, returning the two beers she'd just had, and someone knocked on her stall.

She exited the interstate onto WI-25 heading north, and Katie's memory came back in a rush...

        .   .   .

Seeing the feet under the privacy door, Katie thought a man had come into the washroom. Black jeans and black Doc Martens. But the voice that accompanied the knock was definitely female.

"Katie? Can I have a second of your time?"

Katie wondered WTF was happening. "I'm pissing."

"You can't multitask? It's about Duncan."

Katie finished and pulled up her underwear and skirt. She peeked through the crack in the door and saw a blue eye staring inside.

Katie opened the door—

—and saw a girl she hadn't seen in a long time.

"Kelli Lyons?"

"I just use Lyon these days. You're Katie, right? Katie Greers?"

Katie didn't acknowledge it.

"You remember me?" Lyon continued. "From middle school?"

"Sure."

Everyone in middle school remembered Kelli Lyons. Shy, kept to herself, and was pulled out of school after smashing the class gerbil, Oprah, with the class *Webster's Dictionary.*

No one saw it happen. But rumors were plentiful.

Some claimed she placed the book on it then jumped up and down.

Some said she ate Oprah's guts after it died.

Some said she ate Oprah's guts while Oprah was still alive and squealing.

Kelli never returned to school, but the general consensus was she was sent to military school, or a mental hospital. Her mother, a known hoarder and recluse, never left her house and never spoke of it to anyone.

The girl had changed a lot in the past sixteen years. No longer a thin, tiny blonde, she'd grown body-builder size. Her hair was dyed blue and pink, and she had a nose ring, two eyebrow rings (though her brows were shaved), and both ears were pierced multiple times, including lobes that had been stretched out to fit in tribal rings wide enough to fit a finger through.

Lyon was smiling, but the smile didn't reach her eyes.

"You're seeing Duncan."

It was more like an accusation than a question.

Katie had dealt with enough threatening passengers to recognize hostility. She'd been trained how to de-escalate.

Stay calm.

Be respectful.

Remain attentive.

Show apathy.

"We've been going out together," Katie answered, keeping calm.

"Did he ever mention me?" Lyon asked.

"We don't talk about the past much."

Lyon's voice was as neutral as her expression. "How do you know Duncan?"

"Have you asked Duncan?" Katie replied.

Lyon laughed, which came out like a bark. "Duncan and I have a… *complicated*… relationship."

Katie tried to slip past her, but Lyon blocked her exit.

"What can I help you with, Lyon?"

"Can't two ladies discuss boys in the ladies room?"

"I feel like you're standing in my way, Lyon."

"That's cute. I feel the same way about you."

"Duncan's tending bar right now," Katie said. "How about I buy you a drink?"

Her flight attendant training, kicking in hard.

"Do you suck his cock, Katie?"

This time Katie pushed past, even though Lyon gave her a shoulder bump. She went straight for the bathroom exit, pushing it open as Lyon snagged her purse strap and almost pulled Katie off her feet.

Katie turned, her feet planted wide, her hands in fists. She'd dealt with bullies before, and Lyon was about to get popped in the mouth.

Lyon immediately let go of Katie's purse and raised up her palms. "Easy there, tiger. Just got my arm tangled up."

"What is it you want, Lyon?" Katie hated that her voice didn't sound as strong as she wanted it to sound.

Lyon smiled wide, her eyes dead. "I got what I wanted. Good to see you again, Katie."

Katie turned and left the bathroom. When Duncan saw Katie he smiled, then his smile immediately faded when he noticed who came out the door behind her.

"Lyon!" Duncan said. "Out! Now!"

Lyon began to laugh in a way that was both hysterical and fake at the same time. "Your latest piece of ass is scrawny, Duncan."

"You want me to call Stoker?" Duncan said.

Everyone knew Stoker was Spoonward's police chief.

"Don't be such a pussy, Duncan," Lyon said. "I'm leaving. Just stopped in to use the shitter. See you around, Katie."

Lyon left the bar, and a shaken Katie sat at her stool.

"You okay?" Duncan put his hand on hers to steady it.

"Want to tell me about that?"

"She started coming around here a few months before I met you. Once got really trashed, and tried to drive home. I was closing up, so I offered to drive her. While I was taking her to her place she tried to blow me. Really pushy about it, grabbing and squeezing my balls, trying to get my pants off. I told her no, a bunch of times. She got really pissed, and tried to claw my face off. I had to pull over and yank her out of the passenger seat. Parked on the side of the road and called the cops while she kicked my door and broke two windows."

"Jesus. Why didn't you leave her there?"

"She was wasted. Could have gotten hurt. Better to let her beat on my ride and the police could escort her home."

"Did you file charges? Sue?"

"Neither."

"Why not?"

Duncan scratched his nose. "I guess because I've gotten drunk before, done stupid shit. I wouldn't want one bad day to follow me around for the rest of my life."

"Seems like she's still following you around." Katie glanced back at the exit to make sure Lyon was still gone.

"Gets better," Duncan said. "She kept coming to the bar, harassing me and other customers. I had to actually get a restraining order."

"Doesn't seem to be working too well."

"Captain Stoker keeps cutting her slack. I think he knew her mom, felt bad for her." Duncan shrugged. "Small town problems, right?"

Katie smiled, trying to make light of it. "Is that why you gave me a pepper spray keychain on our second date?"

Duncan smiled back, sheepish. "Yeah."

"I thought it was for when you got too frisky."

"I can get frisky," Duncan said. "But that woman is flat-out crazy."

.   .   .

"That was an understatement," Katie mumbled to herself, directly addressing that first-meeting memory.

She checked her gas gauge.

Quarter of a tank. Forty-mile range. I should be able to make it to Duncan's parent's place without having to stop for gas.

Her cell buzzed, and she hoped it was Duncan while dreading that it could be Lyon again.

It was Lyon.

She'd texted a picture of Duncan and Katie. A familiar one, a selfie Katie had taken the first time they'd put his pontoon in the water. Duncan sitting at the captain's chair, Katie in his lap with his arm around him, both smiling wide with a tinged-sky image of Big Lake Niboowin in the background.

How did Lyon get that pic?

U THINK DUNCAN CAN BE HAPPY WITH A UGLY WHORE LIKE YOU?

Dividing her attention between the road and her phone, Katie dialed Duncan again.

It went to voicemail.

He's fine. Duncan's got to be fine.

There are dead spots on the lake where phones don't work.

He's fishing with his boys.

Lyon is probably hiding in a tree like some rabid raccoon, spying on him.

She's not a real threat.

She's just some crazy, jealous psychopath who is addicted to drama and facial piercings.

Katie's phone buzzed again.

U WON'T GET HERE IN TIME.

It was followed by an audio message. Katie stared at it, not wanting to hit play, knowing that she had to.

I need to listen to it. Save it as evidence. If it's Lyon threatening me, maybe I'll actually get Captain Stoker to take this situation seriously.

Katie tapped her screen, expecting to hear Lyon's voice.

Instead she heard her own.

"Duncan, it's me. You have to call me back. Lyon is harassing me again, and I think she may be somewhere on Lake Niboowin, watching you."

How did Lyon get a copy of the recording I'd left on the voicemail? Does she somehow have access to my phone? Or...

The answer hit Katie like a slap.

She got that recording the same way she got that picture of me and Duncan.

She isn't hacking my phone.

Duncan has that pic, hanging next to his bed in his room at his parent's house.

She's there. Lyon isn't just on the lake, watching Duncan.

That crazy bitch is there at the house.

LYON

Kelli Lyons set down her phone and undressed. Naked, she climbed onto Duncan's bed and squatted.

She clutched Duncan's pillow against her chest, sniffing it hard, remembering his scent from that car ride he gave her.

It seems so long ago now.

Why doesn't he know we're meant to be together?

Why is he dating that stupid whore, Katie, and not me?

Doesn't he know I'm perfect for him?

Doesn't he see how much I love him?

She removed the pillowcase, intending to keep it for her hope chest. Lyon had been collecting little things that Duncan had owned, or merely touched, as a placeholder until she had him.

After folding it up, she pissed on his blankets, moving her butt to get wider coverage, soaking his blankets and mattress and emptying her full bladder. When Lyon finished she climbed off the bed and put on her jeans, socks, and boots. Bare chested, she stared at herself in the oversized mirror on Duncan's dresser.

Years ago she considered getting tattoos, but Mother would have never allowed it. She got away with the facial piercings because she was able to take them out when she was home. Mother lost her eyeglasses in the horde years ago, misplaced among all the thrift store crap and garbage she lived with, floor-to-ceiling. But she would have noticed full sleeve artwork, or a back tattoo.

So Lyon went another route to modify her body.

She lifted her arms, admiring the network of scars crisscrossing her torso. Seventy-seven X-marks, each several inches long, covering her breasts, stomach, shoulders, arms. She had more on her thighs and legs.

Everywhere she could reach on the body with a razor blade, Lyon marked with an X.

She fished a blade out of her front pocket and returned to Duncan's bed. Raising her left arm and flexing her bicep, Lyon cut a deep X underneath her elbow.

Hello, X number seventy-eight.

X marks the spot.

She held her arm over Duncan's bed, letting her blood drip down and mix with the piss.

It hurt. But it's a good kind of hurt.

The kind of hurt I can control.

Lyon understood, from a young age, that life was pain. Mother, who was all kinds of crazy, hurt Lyon in hundreds of ways.

But Mother could never break her.

Because, from a young age, Lyon learned the secret.

Nothing in the world can hurt me more than I hurt myself.

At first, she restricted the cutting to her buttocks. Even as a kid, there was ample fat there so she could go deep without permanent injury. Also, it was hidden from everyone. But Lyon was reminded of her mastery over misery every time she sat down.

As she got older, and Mother's eyesight got worse, Lyon began marking more of her skin canvas.

Pain can be beautiful, if you embrace it.

The blood eventually stopped, as it always did, and Lyon went to the bathroom and washed her arm. She put her Plasmatics T-shirt back on, then went to her phone to check her trackers.

All four of them pinged locations.

The one in Duncan's car was stationary, the car parked out back next to his friends' cars.

The one on Duncan's boat was still on the lake.

The one in Duncan's jacket was back at his apartment, still in his jacket.

The one she'd slipped into Katie's purse, back when she'd first confronted her in the bathroom at Cooper's, was heading east on I-94.

She's moving fast. Maybe an hour away.

Lyon quickly sent her another text.

CALL THE COPS AND HE'S DEAD.

Which, of course, was a lie. She couldn't ever kill Duncan. He was her soul mate.

And she couldn't kill Katie, either.

A dead Katie would mean a mourned Katie. Lyon didn't want Duncan mourning. She wanted Katie to dump him, so Lyon could be there for him on the rebound.

I want him to have a choice, and to choose me.

I'll help him get over his heartbreak.

All I need to do is push Katie until she snaps.

Which shouldn't take much longer.

Lyon wasn't sure what would make that happen. Maybe Katie would get so scared she moved away. Maybe she would tell Duncan he wasn't worth the trouble.

Maybe it's as simple as getting Katie so freaked out she becomes a shitty girlfriend, and Duncan will be the one to dump her.

And if I can't make him dislike her personality, I'll make him dislike her looks.

Some scars are beautiful. But losing a nose? Ears? Lips?

If Katie were disfigured badly enough, Duncan would leave.

You can't have a girlfriend who is too mutilated to kiss.

Lyon didn't sweat the details.

I'm not in any rush. No one is missing Mother. I can keep cashing her government assistance checks with no one ever knowing that she's dead and rotting under a pile of old magazines in the living room.

I can play the long game.

I can play it as long as it takes to drive Katie and Duncan apart.

Drive them apart, and drive him into my arms.

Maybe that's crazy.

Maybe I'm crazy.

But love is crazy, isn't it?

She walked outside, feeling the sun on her face, and went onto the pier. Her cell phone's zoom lens was ridiculously good, and she pointed it at Duncan's pontoon and took a look at what was happening.

Still in the weeds, tougher to see what's going on.

Duncan and his two friends were jumping around.

Dancing, maybe?

He's too adorable.

She snapped a pic.

Lyon didn't hear any music; they were too far away.

I wonder what they're listening to. What kind of music would make them dance like that?

It intrigued her.

Her plan had been to hang around on the property, take some of Duncan's things, leave him a present, spy on the boys from a distance and take a few pictures, and scare Katie.

But seeing the canoe tied to the dock gave Lyon an idea.

Lyon liked making spontaneous decisions. They usually led to interesting places and situations. Too many human beings were sheep, following schedules and routines, never living in the spur of the moment. Risk averse and boring.

She went to Mother's car, parked in the woods near the property line, placed Ducan's pillowcase in the passenger seat, and took the 9 mm Glock from the glove compartment, tucking it into the back of her jeans.

Then she got in the canoe, detached the mooring lines, and began to paddle away from the pontoon, deciding to make a big loop and come up on it from a side angle.

I won't get too close. Just close enough to hear the music, and get some more pictures.

I'll be careful.

This is still the long game.

I'll be back with plenty of time for Katie's arrival...

DUNCAN

SAME TIME...

The panic came so fast and hard that it completely took over, making Duncan a slave to his reactions. He could no longer think. He could no longer control his movements. When the flies attacked, thousands of them swarming, all he could do was hop around like a monkey, flailing his arms, terrified of getting stung.

He smacked them off his skin as fast as he could, and though they went for his bare arms and legs they seemed most interested in attacking his face.

Especially his eyes.

"They're going for the eyes!" Stu yelled. "Close your eyes!"

But that made a horrible situation even more horrible. Even though Duncan couldn't form any rational thoughts, his reptile brain knew at a base, primitive level that if his eyes were covered, he couldn't see. And if he couldn't see, he couldn't swat the flies as effectively.

"My mouth!" Chuck wailed. "In my mouth!"

Duncan smashed his palm against his face as a fly climbed up his nostril, and through squinty eyes he caught a quick glimpse of Chuck leaping off the boat, hitting the water with a splash.

Slapping at the flies tangled in his hair, Duncan noticed Stu frantically spraying the aerosol can of bug repellent at the bugs themselves, which wouldn't do a damn thing because it was meant to be sprayed on the skin.

But the sight of it made an idea pop into his brain, an idea as old as mankind.

All animals fear fire.

He tackled Stu, who fought him as the two fell to the floor of the pontoon. Stu was in full attack mode, hysterical and treating Duncan as a threat, and Duncan took the punches and kicks and focused on taking the bug spray away from his friend, and then screaming loud as he could, "LIGHTER! LIGHTER! LIGHTER!"

He managed three times before flies filled his mouth, which Duncan responded to by chewing them before they could sting and spitting them out as fast as he could, and as he got to his knees he saw the most beautiful thing he'd ever witnessed...

Stu, his arm straight up in the air, the Zippo blazing.

Duncan aimed the aerosol can and sprayed, turning the bug repellent into a makeshift flamethrower.

He waved the flame around, turning flies into burning raindrops, frying hundreds of them.

The bugs backed away, still buzzing angrily around the boat, keeping a safe distance from the fire. Duncan took the fight to them, leaning over the gunwales, climbing onto the pontoon floats, killing as many as he could as the can got hotter and lighter.

As the panic faded to simply terror, Duncan considered making some torches with fishing poles, rags, and gasoline. But just as the bug spray ran out, the swarm retreated, flying off to the east, the black cloud eventually dispersing into reddish sky.

Duncan dropped the can and opened a bench seat, throwing Chuck a life jacket. He reached for it, his face gray with muck and dirty water. He appeared to be standing on the lake bottom, but Duncan acutely remembered how impossible it was to move.

"You okay?" he asked Chuck.

"They got me a few more times. Dude... your face."

Stu was staring at his arms and legs, covered with raised welts. Dozens of them. His face had at least ten more, and one eye had already swelled up.

Duncan checked himself, seeing just as many stings on his own body. He then dared to feel all the hot bumps on his face.

Does each one have a larva inside?

Am I infested with maggots?

He pushed away the thought, focusing on the course of action.

"Stu, put on a life jacket. We're going in the water."

"If we get to the shore, then what? No one lives on this side of the lake. You want to walk through the woods? How many flies are out there? In the forest there are millions of bugs per acre. Millions, Duncan."

"We need to swim for it, Stu." Chuck said from the water, struggling to get into the life jacket. "We need to get to a hospital."

They aren't thinking this through.

What's happening to us could be happening to others. Certainly on this lake. Maybe the lack of activity isn't the air quality, it's bugs. But maybe this is even bigger. Maybe all of Safe Haven and Spoonward is being attacked by these flies. That could mean the hospital is overrun.

We might be on our own.

Luckily, my parents, and their neighbors Sun and Andy, are preppers. They have safe rooms, weapons, medical supplies, and enough food and water to withstand a siege.

We need a way to get back to the house.

"We're not going for the shore." Duncan pointed. "We're going for that guy's boat."

The bass boat that had drawn them into the reeds hadn't moved since Duncan had first spotted it.

I can guess why. The flies got him.

But we can use his boat to get home.

"How about we swim to your house?" Stu asked.

Duncan shook his head. "We're a few kilometers away. And if the flies attack again, there's nowhere to go. You want them laying eggs in your scalp and ears while we spend four hours doggy paddling back?"

"Vote on it," Chuck said. "I say go for the boat."

Stu's face bunched up, and he seemed about to lose it.

Duncan clapped him on the shoulder. "We need to stick together, Stu. But we all need to agree on this."

"We could stay on the pontoon," Stu said. "Make torches out of fishing poles and towels. Wait for the wind to come back and blow us to shore."

"And what happens if we're stuck here until night? You want to be stuck in the dark with those flies?"

"Come on, Stu," Chuck said. "Water is actually pretty nice."

Stu sighed. "You win, Captain. We swim for the boat."

They put on their life jackets, Duncan unlatched the aluminum boat ladder next to the motor, and they climbed down the four steps into the lake.

The water was cool, instantly soothing Duncan's many stings. He could still touch the muck bottom with his toes, so he leaned forward and began an awkward breast stroke as he bobbed, cutting through the reeds and heading for the boat.

Swimming while wearing a life jacket and shoes wasn't easy. Especially through bullrush and cattails jutting up through mucky water. Duncan kept getting hung up on weeds, and his toes kept catching the lake bottom and getting stuck. He also had serious concentration issues, his mind obsessing over the eggs that had been deposited in his many stings, and the paranoia of it happening again.

Chuck managed to keep up, staying on Duncan's heels. But Stu kept pausing to rest.

Maybe he's sick. From the leech bite.

He considered calling out to him, checking on his well-being, but had no idea if insects were attracted by noise.

As they crept closer to the stern of the bass boat, Duncan noticed that the sitting occupant was slumped forward in his captain's chair, head down, wearing a red and black flannel shirt, completely still except for his shirt ruffling in the breeze.

Duncan paused, holding his breath, listening for the telltale buzz of swarming flies.

The lake was oddly silent.

He floated closer, blinking away the dirty water in his eyes, trying to fix his vision because the boat captain's shirt was badly out of focus. Fuzzy.

Maybe I'm sick, too.

That shirt is ruffling in the wind in a really weird way.

Duncan placed his hands on the port side gunwale pulling up to look inside the boat, and with horror he realized his unforgiveable mistake.

There is no breeze.

The shirt isn't blowing.

That isn't a shirt at all.

The boat's captain was completely covered with a thick layer of ants. They marched over him like an undulating wave, crawling in and out of his hollow eye sockets, his open mouth.

And he wasn't the only one. Another passenger was on the floor of the bass boat, ants covering him like a carpet, one skeletonized hand jutting up from the mound, completely stripped of flesh.

A fraction of a second later, the ants were all over Duncan's hands, pain like he'd just touched a hot stove while getting his fingers pounded with a hammer.

Duncan yelped and pushed against the boat, rubbing the insects off of his hands, kicking to swim away from the floating abattoir, his mind screaming white hot with pain and fear.

He backstroked, bumping into Chuck who caught him by the life jacket.

"What's the problem, bro?"

Duncan raised a swollen hand and pointed a puffy finger as the ants poured over the side of the boat like liquid—

—and then floated on the top of the lake.

They began to spread out, a growing ant oil slick, extending past the bow and stern and blacking off the near shoreline.

"Are those fucking ants?" Chuck asked.

"It's an ant raft," Stu wheezed, paddling up behind them. "Jesus, how many are there?"

"They filled half the boat," Duncan said. "They ate two people. Maybe more."

"Be quiet, hold your breath, and paddle slowly away," Stu said. "Insects are attracted by sound, carbon dioxide, and movement."

Duncan wanted to ask what didn't attract insects, because it sounded like they were attracted to damn near everything, but he didn't want to make any sound. The trio slowly swam away from the bass boat, toward the pontoon, trying not to splash.

Incredibly, the ant raft continued to grow, until it was twice the length of the boat.

And it's stretching out in our direction.

"Faster," Chuck whispered. "We gotta go faster."

They kicked harder, and Duncan glanced behind him. The pontoon seemed impossibly far away.

Looking back at the ants, their roundish shape floating on the water had become a triangle, with the nearest point reaching like a finger, closing in on the trio's legs.

A bridge. They're making a bridge to get to us.

And they're only a few meters away and closing the gap.

Noise be damned, Duncan began to paddle and kick like his life depended on it, which it did. Chuck kept up. But Stu floundered, flopping around without getting any momentum.

"Chuck, grab one of his arms."

Duncan reached for Stu, aiming for his wrist, surprised how slimy his friend felt. He managed to get a firm grip and the duo tugged Stu through the water as the ant bridge stretched closer and closer.

The flies were awful.

But being devoured by ants would be even worse.

Though a fraction of the size, their stings hurt Duncan just as much, if not more.

And did they lay eggs in me? Like the flies?

I can't comprehend them being all over my entire body.

It would be worse than being burned alive. Going insane with panic while in absolute agony.

Fear-induced adrenaline gave Duncan a huge spike of energy, and he stroked and kicked so hard he was pulling both Stu and Chuck.

The next minute whirred by, humans racing ants in a deadlock, and then finally, blessedly, they reached the pontoon. Duncan climbed the ladder first, and then Chuck pushed Stu from underneath while Duncan pulled his exhausted buddy on board.

Stu was covered in big hunks of weeds and slime. Duncan sat him on the green carpet in the captain's chair, then helped Chuck up.

Chuck squinted at the lake with his one good eye. "They're almost on us."

"Pull up the ladder. Maybe they'll have trouble getting on the floats."

"Didn't seem to have any trouble getting on that bass boat."

Good point. "Soak a beach towel in gas. Maybe we can set the ant raft on fire."

"Shit, look at Stu!"

Duncan glanced back at his friend, and realized he wasn't covered with weeds.

He was covered with leeches.

"I should have used the Celox," Stu said, smiling weakly. "They were attracted to the blood."

Duncan felt his knees start to give out and his vision go wonky.

Vasovagal syncope. I'm going to pass out.

Stu met his eyes, looking desperate.

Duncan glanced at Chuck, and saw he seemed beaten, and something else.

Pity. He pities me.

Duncan gave his head a big shake, forcing away the nausea.

He gave it another shake, pushing back the weakness.

Fuck you, vasovagal syncope. I got this.

Duncan reached down to start pulling the leeches off of Stu, and noticed his own swollen hands. It looked like he wore a pair of bumpy red gloves. Seeing his injury made the pain even worse.

But it's just pain. I can handle the pain.

I can handle the pain, and handle the blood.

I can handle anything.

I need to help my friend.

Making two tight fists, squeezing specks of blood from all of his stings, Duncan again went for Stu's leeches.

Stu shook his head. "If you take them off, the wounds will still bleed. Plus the shock makes them vomit."

"I've got Celox."

"You got a pound of Celox on this boat?" Stu lifted up his arms, and they looked like crow wings.

He had at least thirty leeches hanging on him. Probably more. Long ones, a foot long each.

"So what do we do?" Duncan asked, feeling helpless.

"Let them feed. Pulling them off runs the risk of them vomiting the contents of their stomach into my bloodstream. All sorts of bacteria and parasites could get inside."

"Why'd you pull the last one then?"

Stu offered a sick smile. "I was showing off. I should know better, right? I'm a freaking entomologist."

"What if they… take too much?"

"What's the most they can drink? Two pints? I can survive that. Plus, there's a bonus."

Duncan raised an eyebrow in question.

"When we all get back to your house, I can get drunk a lot faster."

"Ants are almost here, Duncan," Chuck told him.

"Zippo is in my pocket, Chuck. I can't reach in." Duncan waggled his hotdog fingers as proof.

Chuck took the lighter, and Duncan picked up the fish net and put the gas-soaked blanket in it.

When the gasoline soaked his ant stings, he screamed louder than he'd ever screamed in his life. Duncan actually saw red, his vision blinded by unbearable, intolerable, unfathomable pain.

He was vaguely aware of Chuck taking the net, setting the towel on fire, and waving it like a flag over the side of the boat, dripping fire onto the ant bridge.

As his vision blurred back to normal, he found himself focusing on the boat's control panel, the key dangling from the ignition. On reflex he pinched the key in his tortured fingers and turned.

Nothing happened. The battery was dead.

For want of a nail.

That was an old parable Josh used to tell him.

The kingdom fell, for want of a nail.

He closed his eyes and remembered the first time he'd heard it. They'd been fishing, and Duncan had lost a bass because somehow the treble hook had come off his lure.

"Bad O-ring," Dad had told him. "One tiny thing wrong can lead to disaster. There was a soldier in medieval times, on a battlefield, and the blacksmith missed a single nail when putting on the horse's shoe. Because of that, the horse lost the shoe. Because it lost the shoe, it threw the soldier. Because the solder fell off his horse, he was killed in battle. Because he was killed in battle, the battle was lost. Because the battle was lost, the war was lost. Because the war was lost, the country was taken over and thousands were killed and enslaved. All for want of a nail."

In Duncan's case, their current predicament all came down to losing the pliers.

If only I had another pair of pliers. Or if the pliers on my Swiss Army knife were big enough to grab the hex bolt.

Or even if I had some duct tape. I could wrap that around the spark plug, then pull on the tape with the small pliers.

But I don't have duct tape. Which is why my damn pontoon railings are held together with zip ties.

Zip ties?

Zip ties!

Duncan used his thumbnail to tease the plastic toothpick from its sheath in the case of the Swiss Army knife. Then, with aching shaking fingers, he went to one of the large zip ties wrapped around the aluminum boat railing and used it as a shim to release the tie. Once it was unzipped he went to the motor and looped the tie around the stubborn spark plug.

Using the Swiss Army knife pliers he cinched it tight—

—and then painfully pulled sideways, lefty-loosey, as if he'd wound a string around a top and was trying to let it rip—

—and his hands felt like they'd been set on fire that was extinguished with hydrochloric acid—

—and every fly sting on his body seemed to flare up—

—Stu was covered with leeches and Chuck dripped flaming gas on floating killer ants—

—and dammit he loved Katie so much and he wanted to spend the rest of his life with her and there was no way that could be stopped because of a damn—

The spark plug moved!

Using trembling, tortured fingers, Duncan carefully unscrewed the loose plug and wiped off the soot and gunk on the threads and electrode using a beach towel and some hand sanitizer. Then he threaded it back into the motor socket, attached the cable, and went to his ignition key.

Please, please, let the battery have just a tiny bit of power left...

Duncan twisted the key—

—and nothing happened.

Son of a—

"Doesn't it have a manual start?" Chuck asked, still hefting the burning towel.

Yes! How'd I forget about that?

Duncan turned the cowl over and saw the pull-start rope in a waterproof plastic bag taped to the inside lid. He removed it, then wound the length around the motor's flywheel assembly above the rewind starter.

This has got to work...

He gripped the T-handle in both hands, took a big breath, and yanked like it was his backup parachute and he was five hundred feet off the ground and coming in at terminal velocity.

The engine caught and held, and Duncan immediately moved to the control box, keeping it in neutral but giving it some gas to make sure it didn't die.

It moved, sluggish, and it felt like the propeller was stuck on the lake bottom. With no battery Duncan couldn't trim up, so he gave it a bit more gas, trying to tear through the muck.

"Ants are on the floats!"

Chuck began to wipe the flaming towel over the port pontoon float like he was swabbing a deck, and the smoke began to block Duncan's vision.

Duncan gave it more gas and aimed high, for the fire tower on the lake's north shore.

Chuck moved to the other float, then did a slow circle of the pontoon just as the last of the burning beach towel slipped off the net pole.

"I think we're clear," Chuck announced. Then he began to laugh. "I think we're clear!"

Stu offered a sleepy thumbs-up and a lopsided grin.

Duncan also became swept up in elation. The lower end was still scraping bottom, and the motor was revving at the max level, but the shore and the tower were getting closer, and it looked like they might actually make it to—

"Flies!" Stu yelled. "Attracted by the smoke!"

Of course they were attracted by the smoke.

Chuck began to swat at the sky, and Duncan did too as the bugs began to swoop in and commence stinging.

Stinging and laying eggs and bringing hell on earth, and Duncan thought about jumping in the water, but the ants were in the water, and then he had a really wild and fleeting thought of taking his Swiss Army knife and cutting his own throat because things couldn't possibly get any worse.

Then things got worse.

The engine siren, warning that it was overheating, pierced the air.

The hysterical laugh bubbled up in Duncan and he knew he shouldn't open his mouth because the bugs would get in but he couldn't help himself, and his peals of insane chortling mingled with the engine alarm and he waited for his mouth and tongue to get stung and swell up and cut off his air and put an end to this ridiculous, horrifying tragedy.

Except no insects flew into his mouth.

Instead they began to pop.

All around them, in the air, the flies burst like little kernels of popcorn and fell onto the lake, onto the boat, onto Duncan and his friends.

Duncan stared, amazed, at the stings on his arms, and watched larva emerge and wiggle free, dropping off of his skin, shriveling up and dying on the floor of his boat.

"It's the alarm horn!" Stu yelled.

Duncan watched as the leeches released Stu and tried to squirm away, but before they could wiggle to the edge of the boat they began to burst like blood-filled condoms.

Duncan's laughter went from unstable to genuine, then back to unstable when he noticed his hands were covered with bloody ants.

He began beating his hands against his life jacket, and Chuck caught his wrists, and Duncan tried to pull away but Chuck yelled, "Let them come out!"

They both watched, transfixed, as the baby ants crawled out of Duncan's sting wounds and then dropped off, dead.

Duncan couldn't believe it.

It's over.

This nightmare is over.

Then the boat motor chugged, and died.

And when it did, the motor alarm faded out to silence.

JAKE

Swollen to three times his old weight, Jake rubbed his distended belly as his consciousness transcended reality, taking him to a hellish landscape of a possible future.

A dark cloud of flying insects shrouding the earth, blotting out the sun.

Dead bodies by the millions, rotting in the crumbling remains of cities.

The rest of humanity, enslaved, a dystopian nightmare of pain and torture and death.

And sitting on a throne of the mutilated dead... Him.

The demon lord. Beelzebub. Curling black ram horns, hooves the size of manhole covers, claws like a bear, teeth like a shark's.

Jake was horrified and fascinated, repulsed and aroused.

It makes perfect sense.

Nothing lives without pain.

Everything alive will die.

But life does all it can to ignore these inevitabilities.

What sense does that make? To spend so much energy trying to avoid what is inevitable?

To suffer and to die is to live.

That is what He means to show the world.

Embrace this fate.

Soon, He shall emerge.

Soon, He shall conquer.

Soon, He shall—

The siren echoed across the lake and drove into Jake's skull like a hatchet, splitting his soul and mind into a thousand fractured shards.

Inside, the demon screeched in agony, and forced Jake to submerge himself in the marsh and burrow into the mucky bottom, vainly attempting to get away from the piercing pain.

The water muted the agony, but only a bit, and Jake's body vibrated, shedding the last of the bugs within his flesh, boiling the one who still grew under his skin.

Jake needed to surface, to breathe, but the demon refused to let him.

So he drowned, choking on water and mud, lungs burning, mind screaming.

But he did not die. He continued to drown, over and over, over and over, until all that existed was pain.

Then, abruptly, the torture stopped.

Jake slithered to the surface, gulping in sweet smoky air, and an overpowering, commanding voice in his head crooned, *"Muuuuuuuurder themmmmmmmm."*

Jake sank to nose level and peered across the top of the waveless water. In the distance, not far from the fire tower, three men on a pontoon.

The cause of my pain. Of His pain.

They must be destroyed.

But something even closer beckoned for Jake's attention. He swiveled his head around and saw an approaching canoe, with a lone occupant.

I'd managed to sneak up on those two men earlier this morning, and set the ants loose on them.

But three men at once, with Him so close to emerging, held some risk.

Maybe there is a better way…

LEO

The Tug continued to propel Leo forward along the highway, one step followed by another step, his legs weak, his arms weak, his thirst quenched by a recent head dunk into a pond, but his stomach empty and crying out for nourishment.

His nose picked up the disgusting yet delicious smell of decaying meat, and he followed his legs to roadkill.

Possum. Still fresh. It had almost made it to the other side, but had been crushed less than four steps from safety.

"Life's not fair," Leo said, unsure if he was talking to himself, or to the dead animal, as he squatted down to eat his fill.

He heard the vehicle coming, and assumed that it saw him crouching alongside the road.

The assumption proved to be incorrect. He righted himself and tried to dodge, a fraction too late, bouncing onto the hood and off the front windshield, then going briefly airborne before gravity won and slammed him back to earth.

Leo cracked open his head on the pavement, and as his vision swam in concussion pain he noted that he'd lost his right arm at the elbow and left leg at the knee.

He began to laugh, blowing blood bubbles from his lips, because for some absurd reason he was thinking of an old Patsy Cline song.

I Fall To Pieces.

Pretty funny.

It's good I still have a sense of humor.

And this possum is good, too.

It's got a salty tang to it. And the consistency of tapioca.

Leo licked some off the pavement, then one eye drifted to the side of the road, where the dead possum stared at him in judgment.

If the possum is over there, what am I eating?

He blinked and was able to focus on the road. On the bloody, gooey mess he'd been slurping up.

My brains.

Some of my brains leaked out.

Good thing I probably won't remember this.

Because I just ate that memory.

Leo began to laugh again.

That's...

That's...

That's the most thoughtful meal I've ever had.

Then darkness dragged him away.

KATIE

SAME TIME...

Speeding north on WI-25 Katie looked at her phone, for just a second, to see the latest text from Lyon.

CALL THE COPS AND HE'S DEAD.

When she glanced up at the road again, a man was bouncing off of the hood of her SUV.

Katie stomped the brakes, her vehicle screeching, and fishtailed one hundred and eighty degrees so she had a clear, terrible view of the person she'd just murdered.

Oh no.

He was lying in a puddle of his own blood, and something else.

Oh no oh no.

His brains. His brains had spilled out.

Oh God.

To the left of him, laid his severed arm.

Oh Jesus.

To the right of him, his severed leg.

Oh no oh God oh Jesus.

What have I done?

Completely forgetting her own problems, Katie exited her vehicle and walked robotically, shellshocked, over to the body, squatting down, reaching for a neck pulse that she knew for sure wouldn't be—

"Holy shit!"

The man jackknifed off the street and turned around, eyes wide, his remaining, bloody hand grabbing Katie's shirt.

"My brains," he croaked.

Katie knew she needed to help him, and at the same time she was so surprised and repulsed her instinct was to pull away. But the man had a grip like channellock pliers.

"We… we need to call an ambulance."

The man blinked, then he turned and stared back at his own chunks of cranial tissue splattered on the street. He released her and reached for them, then tried to shove them back into the crack on his head.

"Don't do that," Katie said, "that's… that isn't right."

He didn't listen, and continued to try to cram his brains, along with some small rocks and dead pine needles, into his skull hole.

"I'm calling 911." Katie looked around for her phone, and realized she must have dropped it in the SUV.

She turned to get it and the man yelled, "Wait!"

Katie glanced back and gaped as the man said the most ridiculous thing she'd ever heard anyone say in her entire life.

"I don't need an ambulance," he said.

"Dude, you're literally in pieces."

"I'm good. I'm not even bleeding."

Strangely, he sounded calm and rational.

Which, of course, is irrational. It must be shock.

He's in shock. Or I'm in shock. Or we're both in shock.

"I ran you over. You're going to die unless you get help."

"I'm not going to die."

"You're spread out all over the road."

"You were also all over the road, when you hit me. Give me a ride, we'll call it even."

"I'm calling 911."

Katie hurried back to the truck, and then she had some weird bad feeling and glanced back just in time to see the guy hopping up to her like a pogo stick attached to a blood sprinkler.

"Holy shit! What are you doing? Are you crazy?"

The man smiled. Not a crazy smile, but more of a gentle one. "Well, I just did lose my mind." He winked. "A little."

"You need to lay down."

"On the street? Where someone can run me over?" He added, "Again?"

"Can you… can you get into my SUV?"

"Sure," he said. "I'll hop in."

Is that a joke? How can this guy be joking?

Brain damage?

Or is he having one of those weird moments of clarity before he dies?

Katie's mother, dead from cancer, battled a long time, the last few weeks in a semi-comatose morphine haze. But the day before she died she sat up and was completely lucid. Calm, rational, loving. Katie had thought it was a miraculous recovery, but the hospice nurses said it happened all the time.

They told Katie that those near death often reverted back to their old self, to tie up any last loose ends and say goodbye.

Is that what is going on here?

She helped him into the passenger seat, then began to look for her phone.

"Can you grab my parts?" he asked. "To stick them back on?"

That made logical sense. Katie had heard that severed limbs can be reattached if you get to a doctor quickly enough.

She jogged back to the accident scene, picking up his arm, which sort of felt like picking up a limp cat, and his leg, which felt more like a warm tree branch.

I can't believe this.

This feels surreal.

When she returned to her vehicle, there was a loud whining sound coming from the passenger seat. Unsure of how any human being could sound like that, she timidly crept up and peeked in the cab to check.

The man was holding a spinning angle grinder to his arm stump, spraying the side window with a mist of blood as he tore into his flesh and bone.

Katie threw the limbs at him and ran, screaming, until she was twenty or so meters away.

Then she stopped and tried to make sense of it.

Is any of this really happening?

Is this a hallucination?

Did I fall asleep while driving, get into an accident, and I'm in a coma, dreaming all of this?

The grinder stopped, and the guy yelled, "It's okay! I'm done!"

"What the hell is happening!" she yelled back.

"It's complicated! I won't hurt you! I have a condition where I heal really fast! My arm is okay now!"

Katie hadn't heard of any kind of condition like that. She had no idea what to do. There hadn't been any other vehicles on WI-25 in the past few minutes.

Do I walk back to I-95?

"See!" the man yelled. "I'm okay!"

He'd opened up the passenger window and was waving at her.

With both hands.

"If you don't come back I'm going to have to steal your truck!" he called.

This can't be real.

And if it can't be real, he can't hurt me.

Which means he can't steal my SUV, either.

Some geese flew overhead in a V formation, and honked as they passed.

So why does this all seem so real?

Katie actually pinched her own thigh to see if she could feel it.

She felt it.

So what in the hell am I supposed to do?

Katie thought about Duncan. And then about Lyon.

I have to get to Lake Niboowin.

Her concern for her boyfriend overpowered her concern for herself, and Katie briskly walked back to the truck. She peeked her head in again, and the man held up both of his hands and wiggled his fingers.

"So you'll drive me?"

"I… guess."

"Good," he said. "I'd hate to take an Uber. They charge an arm and a leg."

Ugh.

I should say something.

"How can you joke around when you're…" She spread her hands out.

"I'll tell you about it while we're driving. I'm Leo."

"Katie."

"I know."

"You know?"

Leo handed Katie her cell phone. "Do you know the person stalking you?" he asked.

Katie snatched her phone back. "Yeah. She's psychotic. And that's private."

I'm feeling a little psychotic myself. What started off as a regular day had become truly bonkers.

"Duncan is your boyfriend?"

"It's rude to look through someone's cell phone."

"It's rude to hit someone with your vehicle."

Touché.

Katie got into the driver's seat, keeping one eye on Leo, realizing this whole situation was ridiculous and tragic and life-changing but not knowing what else to do other than help him.

This whole situation is totally messed up.

"Can you turn around? I think we're both going that way." Leo jerked a thumb over his shoulder.

Katie made a U-turn.

"So... I need to put my leg back on," Leo said. "I have to grind it down first."

"How is that... how is it even possible?"

"Long story. Could call it magic. Could call it science. My tissue can reattach, but it can't be scabbed over. I don't know why. You're taking all of this very well, I gotta say."

"I don't have a choice. I can't abandon you. And I can't drive if I'm hysterical."

"Well this is going to be loud, and gross. You probably shouldn't look."

Katie kept her head ramrod straight, eyes focused on the road ahead of her as a wet grinding sound filled the interior of the SUV, reminding her of a dentist drilling while their patient gargled and whimpered, and her imagination of how awful it must look ran scattershot through her mind, projecting horrifying images until she couldn't stand her own thoughts and had to take a peek because it couldn't be worse.

It was worse.

"Eyes on the road," Leo said, shaving and flattening his exposed femur. "That's why we're in this position."

Katie stared it him, slack-jawed.

"Doesn't that... hurt?"

"Of course it hurts," he snapped. "I'm grinding down my flesh and bone."

"Sorry. Dumb question. I... I guess I don't know how to react to this."

Leo turned off the grinder and seemed to consider her.

"It's okay," he said. "Every time I do this, I lose about half an inch. So I guess I'm saying..."

He began to laugh. A full body laugh that made his shoulders shake.

"What?" Katie asked. "What are you saying?"

"That I'm sorry for getting short with you."

Katie glanced at his bloody pants bottoms and slapped her hand over her mouth, unsure if she was ready to laugh or puke.

"I feel like Napoleon," Leo said, tears of mirth in his eyes. "Because he was de-feeted."

Katie shook her head and focused back on the road. "I don't think I can handle this."

"I don't have any more jokes," Leo said.

"Thank God."

"I'm stumped."

"You gotta stop, Leo. I'm gonna hurl."

"I'll do my best. You probably shouldn't watch this part."

Defying the warning Katie peeked at him as he held his severed leg up to his stump, and then she flat-out stared as all of the red jiggly bits began to sort of melt together. It was disgusting and fascinating at the same time.

"Eyes on the road," Leo reminded her.

Katie turned away. After a few moments of silence she asked, "What happened to you, Leo? Were you always like this?"

"I got possessed by a demon. He turned me into a slave. I was cured. Or I thought I was cured. I don't know why my body is doing this."

"Doesn't seem too bad."

"It was all bad," Leo said, his voice harsh. "He made me do... things. Bad things, that I can't forget."

"Is that why you can heal? You were possessed?"

"I'm not sure. This feels... different. I don't know what's happening. Something's... drawing me north. And it won't let me die until I get there."

"Is it the demon?"

"I don't know."

"Are you still possessed?"

"I don't know."

"What do you know?"

She glanced at Leo, and found him smiling again.

"I know that I'm glad you ran into me," he said.

Katie surprised herself by chuckling.

Likely a stress reliever. Or I'm losing my mind.

"You're taking this pretty well," Leo said.

"I'm sure I'll freak out later. Right now…"

"You're too worried about Duncan."

Katie nodded, a lump forming in her throat.

"I'll help you," Leo said. "With the stalker."

Katie wasn't sure if that was a good idea or a bad one. She stayed mum.

"After all," Leo said. "You picked me up."

"Literally," Katie said, remembering carrying his limbs.

"Now who's the one with the dad jokes?"

They drove in silence for a moment. Katie thought of Duncan. Of Lyon.

"Hazy out."

"Wildfires in Canada," Katie told him. "Flights are getting cancelled. Weather service is telling people to stay inside. Look… I don't want to be rude, but I'm hanging on by a thread here and I just need to drive in silence for a little bit."

"Okay."

Her phone buzzed.

Another picture of Duncan and his friends on the pontoon. They were standing up, and something about their poses seemed distressed.

Like they're being threatened by something.

Even worse, the picture is bigger than the last one.

Meaning Lyon is even closer to them.

Katie managed to choke back the sob, but the tears came anyway.

"Not a dad joke," Leo said, "but here's some dad advice even though you want me to be quiet. I was adopted. My parents, they weren't the best. But my stepfather did tell me this, and it stuck. Sometimes you climb the hill. Sometimes you slide down the hill. As long as you're staying on the hill, you're doing okay."

I have no idea if I'm climbing or sliding. But I'm headed to the man I love. So I'm still on the hill.

And maybe I can use some help.

Katie wiped away the tears and made her decision.

"Okay," she said, getting her emotional shit together. "I accept. Apparently we both need each other. And we happened to meet at the perfect time."

"It's practically predetermined," Leo said. "You take me where I need to go, and I convince your stalker to stop bothering you and Duncan."

"You really think you can do that?" Katie asked.

"She can't text you if I break all of her fingers."

"What? No! I want her to stop bothering me and Duncan, but she's messed up in the head. Violence isn't the answer."

"Fine. I can be persuasive without hurting anyone."

Katie was dubious about that.

"What are you worried about?" Leo asked. "That if things get tough, I'll fall apart?"

Double ugh. "I thought you were out of dad jokes."

"I'll work on that. Got anything to eat?"

"Check my carry-on. One of my job perks is unlimited packs of airline peanuts."

"I love airline peanuts."

Leo swiveled around, reaching for her suitcase, and Katie wondered if her luck had just improved, or if things were now spiraling completely irreversibly out of control.

SUN

"Mom! Dad!"

As her husband's airway closed up from anaphylactic shock, and killer—possibly demonic—wasps pelted her from every angle, Sun's fears burst all previous records when she heard their son, Francis, call for them outside.

Sometimes the bus driver honked the horn and waited for her or Andy to come to the porch before letting their child off in front of their house.

Other times Francis just appeared in the house, having walked up the driveway himself.

Today had to be one of those times.

Sun's face lit up with agonizing stings, with several more on her various limbs where the hornets managed to penetrate her bee suit, but her first concern was for her family's safety.

Andy needed an EpiPen injection. They kept one in the garage, on a shelf with a spare medical kit, but even though her husband couldn't breathe he wasn't the priority in this situation.

The priority was Francis. Venom toxicity was dependent on body weight, and there were over a thousand insects buzzing around. If Francis got in the garage, or the hornets got out, their son—without a bee suit—was at a greater immediate risk of death than Andy, even with Andy's allergy.

So Sun's first order of business was to lock the side door so Francis couldn't get in.

After doing that, Sun scanned the floor for the flint spark torch striker that Andy had dropped. She found it under the work bench, bent down for it, and received a series of stings across her back as her bee suit stretched and conformed to her body.

It felt like getting tazed, and her muscles seized and she dropped onto all fours. She managed to crawl next to her husband and pick up the backpack brush burner he'd been carrying, switching on the propane and picking up the torch by the hand grip.

One squeeze of the striker in front of the nozzle, and a blue flame ignited with a jet engine *WHOOSH!*

"Mom?" The knob on the side garage door jiggled, Francis trying to get in.

"Francis, wait in the house!" Sun yelled at him.

Then she wielded the garden flame thrower and faced the swarm.

Waving the torch around her, the fire pointed upward, Sun burned a few hundred converging wasps who curled up mid-air and dropped. But they quickly backed away, keeping their distance from the flame, which Sun didn't hold in one spot for more than a second in fear she'd light the wood joists in the unfinished ceiling.

She did, however, make her way to their huge, paper nest, and give it a nice long fire bath. It went up fast, and smoke quickly rose to eye-level, filling the top of the garage.

Sun set down the torch as the fire alarm began to beep, and keeping low under the smoke, headed for the cabinet with the first-aid kit while Andy rolled on the floor with both hands on his throat in the universal symbol for choking.

As she made it to the cabinet, Sun heard a horrifying sound.

The automatic garage door engaging.

Francis punched in the code and is opening the garage door!

Sun ran to the overhead track and jumped for the emergency release cord, giving it a yank and releasing the rolling door from its lifting mechanism.

"Go in the house, Francis!" she yelled again.

Back to the cabinet, dizzy from smoke and pain, Sun found the first-aid kit, grabbed the EpiPen, popped the cap, and crawled to her husband as the smoke continued to descend and the fire alarm assaulted her ears.

Coughing, she jabbed Andy in the thigh using a hard stabbing motion to get the spring activated needle through his suit and deep into his muscle tissue.

Keeping low, she got to the fire extinguisher hanging on the wall, pulled the pin, and put out the burning bug nest with a few quick bursts of CO_2.

That's when she noticed something unusual. The hornets had all gathered in the far corner of the garage, flying in tight circles. It was extremely odd behavior, but convenient for Sun who once again picked up the brush torch and easily burned them all at once.

They didn't even try to get away from me.

Checking the smokey room for stragglers and not seeing a single wasp, Sun dragged Andy to the side door, unlocked it, and tugged her husband outside, slamming it shut behind her, coughing inside her visor while searching for her son.

"Francis!"

Francis appeared on the front porch.

He seemed fine, but confused.

"Stay there! There are bees in the garage!"

"Is Dad okay?"

Dad, lying on his back, managed to raise a hand and offer a thumbs-up.

"Close the door, you don't want to get stung!" Sun ordered.

The child obeyed.

Sun tugged off her bee hood, her face burning. She pulled Andy's off as well, and saw swelling on his cheeks and neck.

"Thanks," he wheezed.

"Can you breathe?"

"I can now. That stuff works fast."

Sun cleared her throat, spat sooty saliva.

"Did you notice the wasps?" Sun asked.

Andy croaked a laugh. "Of course I noticed the wasps."

"I mean at the end. They were all in one spot in the corner. Like they were hiding."

"Trying to get away from the smoke?"

Sun wasn't sure.

She thought she heard something in the distance, some sort of horn, but she couldn't discern it over the shrill beep of the smoke alarm in the garage.

"They got you too," Andy pointed to Sun's face. "Those little bastards hurt. How many times did they sting you?"

"I can't tell. Over a dozen."

"Me, too. Do you think they…"

Andy let his voice trail off, but Sun knew what he meant.

Did they lay eggs in the stings?

"We need to check," she said. "But first I need to make sure the fire is out and I got them all."

Andy sat up. "I'll do that. Go to your office, check to see if we've been parasitized."

Sun nodded. She watched Andy put his hood back on and then go into the garage. She went into the house.

"Mom! Your face!"

Francis ran to her, and Sun kept him at arm's length because hugging would have been too painful. "I got stung, son. It really hurts."

"How bad?"

"Bad. How was school?"

"We had a test on the Founding Fathers, and it sucked, but your day was worse."

"Homework?"

"Art. We gotta draw the American flag. It's impossible, Mom. It has fifty stars and thirteen stripes. How am I supposed to color all that?"

"I'll help. First I need to take some medicine for these stings. I'll be in my office."

"Can I have a snack?"

"Fruit."

"How about fruit and three cookies?"

"One cookie."

"Two cookies."

"One cookie."

Francis seemed to consider it, then said, "Okay," and bounced off toward the kitchen.

In her office, Sun carefully peeled off the bee suit and inspected her body for stings.

It was ugly.

Eight on her back and thighs. Six on her arms. Four on her face and neck.

She sat on her examination table and pulled over the 3X magnifier light, positioning the articulated arm so she could see a sting on her knee.

The lump was raisin-sized, an ugly red color with a white dot on the pointy peak. Hot to the touch, and agonizing when Sun put even the slightest bit of pressure on it. She prepared a sterile syringe of lidocaine, wincing as she jabbed around the sting to numb the area, and then snapped on some nitrile gloves and unwrapped a new scalpel.

Properly anesthetized, she pressed the blade into the center of the sting, prompting a squirt of blood and milky fluid. She spread open the slice with her fingers, blotted it with gauze, and adjusted the magnifier.

Something wiggled in the wound.

Sun probed it with some Kelly forceps, digging in, grasping the foreign body.

It was a larva, already several millimeters long.

How could an egg hatch that quickly?

Such an accelerated growth rate could only mean one thing…

Sun pinched the grub hard enough to bisect it, pleased that it seemed to die. She placed both halves on a fresh slide and gave the specimen a look under the microscope.

Wasp larva usually had no visible eyes, or simple eyes known as ocelli.

But this had large eyes. Large eyes with elongated pupils.

"How's it going, babe?"

Sun glanced up from the scope and frowned at Andy.

"We're infested," she said. "And I'm pretty sure it's Bub."

LYON

Rowing the canoe was harder than Lyon expected. She hadn't had much boating experience, and the combination of balancing and pointing in the right direction frustrated her.

For a length she'd been going in the completely wrong direction, and then when she turned around she'd completely lost sight of Duncan's pontoon.

Fail. Total fail.

Lyon eventually reached the shore and headed west, moving slowly along the shoreline, heading toward the fire tower. This side of the lake, due to all the marshland, didn't have any houses, so Lyon didn't fear witnesses.

I don't need more trouble with the cops. That's why I'm being so careful.

She shifted her weight, almost tipping the boat over, the Glock dropping out of the back of her waistband and falling onto the aluminum hull.

A dull *CLANG!* echoed out over the still water and Lyon set down her paddle to reach for the gun. It was near the rear of the boat, and when she tried to twist around to get it the canoe rocked so badly she had to grab the sides to stay in.

Lyon decided to leave the weapon where it was until she found a pier, or shore, and could pick it up without capsizing. She picked up the oar again, looking for a spot to beach the boat, and noticed something swimming in the water thirty meters ahead of her, just under the surface.

It was so large that Lyon thought it was maybe a small deer, or even a bear, who had waded into the lake. But the way it moved, and its shape, had a weird sort of irregularity. Messed up. Like a jerky, man-sized marionette being yanked through the shallows.

Or a shark. Do lakes have sharks?

Whatever it was went from object of curiosity to threat as it headed right for Lyon's canoe. She reflexively turned, once more reaching for the gun, once more rocking the boat, once more trying to find balance. Lyon didn't reach the gun, and when she turned back to the lake to see how close the swimming thing was getting to her, she no longer saw any movement in the water. Only ripples, five meters away.

Lyon tried to stay completely still, which proved really difficult when she wasn't moving forward because her core made the boat shake. She braced her hands on the sides, holding her breath, waiting to see if that swimming thing came back.

Then, at the front of the boat, something silently poked out of the water.

A human head, wearing some sort of monster mask—a zombie or a swamp creature—raised up to neck level and watched her.

The mask was designed with greenish flesh, hanging loose, pockmarked with dozens of dark black slits. The eyes dull black. Patches of wet hair, like a dog with mange.

It stared at Lyon.

Lyon stared back.

What the hell is that?

A survivor of abuse, as well as an abuser, Lyon remained calm, waiting to learn more before proceeding. A child who was regularly beaten could keenly observe and predict the warning signs before the violence began. Likewise, choosing someone to bully, and knowing when to bully, required a careful analysis of the potential victim.

Her heart rate kicked up a bit, but outwardly Lyon remained calm.

The head blinked, then sank back into the lake.

Okay, that wins the weird event of the month. And I just pissed and bled all over my boyfriend's sheets.

Lyon continued to stare at the spot where it submerged.

Then she heard something faint, coming from the bottom of the boat.

Scratching. As if something was directly beneath it, running fingernails across the aluminum.

Are they trying to frighten me?

What sort of weird shit is this?

The sound stopped.

Lyon waited. And watched.

The lake stayed still and silent, like a cemetery on a winter's night.

"Aren't you afraid?" a man asked, deep and gurgly.

The voice came from the other side of the boat. Lyon turned around, slow and easy so she didn't rock.

"It takes a lot to scare me," she answered, staring at the head again.

Five meters away, the head began to slowly move toward her.

It made a wet, snorting sound, similar to a pig snuffling.

"You're bleeding," said the head.

Four and a half meters, and closing.

Not a ripple. Not a sound. As perfectly still as one of those Olympic synchronized swimmers.

"You're ugly," Lyon countered.

The head had gotten close enough that Lyon could tell it wasn't a mask.

This is actually some kind of lake monster.

And I'm fine with it.

"Did you do that to yourself?" the head asked. "The bleeding?"

"Did you do that to yourself?"

The head sank again.

Did I piss it off?

Am I hallucinating?

Was I somehow teleported into some effed-up horror movie?

Lyon sorted her thoughts, trying to find some truth.

Either I'm crazy, which is possible, dreaming, which is also possible, or this is some sort of magic or space alien or ancient creature or the most elaborate practical joke in history.

Or a ghost.

The head broke the water right next to her canoe. Lyon could smell it, now.

Rot. It smells like Mother in the dining room, under all the magazines.

So many magazines fallen on top of her she couldn't get out.

A true hoarder's death. Buried alive by your own trash.

Mother screamed for hours. Then moaned for days.

I watched the pile until the noises stopped.

I sat there, every day, wondering if Mother could somehow come back.

I sat there until the stench came.

A terrible, wonderful stench.

A stench that meant it was the end.

A stench that made me glad I pushed the wall of magazines on top of her.

"You really aren't afraid." The head smiled. Its teeth behind mottled lips were black and seemed to move, like crawling bugs. "He is impressed."

"Who are you?" Lyon asked the rotting head.

"I'm a vessel for the ultimate power. Do you wish to have power?"

"I have power," Lyon said.

"I mean real power. The power to burn down the world. To kill billions. To enslave mankind."

Lyon found that amusing, and laughed. "You look like a rump roast left out in a dumpster on a hot day," she said. "What power do you have?"

"Not me. Him. The power is in Him."

"And who is He?"

The head slowly sank again.

Lyon shivered, in an excited way. Like when she killed an animal. Or when she cut herself.

I'm not sure what's happening, but I—

The huge *SPLASH!* coincided with the boat tipping to the side, and a moment later the head, attached to a rotten black body that seemed to have been run over by a tractor and then left to putrefy in filthy water, covered by torn clothes, mud, and weeds, flopped into the front of the canoe and splashed Lyon with muck and bits of rancid flesh.

Lyon fell backward, onto the Glock, and she scrambled for it and picked it up and aimed it at the zombie—by this point she was sure it was a ghost or a zombie—and racked a round into the chamber.

The boat rocked for a few seconds, and then became still as Lyon and the thing stared at each other.

"He likes you," the thing said.

"Who?"

It smiled again, and this time Lyon was sure a bug ran out of its mouth and quickly crawled up its mottled nostril.

"What is your name?"

"Lyon."

"He likes you, Lyon. He senses you are strong. Like your name is strong."

"Who likes me?"

The monster's head bent at an odd angle, making a wet, cracking sound. Its mouth opened and a wiggling black tongue came out.

And kept coming out.

And kept coming out until it dangled down to its shoulder, then slurped out of its mouth and plopped onto the bottom of the boat, where it squirmed like a live bratwurst.

Not a tongue. A leech.

"You're the devil," Lyon said.

"You believe in the devil?"

"I used to pray to the devil. God never answered, so I begged to Satan."

"He prefers Beelzebub. Or just Bub. What did you beg for?"

"I wanted to destroy my enemies."

"Who are your enemies, Lyon?"

"The world."

The vessel smiled, and drool came out. Cloudy drool, filled with maggots.

"He can help. Bub can help. Do you wish to accept His help?"

Do I get to actually sell my soul to the devil?

For the first time in my miserable life, could I actually be that lucky?

"Yes. I want His help."

"Take off your clothes, Lyon."

Lyon didn't hesitate. She set down the gun and carefully stripped while trying to keep the boat steady. Shoes. Socks. Shirt. Pants. Underwear. When she was naked she sat proudly, defiantly, her knees open slightly.

"You are no stranger to pain," the vessel said.

"Life is pain."

The vessel leaned forward, its black eyes widening. "He sees Himself in you."

"What do I have to do?"

"One small thing. Survive the pain."

The sound reminded Lyon of microwave popcorn as holes in his flesh opened up like hundreds of tiny mouths.

Flies, hornets, ants, worms, and leeches were wetly and violently birthed out of his body, and they swarmed over her bare skin, crawling and biting and stinging and wiggling, and she couldn't stay still, she had to fight back and try to slap them and get away but there were too many and the vessel was on top of her, pinning her down, and as white hot agony spread over Lyon's nude body, igniting every nerve, driving her past insanity with unrelenting, continuously building pain, her screaming mind completely understood the comment; "He sees Himself in you."

Because every hole in her body, large and small, was violated and filled to bursting with bugs.

CHUCK

SAME TIME...

After the motor died, the pontoon coasted to a stop twenty meters from shore. Chuck squinted at the fire tower on the shore's edge and guessed it had a road, or at least a trail, leading up to it. Even though the structure was abandoned by the DNR, it must have been accessible at some point.

But if we can even get there, will we have to battle more bugs?

There are no houses on this swampy side of the lake.

Will we need to walk through the woods while being attacked by flies and ants? What if they're even worse than on the lake?

Chuck felt drained, maybe 60% of his usual self. His eye was swollen shut and throbbed with his heartbeat. With his remaining eye he examined himself, and appeared to be peppered with birdshot. He had bleeding welts everywhere, bleeding holes everywhere, some still filled with popped maggots, and they all hurt.

Duncan fared about the same, maybe slightly worse, boasting hands that looked like he'd dunked them in strawberry jelly.

Stu, lying on one of the seat benches, was covered in welts and pink powder. Duncan had managed to dump six packets of Celox on Stu's leech bites without passing out. While Stu's bleeding seemed to be slowing down, he looked like he'd been dunked in pixie sticks and grenadine.

If our team is 'ride or die,' we all seem closer to the 'die' part of that expression.

Shore remained ten meters away, and the damn lake still lacked a damn breeze. As if fate devised a master scheme to not give them any kind of break at all.

The plan was to decide who would hop out and pull the boat to shore. No one was anxious to get into the water again. Stu was too weak to do it, and Chuck and Duncan hadn't figured out who would go. They were both bleeding, and neither wanted to join Stu in the Leech Feeding Club.

So for the moment everyone stayed put, keeping their eyes out for approaching bugs, racing to figure out their next move while waiting for a drift.

Chuck swallowed, throat dry, and searched around the pontoon for water bottles. He found an empty one near his feet, picked it up, and let the last few hot drops coat his mouth.

He let it drop, found another bottle, and repeated the gesture.

Not enough to quench my thirst. But as my grandpa used to say, it wet my whistle.

Chuck found a third empty bottle. Just as he lifted it to his lips, Stu croaked, "Stop!"

Chuck paused.

Should I be sharing these final drops with my boys?

I probably should. They must be just as thirsty.

He offered it to Stu, and Stu weakly shook his head. "The maggot that I pulled from that dead bass's eye... I put it in one of the bottles."

Chuck's stomach did a backflip. He squinted into the plastic bottle, and didn't see a maggot.

He quickly found the two he'd sucked dry.

No maggots.

That left three more empties.

He checked one.

No maggot.

He checked another.

No maggot.

He checked the last one...

No freaking maggot.

"Damn it, Stu. I think I swallowed your damn bug."

"I chewed up and ate a bunch of flies," Duncan offered.

"But they were dead," Chuck said. "Stu, was that maggot alive?"

"The boat siren probably popped it, like it did the flies and ants," Stu said. "Probably."

Chuck checked each of the water bottles once again for popped maggot guts. They all looked clean.

He held his belly, wondering if he had a live worm in there.

"Maybe your stomach acid will kill it," Duncan said.

"Stu? What do you think?"

"Parasites can survive inside bodies. Even stomachs. And parasites can have parasites. Hyperparasitism. So a leech or parasitic wasp can have flukes, protozoa, tapeworms. And those hyperparasites can have bacteria and viruses inside of them. It's like multiple layers of infection."

"You're an asshole, Stu."

"Let's forgive each other. You forgive me because you ate my maggot, I forgive you because you ate my maggot."

Asshole.

Given their situation, Chuck chose to forgive and forget.

Well, maybe not forget. Especially if I start throwing up maggots.

But I am interested in something we haven't discussed yet. Something Stu might know.

"So… what's going on with these bugs, Bug Lord?" Chuck asked. "Why are they acting like this?"

Stu shrugged. "No idea. Maybe something to do with all the aquatic herbicide they used to control the weeds, accelerating mutation. I don't know. Pick a topic. Global warming? Deforestation? Pollution? Someone dumping nuclear waste in the lake? Cosmic rays altering DNA?"

"What do you think, Duncan?"

"It's the devil," Duncan said.

"The devil," Chuck repeated.

Duncan stared out over the water. "Our neighbors, Sun and Andy, came over once, for a BBQ. We were all drinking. They said they met the devil. That one of the devil's minions even came to Lake Niboowin. I thought they were being funny. Or drunk and stupid."

"It's not the devil, Duncan," Chuck said. "There's no such thing."

Duncan turned to face him. "Do you believe in evil, Chuck?"

Chuck shook his head. "I sure don't. Life is shitty. People do shitty things. But those are choices. They begin as thoughts, and then become actions. It's selfishness. It's harm. We can call it evil, but it's just a description, not an actual, tangible thing."

"Pretty deep for a Quickie Lube mechanic," Stu said.

Duncan stared at his hands. "I've seen evil. It's deeper than human nature. Evil has its own life. It's own force, outside of humanity. Maybe it's tangible. Maybe it's real."

"Satan is said to be the embodiment of evil," Stu said. "But I'm voting for cosmic rays."

No one laughed.

"So do you also believe in good?" Chuck asked Duncan. "That people can embody good?"

"I'm not sure," Duncan said. "Maybe, when evil showed up, good left town."

They were all silent for a bit.

The quiet was broken, almost predictably, by the buzz of a black fly.

Chuck swatted it away. "We gotta get to shore, guys. Duncan, rock-paper-scissors for who goes in the lake?"

"Naw," Duncan said. "I'll do it."

"You sure?"

"My boat, my fault. Captain's rules."

Duncan stood up, opened the vinyl seat panel, and grabbed a roll of nylon rope with the anchor attached. He also grabbed a rusty air horn can.

After handing the can to Chuck, he said, "I'm going to swim us to shore then pull the boat in by rope. Use that if any flies get closer."

"Does it still work?"

"I never tried it."

Chuck removed the plastic safety bit and gave the horn button a quick press. The sound trumpeted loud as an AC/DC rock concert and spread out across the mirror surface of the lake.

"Bug Lord, watch for bugs."

"Aye aye, Captain."

"Chuck, I'm tying the rope around my waist. If I get into trouble, pull me in."

"Roger, Captain. Be careful."

"Just a quick dip in the lake." Duncan winked. "What could go wrong?"

Chuck's stomach churned, and he didn't know if it was worry for his friend or maggots breeding in his digestive system.

Duncan buckled on his life jacket, cut the rusty old 15-pound anchor off the nylon rope, then wrapped the rope around his waist and cinched it with a bow knot. He handed the other end to Chuck, opened the gate, and folded down the port ladder. After carefully descending into the lake, letting Chuck hold the slack, Duncan began to breast stroke toward the shoreline.

He made it five strokes, and then the screaming began.

Duncan thrashed as if he'd been dropped into a cauldron of boiling oil, swinging his arms, kicking his legs.

Adrenaline overtook Chuck, and he immediately and viciously yanked on the rope, pulling hand over hand, the nylon biting into his palms and knuckles, twisting and wrapping it around his wrist and leaning back, digging in and moving toward to the bow like he was gaining ground in a tug of war.

Stu managed to get onto all fours and crawl to the stern, helping Duncan up the ladder. Duncan dropped to his knees next to the motor and began to slap his body.

Or more precisely, the black things all over his skin, biting his body with little spurts of blood.

Chuck stood there for a moment, transfixed, then Duncan's next wail spurred him to action, and he held the air horn in front of him like Van Helsing warding off vampires, pressing the button and letting it blast.

The horn made the biting things stop biting and drop away, and as Chuck moved closer some of the things even burst open. Duncan scrambled backward, undoing his life jacket, slapping his bare chest while he continued to hyperventilate. After Chuck waved the air horn all over Duncan like it was a can of bug spray (which it sort of was), he released the button and knelt next to his friend.

Duncan's face was a mix of pain and panic. "Shit, those things hurt like hell."

"What are they?" Chuck asked.

Stu squinted at one Duncan had slapped to death. "They're way too big, but they look like dragonfly nymphs. They have the labrum; the hinged jaws that grab prey."

Chuck was confused. "I thought dragonflies don't attack humans."

"They don't. They don't have ovipositors, either. But these do."

Duncan moaned. "You mean they laid eggs in me?"

"I have no idea. But if we're going by what we've seen so far, it's a good assumption. They tore into your skin with their mouth parts and then stung you in the wounds. A genetic combination of bot flies and parasitic wasps. And dragonflies, of course. Those nymphs are the babies. I'd hate to see them all grown up."

"Gimme the horn." Duncan held out his hand. "Maybe that can drive them out of me."

Stu passed Duncan the can, and he held it to some of the new bites on his arm, which stood out from all the older stings on his arm because they were jagged lines instead of round bumps, and Duncan pressed the button.

Sure enough, little whitish rice-sized things wiggled out of the fresh wounds and then burst.

We're all going to need some serious antibiotics after this.

Chuck thought it rather than said it because the horn was too loud to talk over. Until it wasn't.

The trumpet became a whistle, which became a hiss, which became dead silence.

Duncan gave it a shake and tried again. Nothing.

"It's empty."

Duncan began to laugh. Stu joined in.

Chuck thought they were both freaking nuts.

They eventually calmed down. Then Stu threw up blood.

"Keeps getting better and better." Stu wiped his mouth with the back of his arm, leaving a red streak.

"Remember fishing this morning, when we complained nothing was biting?" Duncan asked, prompting those two morons to start another laughing fit.

Chuck turned away, irritated, his eyes falling on one of their fishing rods.

It's a thirty-pound test braided line. Maybe if we could cast far enough we could hook the shore and reel the boat in? Every angler working the shoreline has accidentally cast too far and wrapped their lure around a tree. With modern line, and a quick drift, the pole would break before the tree or line did.

I bet I could hit a leg on that fire tower with a big lure. With a slow, steady retrieve, and the drag set to max, and no wind, it should be possible to reel the pontoon to shore. And with all three of us doing it at once, going nice and easy, it would only take a few minutes to—

"Damn, Duncan! Gross!"

Chuck made the mistake of looking at his friends.

Stu seemed ready to barf again. He was gaping at Duncan, who was using a trailer hook to dig into his own wounds and fish out dragonfly grubs.

"I think I've cured my vasovagal syncope," he said through a clenched jaw as he yanked a squirming grub out of a bleeding gash in his arm.

"Jesus, dude, doesn't that hurt?" Chuck asked.

"Yeah it hurts. But I want to get them out before the wounds close up and the bugs start growing."

Chuck leaned over the gunwale to vomit, but nothing came up but dry heaves.

Disappointing.

Motion in his peripheral vision caught Chuck's attention, and he turned to see a small black bird land on the motor.

But, of course, it wasn't actually a bird.

"Hey, Bug Lord," Chuck interrupted his gagging. "How many wings do dragonflies have?"

Stu held up four fingers. "Four. Two pairs."

Chuck counted four translucent wings on the insect, attached to a black body as long as a hot dog.

And its eyes…

Big and bulgy and wet, like a bullfrog's.

And its mouth…

It had its own little arm, like a crab claw.

Chuck slowly picked up the rod and reel, raising the lure up behind his back.

"You going fishing, buddy?" Duncan asked.

Chuck performed a casting motion but didn't take his finger off the spool to release any line, so the lure stayed at the end of the rod, lashing out like a barb on the tip of a whip.

The treble hooks caught on the dragonfly, which immediately tried to shake itself free, buzzing and flailing around in an angry, frightening blur, attacking the pole.

The trio watched, transfixed, as the insect somehow bit the first four inches of the pole off, along with the thirty-pound test line, and then flew away carrying a 5/8 oz lure with it—

—into a hovering black mass of more giant mutant dragonflies.

And that was enough for Chuck. There wasn't time to cast a lure out to shore. He dropped the pole and grabbed the rope.

We need to get the hell off this lake, right now.

"Maybe evil exists," Chuck said to his buddies. "But good exists too."

He went to the stern and tied a bowline knot around the float cleat and the other end of the rope around his waist.

"Chuck!" Duncan warned. "You don't want to—"

Chuck dove into the shallow, mucky water.

Then we swam for his life.

At first, he made fast, painless progress, halving the distance to shore in just a few seconds.

Then, all at once, he felt like he was swimming in a blender. The water churned around him with insect attacks, dragonfly nymphs darting from all directions and latching on with their beartrap mouthparts.

Fighting the instinct to try and brush them off, determined to save his friends, Chuck continued to dig in, kicking hard, stroking hard until his hands began to scoop up muck on the shallow lake bottom, seeing the shore only five feet away, screaming into the filthy water, and then no longer being able to swim in the mire and reeds and instead crawling and clawing and pushing his way through it, coating his body with mud but not stopping the relentless attack of the nymphs, finally FINALLY making it to the coast and pulling up onto the shoreline and rolling through the dirt and rocks and scrub grass to shake off the biting, stinging horde trying to strip him of all his flesh.

He rolled until he hit a chain-link fence and there, above the barbed-wire top, was the looming fire tower, and Chuck blocked out his own pain long enough to push himself onto his feet, reaching for the rope to pull the pontoon in before the dragonflies attacked Stu and Duncan—

—and realizing the rope had fallen off.

Chuck turned to face the water, and saw the yellow length of nylon rope floating just two meters away. On the boat, his friends each wielded fishing poles, swinging lures at dive-bombing dragonflies. He watched as one of them swooped down on Stu and attacked his neck, prompting an animal-like squeal.

Gotta save them.

I gotta save them.

His legs didn't want to move, but Chuck forced them to, stumbling and splashing back into the water, more nymphs attacking him, the pain worse than being scorched with a hundred blowtorches all over all at once, and Chuck stretched for the rope, stretched for the rope, stretched for the rope—

—and then sank face first in the muck and couldn't free himself.

LEO

So perhaps destiny is real.

In some weird, coincidental, practically unbelievable twist of fate, the Tug wanted Leo to go to the same house Katie drove to.

Leo didn't know where he learned the term *superdeterminism*, which referenced the quantum mechanical principles of measurement. In short, it postulated that everything that happens has already happened and cannot be altered, so free will doesn't exist. The concept wasn't popular.

But it was related to the currently en vogue idea of *Invisible String Theory*—metaphysics not physics—which basically said everything is connected and what happens is meant to be.

Leo also didn't know where he learned that tidbit, but if fate was a real thing he really seemed fated to go on this journey and meet Katie.

He also knew that fate wasn't finished with him yet.

"We're here."

After taking a side road, and an even smaller side road through the deep woods, Katie stopped at a nondescript house on the south shore of Big Lake Niboowin, on a property enveloped by white spruce, red maple, green ash, and paper birch. She parked on the driveway and Leo followed her out of the vehicle, backpack on his shoulder, moving slow and careful to test the strength of his joints.

Katie hurried into the house, banging on the front door.

I don't know how formidable a person Katie is, but everything she told me about her stalker points to Lyon being unhinged. You should typically approach unhinged people cautiously, and possibly armed.

When no one answered, Katie checked the knob and discovered it unlocked. Leo followed her inside, feeling curious and also feeling protective.

Prior to all the current craziness, there had been past craziness, and Leo had worked as a bodyguard-slash-boytoy for an unhinged woman. Protecting her had become second nature, and he recognized the feelings when they returned.

It's been a long time since I cared about anything. Including myself.

Whatever is goading me internally may know I needed to do this.

But is this my destiny? To protect a young girl from another young girl?

Is this what the Tug called me to?

The house was well-maintained and clean, upper middle-class furnishings, and uncluttered to a degree that Leo sensed was functional over stylistic. The front door, though unlocked, was steel, the lock formidable. Leo checked the nearest window and found security bars and reinforced glass. While Katie hurried down the hall, Leo followed a hunch and checked the top of the refrigerator, his fingers brushing a handgun.

The occupants here have placed a priority on security and personal safety. There are likely many hidden weapons, and cameras, on the property.

Leo borrowed the gun, a Colt Detective Special loaded with six rounds of .38 cartridges, and stuck it in his trench coat pocket.

"What in the actual fuck?"

Leo followed Katie's voice to a bedroom. She stood next to a bed, which had been soaked with blood, and by the odor, urine.

Blood is still red. Recent. It turns brown, then black, as it dries.

"Your boyfriend needs to buy a new bed."

"Why would she do this? It's insane."

It didn't seem insane to Leo. "She's staking her claim."

Leo wasn't sure how to explain that he knew what a territorial mark smelled like, or how he even knew what one was.

I just know. The same way I know the Tug wanted me to come to this lake.

The same way I know that something big is going to happen.

The same way I know that when this is all over, I'll finally find peace.

Katie hurried out of the bedroom, and Leo listened to her footfalls as she searched the house, eventually exiting through a sliding patio door.

Leo didn't feel the need to go after her. Instead he felt drawn to the back door, through the yard, to the pier. He stared out over the lake, a huge flat mirror that reflected the hazy sky and oppressive sun.

At first glance, no boats.

Strange. I would have expected water skiers, fishermen, people out for pleasure cruises.

He squinted and his vision focused a little, and he was able to see a bit further.

A canoe. On the opposite shore. Abandoned in the reeds.

Further to the west, near a steel fire tower, a pontoon.

That's where I need to be.

That's where the Tug is leading me.

"Lyon's car is parked in the woods." Katie had run up behind him. "Both the boats are gone, the pontoon and the canoe. I bet that crazy bitch took the canoe."

"They're on the other side of the lake."

Katie stood next to Leo and shielded her eyes with her hand. "How can you see that far?"

"We need a boat," Leo said.

"The neighbors, Sun and Andy, they have a boat. Maybe they can help."

Leo cocked his head. "Sun and Andy Dennison-Jones?"

"Do you know them?" Katie asked.

"No."

"How did you know their names?"

"I don't know."

"You don't think that's weird?"

"I once shit out my own intestines and then ate them out of a public toilet with a fork. My definition of weird is probably different than yours."

"First, yuck. Second, yuck and yuck. Let's go to their house. Don't mention grinding down your limbs, or eating your organs. Or anything. In fact, don't talk. Don't talk, and don't do anything. Just try to be a decent person. Got it?"

"Got it."

Katie's face scrunched up. "I've hung out with them a few times. They're good people. They like Duncan and his parents. They'll lend us their boat. They have to."

That really didn't matter to Leo.

If they have a boat, I'm taking it. Whether they approve or not...

STU

A MOMENT EARLIER...

Anisoptera.

  Nature's perfect predator.

Stu stared, in awe, as over a dozen gigantic dragonflies approached the pontoon while Chuck thrashed and screamed in the water between the boat and the shore.

Three hundred million years ago, the ancestor of dragonflies, griffin-flies, could grow up to a pound in weight, with a wingspan over two feet. These *Meganeuropsis permiana* were able to get so large because there had been more oxygen in the prehistoric atmosphere. Either more O_2 allowed them to better utilize oxygen, or a competing hypothesis postulated that they grew larger to avoid oxygen poisoning. Either way, the insects were enormous. This superpredator, hunting in packs, could have killed and devoured dinosaurs.

Stu knew they'd have no problem devouring him. Especially in his weakened condition, likely due to some disease or parasite the leeches had bestowed upon him.

  At least it will be a spectacular death.

He turned to Duncan and saw his friend drop the hook he was using to fish larva out of his open wounds, then threw open his tackle box, digging through it. He quickly unsnapped his leader and replaced the bait on his fishing rig with one three times the size; an eight-inch Believer lure with three massive treble hooks.

  He's going to use it like a mace to defend himself.

  Pretty good idea.

Stu rummaged through Duncan's open lure box and found a large lure for his own pole, attaching it to the end of his line. He then looked to Duncan to mimic his stance, and a dragonfly divebombed and latched its labium—a claw pincer the length and shape of a staple remover—onto Stu's neck.

The pain was instant and the fear was all-encompassing.

Stu screamed, releasing the rod and slapping at the creature with both hands, ultimately gripping its long, segmented abdomen and trying to tear it away.

The skin on Stu's neck stretched, then tore, and Stu tossed the insect aside and probed his wound to determine the damage.

A gash, but no veins or arteries, and not deep enough to open up a hole in my throat.

He turned to Duncan again, to see if he'd been similarly attacked. But instead of facing the oncoming swarm, Duncan was facing Chuck, who'd made it to shore, bleeding like his skin had leaks, and then for unknown reasons jumped back into the water, where he flailed, cried out, and sank.

Stu batted away another attacking dragonfly and watched, aghast, as Duncan cast out his big lure directly at Chuck.

The bait sailed beyond him, almost reaching the shoreline. Duncan began a quick retrieve, the lure diving under the water. Then Duncan's pole bent, and Duncan pulled back hard—

—setting the hook on Chuck.

Duncan grunted, continuing to reel in, and Chuck popped back to the surface, coughing and gasping and clutching Duncan's lure, lodged deep in his shoulder.

Stu reached for his dropped pole, then wielded it as a weapon, whipping it at dragonflies, catching one on the barbs with a wet crunch followed by a screeching buzz. The hooked bug pulled, and Stu's muscle memory reflexively triggered and he tried reeling in, accidentally hitting the cast bar, releasing the line which whirred out as the insect flew off with the lure.

As Stu fought to reel in the dragonfly darting over the boat in a quick figure eight, another darted in and landed on his face, grasping his cheeks with six barb-covered legs, its mouth parts clamping onto the bridge of Stu's nose.

Stu furiously shook his head, trying to dislodge it without dropping his fishing pole, tripping and almost falling over the anchor Duncan had cut off the nylon rope, and the insect curled up and poked its long, black abdomen at Stu's lips, trying to force his mouth open.

Ovipositor. It wants to lay eggs down my throat.

I've had enough.

I've had enough of this.

In a moment of crazed clarity Stu screamed, feeling the rough tail force itself inside, past his teeth, poking his quivering tongue, and Stu immediately bit down, the sound similar to stuffing your face with corn chips, the dragonfly electrified with a frenzy of pain and anger, its wings beating and slapping Stu's face in an effort to get away.

Who's eating who, motherfucker?

The abdomen leaked gooey hemolymph—*Anisoptera's* greenish blood—and Stu spat it out, releasing the insect, which flew off as he finished reeling in the one flying around the boat, slamming it down on the floor of the pontoon, stomping on its giant bulbous head with its huge black eyes, crushing it like eggs, and turning to see Duncan at the stern, pulling hard to help a wheezing, sputtering Chuck get out of the water and back on board. Chuck's wrist was hooked to his opposite shoulder with Duncan's lure, impossible to know how deeply because there was blood everywhere from all the nymph bites.

Stu faced the swarm again, raging at them, swinging his fishing pole, and they kept their distance but continued to zip around the boat.

Feeling his energy drain away, Stu stared out at the shore, so close but so very far, wondering how it could even be possible that there hadn't been even a faint breeze for hours.

It's like we're anchored here.

Anchored…

The anchor!

"Duncan! Take my pole!"

He looks as bloody as Chuck and as weak as me.

But we can do this.

Duncan seemed confused but took the rod and reel that was shoved into his hands, and Stu went to the stern and reached for the nylon rope tied to the float cleat, pulling it in from the lake where Chuck had dragged it. After grabbing the end he crawled to the anchor, the lovely, perfect, rusty old anchor, and quickly tied in on using a fisherman's knot.

As Duncan continued to swat at the horde, Stu picked up the anchor line and began to swing it by his side, like a pendulum, aiming for the shoreline. When he got the motion waist-high, he released the rope and threw the anchor into the lake.

It sailed about five meters, then quickly sank.

Stu got on his knees and began to pull at the weight, slowly.

Anchors were really tough to get off of mucky bottoms. On a lake without waves, Stu succeeded in pulling the boat toward the anchor, and therefore toward the shore.

"That's genius, Stu!" Duncan yelled. "Keep going!"

So far, so good.

Suction is keeping it rooted in place.

It'll be a PITA to lift, but maybe we'll make it after all.

"Nice work, Bug Lord," Chuck told him, still lying down but giving him a weak thumbs-up with his free hand.

When he finished tugging the pontoon to the anchor's location, Stu bent at the knees, wrapped the wet line around his elbows, and tried to deadlift the weight off the spongy bottom.

He strained, and the suction slowly broke. He brought the anchor up, hand over hand. As expected, mud, dead leaves, and weeds clung to the rusty metal. A few nymphs had also taken a ride, springing themselves off and flipping around like landed fish.

Stu wiped the anchor clean, stood up, and again began to swing it.

A few meters to go. Maybe I can reach land on this try.

For some reason, instinct maybe, he quickly glanced at Duncan, who managed to be keeping the dragonflies at bay with his fishing pole.

Then he checked the water, behind Duncan, and saw—

A raft.

A reddish, blackish, amorphous raft shaped like an irregular puddle.

Moving across the water without any wind or waves.

"Ants!" Stu yelled. "It's an ant raft! Two meters away from the boat!"

Two meters, and moving closer.

Those little bastards aren't just floating. They're swimming.

Stu continued to swing the anchor, shoulders aching, lungs burning, vision swirling, knees wobbling, but resolve hard as steel.

"Throw the damn thing, Stu!" Duncan ordered.

"I'm adding momentum so the oscillation reaches its apex amplitude!" Chuck yelled, "Fuck the science and just throw the fucker!"

Stu threw the fucker—

—which arced through the air on a perfect trajectory and landed only a meter short of the shoreline.

He knelt down and once again began to pull.

"Ants are gaining," Chuck told him. "How the hell can ants swim, Stu?"

Stu grunted. "I don't know, Chuck." His breath was labored, and the poor air quality didn't make it any easier.

Something landed on Stu's back, and he held the line and tried to swat it off with his other hand. When he couldn't reach, and the biting began, he called for Chuck.

Chuck yelped, but didn't come to his rescue.

Stu scooted over, pressing his back into one of the pontoon benches, hearing the crackly *CRUNCH!* of a crushed dragonfly, and then turned to berate Chuck—

—and stared, appalled, that Chuck was hooked to the green pontoon carpeting and straining to free himself.

Chuck met his eyes, frantic.

Stu glanced back at the ants.

They're so close.

Stu went back to pulling on the anchor, slowly, inexorably, dragging the big pontoon to the shore.

"If they get on board," Chuck said, "I want you to kill me."

Stu didn't reply, but he noticed Duncan kneeling next to Chuck.

"Guys, promise me—"

"Shup up!" Stu screeched. "No one is killing anyone!"

"I don't want to die like that. I don't—"

"No one is dying!"

Hands slick with water and lake slime and blood and sweat, Stu once again wrapped the rope around his butt and walked it backward, and then he went hand over hand back to the stern to do it again when his ankles became wrapped in hot electric bolts.

The fire ants had come aboard.

Stu didn't think it through, he just acted on instinct, jumping into the lake, the shore just two meters away, the stinging of the ants replaced by a full-on assault by dragonfly nymphs, and Stu's feet sunk into the muck but he was absolutely crazed with a burst evolutionary fight-or-flight energy and he pulled and pulled and pulled and he got to shore and dragged the pontoon in behind him and it was almost there almost there almost there and then Duncan cried, "I'm so sorry, Chuck!" and Stu watched as he raised his Swiss Army knife over his head, the blade pointed down.

JAKE

The woman in the canoe somehow survived.

Lyon's flesh rippled with life, flies and wasps and grubs poking their heads out of the thousands of tiny holes honeycombing every inch of her body.

Her epidermis is their new home. Like thousands of small, biting pets who have just moved in.

They await her command.

Each pore in Lyon's skin had been stretched and torn to accommodate one of His creatures. She appeared to be wearing red, shimmering armor.

The shimmering was the wiggle of insect legs and antennae and the snapping of mandibles.

The red was Lyon's blood.

This infestation came with a high cost.

The shock should have killed her.

But the expression on her face is one of elation. Even ecstasy.

She smiled, even as maggots wiggled in her gums and black ants swarmed over her teeth.

The woman shall now serve Him.

He has chosen wisely.

Jake's stomach rumbled and stretched, distending to the size of a twenty-month pregnancy. His belly button opened like a small mouth, rimmed with thorn-like teeth.

Without prompt, Lyon pressed her hand into Jake's stomach, all the way to the wrist.

The sound of munching and slurping ensued.

"He has enemies," Jake told her.

"I can feel them."

"This lake is His outpost. He only controls a portion. After His enemies are absorbed, He'll finish taking over the lake."

Lyon laughed, spitting up nematodes like canned spaghetti. "The lake, the town, the state, the country... the world."

"You wish to go to the boys on the boat."

Lyon nodded.

"He will allow it."

"I know. I hear Him. I feel Him."

Lyon whimpered, then quickly withdrew her hand from the gaping mouth in Jake's stomach.

Her fingers had been stripped of flesh, and the bugs swarmed to feast on the remaining scraps still stuck to the bone.

Yet, somehow, she could still clench her skeletal fist.

"Go to them," Jake said. "Bring the boys into His flock."

Lyon slipped over the side of the boat and vanished under the water.

Jake looked to the south, to the opposite shore, toward the home of Sun and Andy Dennison-Jones.

It's finally time for vengeance.

It's finally time to deal with the enemy.

SUN

"How much lidocaine do you have?" Andy asked.

She had numbed both of them up with dozens of shots and had been extracting wasp eggs from her husband's face, which was about as sexy as it sounded.

"I bought in bulk for special occasions like this one." She raised her voice, yelling through the closed lab door, "Francis! Are the animals all okay?"

"Yeah, Mom! They're in my room. We're watching *Little Witch Academia.*"

Andy winced. "Should we let him watch that supernatural stuff?"

"A demon put a giant wasp hive in our garage so it could grow larvae in our bodies."

"Point taken. Is it time to call Frank Belgium?"

Sun considered her answer carefully. "Frank... hasn't been himself lately."

"That's putting it lightly."

"I think we need to do some more exploration, see if there is anything else around. Every time Bub shows up, he changes his tactics."

"He learns from mistakes," Andy said.

"Maybe. Or maybe he has a playbook. Sort of a counterpart to Sun Tzu's *Art of War.* If one battle-tested plan doesn't work, he tries another."

"And this one is possessing insects?"

"Possessing. Or mutating their DNA with that reformant serum he secretes. Or building a slave army. Whatever it is he does. He keeps adapting."

"But so do we."

Sun nodded. "That's why he hasn't won."

Yet.

The bulldog began to bark, and the goat began to bleat, and the pig began to oink. A moment later, the doorbell rang.

We have an electronic alarm system, but sometimes nature's alarm system worked even better.

Sun checked her cell phone and opened up the surveillance camera app.

"It's Duncan's girlfriend, Katie," she told Andy. "And a man."

"Mom! Someone's at the door!"

"Stay in your room, Francis." Sun pressed the screen to talk through the door speaker. "Hi, Katie. We're kind of busy at the moment."

"We need to borrow your boat. Duncan's in trouble."

Andy squinted at the screen. "That guy seems sort of familiar. Is he…?"

Sun reached under the examination table where Andy sat, and used her fingerprints to open the gun safe. They had a biometric weapon stash in every room in the house. She equipped herself with a Sig Sauer MCX-SPEAR-LT loaded with 300 AAC Blackout ammo in an AR-15 mag. Andy took its twin—his and hers assault rifles—and he yelled, "Lockdown, not a drill!" to Francis.

Francis would bolt his doors and windows and use the trap door dumbwaiter under his bed to get himself and the dog, cat, goat, and pig, into the basement, and the panic room. They'd been drilling him since he could walk. In the beginning, Sun thought it was unfair to the child to put him through that, but being at the mercy of evil seemed not only more traumatic, but potentially deadly.

Andy took point and Sun followed behind in practiced stack formation, covering over his head while her husband moved in a crouch. They split up when they reached the front door, bracketing the jamb on either side.

"You okay, Katie?" Sun asked. "Need an angel shot?"

Katie had shared that code word with Sun and Andy during a get together at the VanCamp's not too long ago.

"I'm good, Sun. This is Leo. He's good. Well, not good. He's all messed up. But he's helping me."

Sun and Andy exchanged a look, nodded at each other, and then Sun opened the door and Andy filled the doorway, weapon raised and pointed at Leo.

Leo raised up his hands, but didn't appear nervous. The last time they'd seen him, he'd been a handsome man who lost a fight.

Now he looks a lot worse.

Scarred, bloody, dressed like he came out of a low-budget zombie apocalypse movie.

And is that a cheese grater hanging from his belt?

"Leo," Andy acknowledged him. "Did you come here for us? Or did you know we buy cheese in bulk?"

"I'm helping Katie. I'm still not sure why I'm here."

"Still possessed by Bub?" Andy asked.

"I don't think so." Leo raised a scarred eyebrow. "Are you?"

"I'm good."

"How's your friend? The biologist? I know he had that out-of-body experience."

Leo appeared a tiny bit amused at his own joke.

"He's fine," Andy turned to Katie. "What's going on with Duncan?"

"He's out fishing with his buddies."

"In this smog?" Sun asked.

Katie nodded. "I can't reach him. Remember I told you about his stalker? She's back, and I think she took their canoe and is planning on hurting him."

Andy said, "Did you try the walkie-talkie?"

Katie's eyes got wide. "Shit! The radio! I forgot about the radio!"

"We can call him on ours," Sun said. "Andy, take Katie in the basement and try to contact them. Leo and I will got down to the dock and check the lake."

Andy stared hard at Leo. "Don't try anything stupid with my wife, Eddie Van Halen."

Katie said, "Eddie Van Halen?"

"He's calling me that because I shred," said Leo.

Andy winked.

"What's with old guys and bad jokes?" Katie said.

"It's got something to do with lower testosterone levels as they get older," Sun told her. Katie came inside and followed Andy to the basement door.

She considered the battered, broken man standing before her.

I don't trust this guy as far as I can bowl him.

"Are you armed?" Sun asked Leo.

Leo nodded.

Sun held out her palm, and Leo slowly handed her a revolver. She tucked it into the waistband.

"You and your husband are injured."

"Bub did his DNA thing with some hornets."

"So he's back," Leo said.

"Isn't that why you're here? To come and do your master's bidding?"

Leo appeared strangely calm. "I don't think so. I'm don't feel connected to Bub anymore."

"So it's a coincidence that the last time we saw you, in Oklahoma, you were on Team Bub, and now Bub is here and so are you?"

"I didn't know you were here. Or that Bub is here. Or why I'm here."

Sun moved her finger off the trigger guard and onto the trigger. "And what if I don't want to take any chances and end you right now?"

"You might need more ammo than that." Leo pointed his chin at her Sig. "And burn me afterward. Burn every bit down to cinder, so I don't come back."

"Damn," Sun said. "You got dark."

He shrugged. "Been a rough few months."

"Are you injured?"

"Not exactly."

"Do I want to know about the cheese grater?"

"Probably not. It didn't make Katie happy."

"Okay. The pier is around the house. I'll follow you."

Sun gave him the move along motion with the rifle, and Leo headed across their property, toward the lake. They had four boats moored to the dock; a pontoon, a speed boat, a paddle boat, and a canoe.

Leo walked to the end of the pier and pointed. "There's the pontoon in the pictures Katie showed me."

The boat was way on the other side of the lake, in the marsh area, barely a speck.

How the hell can Leo see that far?

Sun shouldered the Sig and peered down the WHISKEY5 riflescope, adjusting the optics.

She saw Duncan, soaked with blood, and someone on shore, equally bloody.

She also saw something else. In the water, swimming toward them.

It's shaped like a human being. But it isn't swimming like a human being.

This thing is swimming like an alligator, cruising along the top of the water, with its head poking out of the surface.

"I think Katie's stalker just got an upgrade," Leo said.

LYON

The sensation of being a living insect hive was incomprehensible. The feeling existed somewhere beyond pain and pleasure, an intensity so pure it felt as if her nerve cells finally had purpose and meaning.

I've lived my life as an empty shell.

But now I am full.

Lyon swam easily, gliding through the water like an anaconda, nearing Duncan's boat and anticipating their meeting.

Our first time alone together since he gave me that ride home.

I've spied on him from a distance.

I've followed him around.

I've licked his parked truck. The doorknob to his apartment. The throttle on his outboard motor.

I've followed him around. Online. On foot. In Mother's car.

I've called him to hear him say hello, only to hang up immediately.

But now...

Now I finally get to be with him.

But Lyon knew it would be more than just being with him.

More than kissing him.

More than fucking him.

More than killing him.

I'm going to absorb him.

I'm going to consume him.

I'm going to merge and meld with him, until our bodies are tangled up in a twist of tissue and veins and muscles and bugs, bugs crawling in and out of us, through us, biting and stinging and feasting and shitting, and together forever entwined we'll watch the world crumble.

Ten meters away from her man, Lyon let out a wet laugh, swallowing lake water and a variety of insect life, feeling the jaggy bumps crawling inside her throat and into her stomach.

I'm coming, my love...

Soon we'll be one.

DUNCAN

I'm so sorry to do this to you, Chuck...

As the first few ants bit and stung Duncan's knees and shins, he hacked and slashed with his Swiss Army knife blade, trying to cut away the plastic carpeting and pull his friend off the floor of the pontoon.

It meant pulling on Chuck's shoulder to get room under him, which meant tugging on the hooks lodged in Chuck. The poor guy howled and thrashed in pain, making it even harder for Duncan.

The carpet was tough, but even tougher was the glue sticking it to the aluminum.

Come on! Come on!

"They're stinging me, Duncan!"

"Stay still! I can't cut you loose!"

"Give me the knife!"

"Chuck...!"

"Give me the damn knife!"

Fearing what his buddy would do, but also unable to continue kneeling in a growing pool of bloodthirsty fire ants, Duncan pressed the Swiss Amry knife into Chuck's palm and watched, horrified, as Chuck dug the blade into his arm and pried the hook out.

Once free, Duncan helped him up and they both slapped at their legs as they scurried to the port side. Duncan kicked hard, knocking down the rickety aluminum, seeing Stu only a few feet away, lying on the shore on his back, the rope clenched in his bloody hands as dragonfly nymphs still wiggled into his open wounds.

He pushed Chuck out of the boat, next to Stu, and then got ready to abandon ship himself—

—and then stopped.

The ants are here.

My friends look almost dead.

If the ants get on shore, they'll be eaten alive.

So Duncan didn't jump.

Instead he turned back to face the horde, slowly turning the green carpet reddish black as they swarmed over the boat.

Duncan ran over them, to the plastic gas tank, quickly twisting off the cap and disconnecting the line and then pouring good old American 93 octane fuel all over his pontoon, soaking the floor and the vinyl seats, emptying out the container and then reaching for his trusty Ace of Spades Zippo in his front pocket.

"Let's find out if you're really fire ants."

He flicked the flint and dropped the lighter and then watched for a moment as his beautiful, terrible Facebook Marketplace boat became a beautiful, terrible *WHOOSH* of barbeque flames, laying siege to the ant army.

Then Duncan launched off the side of the boat, plopping half onto the shoreline, half in the water, and gave the pontoon float a kick.

As the fire spread, the old boat slowly drifted out onto the lake, a burning, smoking, floating, sizzling, Viking funeral pyre.

Duncan looked at his friends. Chuck was brushing away the nymphs on Stu. He still had a lure in his chest, but his arm was free, albeit bleeding badly.

Stu seems… gone.

Passed out.

Or worse.

Is he even breathing?

Duncan reached for him, tentative, emotion welling up, then awash with relief as Stu's eyes peeked opened.

"Did I hear you actually say…" A chuckle bubbled from Stu's lips. "Did you actually say *let's find out if you're really fire ants*?"

Chuck cackled. "Dude. That's so lame."

It was lame.

But we did it.

We got to shore. We survived.

Survived the leeches, the flies, the ants, the dragonflies and nymphs.

Nature tried her best to kill us, but we got through it, and all that's left is to heal.

Duncan's whole being became lighter, more relaxed, and the joy of being alive prompted an endorphin release that helped to ease his full-body pain and cause him to smile wide.

"Guys…" he said. "We made it."

Through peals of laughter, Stu managed to say, "We made it because you embarrassed those ants with your lame ass one-liner."

"Kiss my ass." Duncan joined in their infectious giggles. "What would you have said?"

"How about, *you're fired*," Stu said.

"That doesn't even make sense," Duncan said. "I'm not the ant boss. How could I fire them?"

"That's a Schwarzenegger joke," Chuck said.

"He used it when he fired a missile. This is an actual fire."

"It's worse than Duncan's," Chuck insisted.

"So what's your tough guy line?" Stu asked.

"I would have said, *here comes a sick burn*."

"Lame," Duncan said. "You're both lame. Mine was best."

"*Here's your burn notice*," Chuck tried again.

"*Get ready for a fire sale*," Stu countered.

Duncan was trying to think of some sort of pun using the word *blaze* when Katie said, "Duncan! Can you hear me?"

Oh my God! Katie!

Duncan slapped at the walkie-talkie still clipped to the waistband of his swimsuit. He yanked it free and pressed the talk button.

"Katie? Babe? Oh man, I love you so much. Are you on the lake? I thought you were on call. Wait… why are you on the lake?" His joy at hearing her voice became shuttered out by panic. "Katie, don't go outside! There are bugs everywhere! And we're not talking mosquitos and deer-flies, these things are really dangerous!"

"Duncan, Lyon is coming for you."

Confused, Duncan looked out over the water. "There are no boats on the lake, Katie. If Lyon comes out here, she'll be eaten alive. We found two dead guys, and we're all hurt bad. Use the land line and call Sun and Andy next door. They have bee suits. Tell Andy to put one on and get in his speedboat and—"

"Duncan, it's Andy. Remember the demon we talked about that one night? It's controlling the insect population."

Duncan considered how ridiculous that sounded, then reconsidered questioning it because of all the hell he and his friends had just endured.

"Demon bugs?" Stu said. "I'm pretty sure that isn't a thing."

Duncan ignored him. "We've been attacked by flies and ants and dragonflies and leeches, and these buggers aren't playing around. They sting and lay eggs in the wounds. You need to watch out for Sun and Francis."

"We're all safe, Duncan. Where are you right now?"

"Right next to the fire tower. Just look for my burning boat."

"Your boat is on fire?"

"We're on shore. We've all lost a lot of blood."

"We'll be there in five minutes. Less."

"Does your boat have a horn?" Duncan asked.

"A horn?"

"The bugs, they hate the sirens. It can kill them if it's loud enough. They—"

Over the sound of his voice, Duncan heard the unmistakable buzz of insects. He jerked his head up, trying to pinpoint the direction the next horror was coming from, and saw a swarm of giant hornets rising up from under the water only a few meters away, popping to the surface like black bubbles and then taking flight and forming a growing swarm of insects.

And following them up out of the water, breaching the surface…

Something unspeakable.

Something unholy.

Something horribly familiar yet horribly perverted.

"Bring weapons," Duncan said. "There's a monster here."

Before they could reply Duncan turned down the volume knob and switched the radio off.

The creature that rose from the lake, soaked in black muck and red blood, had the body of a nude woman, completely pockmarked with clusters of irregular holes. Like those gross-out trypophobia memes on the internet.

But these holes had bugs inside. Wriggling, writhing bugs.

And this nude woman, though brutally disfigured, was recognizable by her pink and blue hair.

"Lyon," Duncan announced.

"That's Lyon?" Chuck said under his breath. "Someone took an ugly stick and beat her ass for weeks."

"She's a goddamn bug farm," Stu added. "Is she the one that did this? Is your stalker some kind of tenth level demon witch bug necromancer?"

Lyon seemed to have no trouble walking on the mucky lake bottom, and as she neared the shore she raised her hands above her head and the cloud of bugs rose up around her, gathering mass.

"Hello, Duncan."

Her voice was low, croaky, straight out of *The Exorcist*.

"I just pissed myself," Stu said.

Duncan forced himself to stand up, not sure what to do but knowing escape wasn't an option.

We're too injured to run. And if she can somehow control the bugs, we won't be able to hide.

"Hello, Lyon."

"Duncan, what are you doing?" Chuck asked, reaching for his leg.

Duncan waved him away and continued to approach the creature—

—and then the creature raised both of her arms, and the swarm of hornets and dragonflies and sand flies and who knew what else buzzed across the water, heading toward Duncan and his friends.

"Stop it!" Duncan ordered, putting up his palms.

Incredibly, the insects paused in mid-air, halting the attack and hovering just above their heads.

"This is inevitable, Duncan," Lyon purred. "It has always been inevitable."

Lyon kept moving forward, and as she got knee-deep in the water he watched, stomach churning, as leeches slithered out between her legs and plopped into the muck.

Chuck vomited. Duncan felt close to doing the same.

"Let my friends go," Duncan said, modulating his voice, getting the fear and disgust under control. "I'll do whatever you want."

A low, wet rumbling sound came from Lyon.

Jesus. She's laughing.

"You're wrong, Duncan. *I* can do whatever I want. I don't need your permission."

She's a crazy stalker. I know that.

Now she's a crazy stalker and a monster who can control killer insects.

What's the play here?

What's my move?

I can't fight.

Which means...

"What if you had my permission?" Duncan asked.

Lyon's head cocked to the side, like a confused dog.

He made himself smile. "What would you rather have, Lyon? You forcing me to do something? Or me doing it willingly?"

"Willingly?" she croaked.

"Call off the bugs. You won. You finally made me understand."

Lyon came up on shore, bringing a stench with her.

Blood. Viscera. Meat going bad.

Her glossy eyes went wide, thin white worms oozing from her tear ducts and squirming onto her holey cheeks, and the bugs hiding in the holes feasted on the worms like noodles. "What do you understand, Duncan?"

Stay cool. Stay calm.

This is like deescalating a bar fight.

Soothing tones. Rational words.

"I was wrong to choose Katie. You're the better woman. You're smarter. You're stronger." Duncan swallowed, then tried his best to flirt. "You're... you're more attractive."

"You like the new look?" Lyon asked. After she spoke, a long red leech slithered out of her nostril and dropped onto her protruding tongue. She slurped it up.

"Jesus Christ, Duncan," Stu said.

"Stu, shut the hell up!" Duncan tried to smile. "You're very powerful, Lyon. Power is hot."

"If you think it's hot, kiss me."

"Oh hell no!" Chuck said. "Just let her kill us, Duncan. I can't watch that."

He whirled on his friends. "Chuck, show some freaking respect." Then he lowered his voice and said, "I'm not going to let you guys die."

They didn't reply.

"Get the hell out of here," Duncan insisted. "Let me have some private time with this girl. Go!"

Chuck managed to get up. He offered a weak smile. "I puked up the maggot I swallowed."

"Help Stu. Get away."

Chuck's eyes got glassy. "Duncan... all we've been through, I can't handle this emotional bullshit."

"Man up and handle it. You're my brothers," Duncan smiled, his lips trembling just a bit. "I love you guys."

Chuck said, "We're ride or die, Duncan."

Stu nodded. "Ride or die."

"Well," Duncan said, "the ride is over."

They stared at him.

"Captain's rules," Duncan ordered. "What the captain says is the rule, right? Both of you, go. Now."

Neither of his friends moved.

"Now!" Duncan yelled.

Looking like scolded children, Stu and Chuck limped away, into the woods.

Duncan inhaled deeply, the sooty air rough in his lungs.

Keep it together until Andy gets here with weapons.

But what could guns do against thousands of insects?

He pushed back the doubt and turned to face Lyon—

— who was standing directly in front of him.

Up close, her condition defied reality, defied sanity. She was a night terror come to life, bugs everywhere, holes everywhere, blood everywhere, her bare, tortured flesh rippling as insects crawled over her, in and out of her, a walking, grinning, gory nest of wasps and ants and hell.

She smiled, revealing pink gums wiggling with slimy grubs, red ants scurrying over her lips and face like runny makeup, the holes in her cheeks filled with flies and hornets, contemplating Duncan with their wet eyes as they poked out their heads.

Lyon stuck out her tongue, a black tongue, and it kept stretching and stretching and it eventually slurped out and fell, not a tongue but another huge leech. The insects buzzing around her landed, finding the gaping holes in her flesh, coming back to their living hive.

"How about that kiss, lover?" she gurgled.

Duncan checked behind him.

His friends were gone.

He checked the lake.

No sights, or sounds, or any approaching boats.

I have my Swiss Army knife.

She has thousands of biting, stinging insects living in her skin.

I only have one option.

Kiss the girl.

Duncan remembered being a kid, a real kid, before the destruction of Safe Haven, when bad dreams were only dreams and evil didn't exist yet and monsters were just fantasies made up to scare children.

It had been third grade. Recess after a rain. Earthworms on the playground, frolicking in the puddles, looking to inch their way back into the mud.

Duncan had been dared to eat one.

The dare included bribes. A new box of crayons. A Transformer toy. A Spider-Man comic book. Duncan held out for more, and eventually his classmates also offered him three dollars, ten videogame tokens for the local arcade, a Braves hat, and a pack of Bubblicious.

Duncan picked up the worm, dangled it above his open mouth, and swallowed that sucker whole.

He won a bunch of stuff, won the respect and awe of his friends, and felt like the bravest kid in the school.

The worm had been covered with mucus, tasted like cold pennies, and had wiggled going down.

It wasn't pleasant, but it was bearable.

How much worse could this be?

Duncan closed his eyes, tilted his head, and moved in for the kiss—

—and the kiss began.

Lyon's mouth was cold, like raw liver.

Raw liver that moved and rippled.

Duncan tensed, feeling the slimy little maggots stuck in her gums caress his lips. He kept his tongue pulled away, waiting for the bites and stings, but what happened next was in some ways worse.

The bugs didn't attack. They invaded.

Duncan's mouth began to fill with crawling, slithering things, like rice pudding that was alive. The taste wasn't too bad, nutty and a bit sour, but the disgust factor got worse as his cheeks expanded, and the nauseating sensation of having a mouthful of living creatures caused his stomach to somersault, but he didn't dare throw up because his tongue was pressed against the roof of his mouth, blocking off his throat so nothing crept further inside of him.

Duncan tried to pull away, but Lyon grabbed the back of his head, pressing into him, her wormy leg rubbing against his bare calf, her tongue—or maybe another leech—tunnelling through the maggots in his mouth and licking the backsides of his teeth.

She moaned, low and deep, and Duncan didn't want to touch her infested body but had to so he could push away, and when his palms pressed against her chest she moaned, louder, and then something in his mouth began to bite him, little electric nips of pain on his gums and inner cheeks and underneath his tongue, and then he had only one defense left…

Duncan began to chew.

The taste turned bitter, acrid, and slightly oily, with a texture like grapes made of raw meat. He continued to bite the creepy crawlies as they bit him, but he couldn't get away from Lyon, she was impossibly strong, and the more he resisted the more excited she seemed to get.

This was the worst decision I've ever made, and the last decision I'll ever make, and I'm going to die in the most horrible way and I'll never see Katie again and oh now Lyon is reaching into my swimming trunks and there is something pushing past my tongue and into my throat and at least I saved Stu and Chuck those ungrateful little—

There was a *THWAK!* sound and Duncan was suddenly freed. He staggered back, spitting and choking, digging his finger into his mouth to wipe it out, and kept hearing *THWAK! THWAK! THWAK!* and noticed Stu and Chuck were beating the absolute shit out of Lyon with large tree branches the size of caveman clubs.

When Lyon stopped moving, her head and chest flattened, blood soaking into the ground beneath her, Stu and Chuck stopped their attack and looked at Duncan.

"Ride or die, Captain," Stu said.

Duncan, overwhelmed by emotion, stretched open his arms to hug his brothers and they both backed away.

"Hell no! You still got maggots in your damn mouth!" Chuck said. "How could you kiss that beast?"

"I did it to save you jackasses."

"You liked it!" Stu accused. "You got wood! That's disgusting!"

"I don't have—" Duncan looked down at his swim trunks, which were sticking out a few inches more than usual.

Sticking out, and wiggling.

He reached in, felt around, and his fist locked onto an enormous leech. He screamed, tugged it out of his shorts, and threw it into the woods.

As he felt his knees giving out, a buzzing sound filled his ears, and he watched, blurry-eyed, as the bugs began to evacuate Lyon's crushed body, crawling out of their flesh homes and taking to the air.

"Run," Chuck said, dropping his club and using his good arm to grab Duncan's wrist.

"The fire tower," Stu pointed. "The lookout room is screened in."

They moved as fast as they could, staggering around the barbwire topped chain-link fence surrounding the tower, and coming to a gate.

A locked gate.

We'd planned on coming here later. We knew there was a padlock.

That's why I brought my lockpick kit.

Having a family into prepping meant learning a lot about a lot from a young age. Starting fires with sparks and tinder. Making water potable. Building a shelter in the woods. Knot tying. Reading a compass. Shooting a variety of weapons. Foraging for edibles. Trapping animals.

And, inevitably, picking locks.

Duncan found himself facing a standard Master Lock 7LF. He wouldn't even need to pick it. With a tension bar and a wave pick, he could rake the lock; basically stick the pick in and out really quick while pressing up against the tumbler pins and applying torsion to the cylinder.

It took three seconds.

But no one had time to be impressed, because the horde of flying insects had found them and the attack had begun. Duncan dropped the lock, opened the gate, and the three injured men hurried to the ladder. The fire tower was essentially a screened-in room with a large siren on the roof, eighty feet above the ground on top of a steel lattice structure. From that height you could spot smoke columns and flames and judge the direction the fire was moving in and how quickly. Essential before 5G became a thing.

They hurried to the first metal staircase, Stu going up first, Chuck behind him, and Duncan bringing up the rear, ascending quickly considering their injuries, only stopping to swat at stinging insects.

By the fourth set of stairs they were exhausted. But the insects weren't, and apparently had no trouble flying and attacking at that altitude. And while the shitty air quality burned their lungs and slowed them down, it didn't slow down the flies and wasps, who kept dive bombing the trio faster than they could slap them away.

With two flights left Duncan passed Chuck and half-carried Stu, making it to the top, opening the unlocked steel door and setting him on the floor, then going back to assist Chuck.

When all three were inside with the door closed behind them, coughing and wheezing, Duncan noticed a few bugs got in as well. The 15'x15' room was nothing more than four walls surrounded by screened windows, overlooking the lake and forest. In a corner was a circuit breaker panel and a metal locker. In the center of the room, a square table with three chairs.

"It's like they knew we were coming," Stu said.

On the table were some old magazines, a deck of cards, a worn out Jack Kilborn paperback, and a dusty pair of binoculars.

"Keep your eyes closed, guys. I'm going to take care of the bugs."

Four gigantic wasps, and three flies, had entered the tower room with them, and as his friends sat in the chairs Duncan hunted down the insects with a June 2012 copy of *Playboy*. In deference to the pretty brunette on the front cover, he rolled the magazine reverse-side out, smacking the insects with the Justin Timberlake Givenchy ad on the back.

Bye bye bye!

And when the NSYNC boy's face smashed the last giant wasp into goo, Duncan sat at the table with the boys.

"Guys…" he said. "We made it. For real this time."

Stu, wiped out and barely keeping his eyes open, gave him an up nod. Chuck, cradling the lure still stuck in his shoulder, also gave him an up nod, but his eyes were locked on the Jaclyn Swedberg magazine cover.

That's when Duncan heard a sound that cut right to his very soul.

From the ground below, screeching like a beast from hell, something roared, "DUNCAN!"

"Oh, shit," Chuck said. "We broke the cardinal rule in the horror genre. Make sure the big bad is dead."

They went to the window and looked down, watching as the actually-not-dead bug-infested Lyon got back up and beelined for the fire tower.

LEO

All three hundred and fifty of his joints aching and threatening to separate, Leo followed Sun back into the house.

The Tug didn't want him in the house. It wanted him on the lake.

He still had no idea why.

Leo also had no idea what to do if he snapped in half. His spine really hurt, and if his lower body fell off he wasn't sure that it could be reattached with an angle grinder, even with the chainsaw blade.

I guess I'll find out when the time comes.

Life is full of lovely surprises like that.

Spending time with Mary the other day had been an interesting experience, but an unrelatable one. He had no idea what it was like to be elderly, so he couldn't fully identify with her worldview. Driving with Katie had also left Leo somewhat detached; while he could remember being that young, his situation had been so far removed from Katie's that he felt more than a single generation older.

But seeing Sun, in an apparently happy and healthy relationship with Andy, stirred regret in Leo.

There was a time when I could have married. Got a house on a lake. Maybe even had kids.

I'd always been too vain. Too angry. Too preoccupied. Too selfish.

Now it seems like I'm getting my nose rubbed in all of my mistakes and regrets.

I know I deserve it. If the Universe is keeping a balance sheet, I'm very much in the red.

This is the destiny I'm due.

Leo let himself dwell on the thought, but felt oddly at peace with it.

Maybe I'm changing mentally as well as physically.

Maybe it isn't all about me.

Marriage isn't in the cards. No house on the lake. No children.

I might not have a future.

But maybe, just maybe, I'll find out how to live with myself before I die.

"Don't touch anything," Sun warned him as they walked through the kitchen.

Leo kept his hands in his trench coat pockets. Sun and Andy's house, like Duncan's, was set up to deal with trouble. Everywhere he looked, security doors and windows and locks, surveillance cameras, weapons likely hidden everywhere.

These people have gone through some shit, and they don't intend to let it happen again.

As they headed down the basement stairs he heard Katie.

"Duncan! Duncan, please answer me!"

She was pleading into a radio handset. Andy stood next to her, staring intently into what appeared to be a fully stocked weapon bunker. The walls were lined with firearms, boxes of ammunition, and shelves of assorted gear, including what looked like land mines.

Andy chewed on his knuckle. "I can't figure out what we can use against bugs, other than that brush burner. Everything we have is for larger targets."

"We have a larger target," Sun told him. "They're at the fire tower across the lake and something attacked them."

"Some… *thing*?" Katie asked, looking up at Sun. "Duncan said there was a monster."

"It was female, had hair dyed blue and pink, and bugs flying out of its body," Leo said. "They knocked it down, but we watched long enough to see it get back up."

Katie went from appearing upset to appearing upset and confused. "I don't even know what that means. Tell me everything that happened."

"You don't want to know." Leo frowned. "But before you kiss your boyfriend again, make him brush his teeth."

As the words left his lips, Leo realized something odd.

How did I know her boyfriend was the one kissing that thing? There were three kids there. One of his friends could have taken one for the team.

Yet I'm 100% sure it had been Duncan.

Strange.

Sun walked into the ammo room and selected a Bullpup tactical shotgun, and one of the mines. On the top were words stamped into the green metal, FRONT TOWARD ENEMY.

"Is that a Claymore mine?" Leo asked.

Sun didn't seem to appreciate his knowledge of military ordnance. "Almost a kilo of plastic explosives, which hurtles seven hundred steel balls at four thousand feet per second. Can liquify anything within fifteen meters."

"Where'd you get it?" Leo asked. "One of those farm and fleet stores?"

"We have a friend named Harry who knows people," Andy said. "Look, Sun, I'm going for Duncan, not you. No argument. I don't want to get into a fight about who's tougher."

"I'm tougher," Sun said.

"You're tougher," Andy immediately admitted. "But I'm bigger."

"Shouldn't the bigger parent be the one at home, protecting Francis?"

Andy said, "Shit. You're tougher, and smarter."

"You're smart and tough, babe," Sun gave Andy a peck on the cheek. "Katie, can you use firearms?"

"I'm a Wisconsin girl. Of course I can."

"This is a Keltec KSG 12 gauge, two magazine tubes each with six rounds, left is lead slugs, right is double ought buckshot. Pump action, this is the safety, this is the magazine selector switch, hold it like you'll lose it, it kicks hard."

Sun handed the weapon to her and Katie shouldered it, sighting down the barrel at the wall.

Andy came over to Leo and clapped him on the shoulder. "Protect them. We're brothers."

"How are we brothers?" Leo asked, genuinely curious.

"We were both possessed by Bub. We're possessed bros."

"Can I have a weapon?"

"Possessed bro does not get a weapon," Sun stated.

"You can have one of those." Andy pointed to the pool table at two cans of aerosol air horns, and then began to unzip his beekeeping suit. "Duncan told us the bugs can be killed by sound. Katie, you're going to need to put this on."

"Does possessed bro get a beekeeping suit?" Leo asked.

"We only have two. Sorry, bro."

Leo shrugged. "No suit, no gun. What am I supposed to use? Threats?"

Sun narrowed her eyes. "I didn't know anyone invited you on this rescue mission."

Leo glanced at Katie, who refused to meet his eyes.

Sun continued, "You said yourself that you don't know why you're here."

A fair point.

"Something is drawing me here. Or more accurately, to the lake. I know I need to be here. But I don't know why I'm here."

"That makes two of us," Sun said.

Leo nodded. "I get it. Trust has to be earned. Just so I know, what will I have to do to get you to trust me?"

"Die saving our lives," Sun told him. "Then we'll trust you."

A high barrier to entry, but it made a warped sort of sense.

Katie dressed in Andy's bee suit, and Sun began putting Claymores into a bag.

"Is that safe?" Leo asked. "Stacking land mines on one another?"

"They aren't armed yet. These are programmed to be command detonated."

"Babe, are you taking chaperones?" Andy asked.

"Do I need chaperones for insects?"

"We don't know the strength of Bug Girl. Or what else is out there."

Sun rubbed her chin, then nodded. "I'll take Mr. Drummond and Mrs. Garrett."

Well. Different strokes.

"How about the brush burner?" Andy asked.

"Keep it here. Protect our family."

Sun strapped something to her wrist, and something to her ankle, and continued to fill her gear bag.

Katie was offered a fanny pack, which she filled with various items.

Leo wasn't offered anything. When he checked the pool table he saw the boat horns were already taken.

Then he noticed a smell.

Dog. Cat. Pig. And something else… a sheep or goat?

He followed his nose to the other side of the room, stopping at a wall lined with supply shelves. Leo crouched down and looked between two boxes of dried potatoes, staring into a pair of young eyes peering from a peephole behind the wall.

"Hi, Francis." Leo spoke softly. "I'm Leo. You keeping your pets safe?"

"Yep. Are you the reason we're playing lockdown?" the boy asked.

"No. I think this time, I'm one of the good guys."

"Good guys do good things. Have you done good things?"

"No," Leo admitted.

"Then do something good," said Francis. "Be the good guy."

From the mouths of babes.

"Hey!" Sun barked at him. "Back away from there!"

"I'll have to convince your mom." Leo winked and stood up.

Andy hurried over, appearing ill at ease. He clapped Leo on the shoulder.

"My wife is a scientist," Andy told him, "so she's firmly on the skeptical side of the evidence vs. faith debate. Don't give her any reason to dislike you more than she already does. Okay?"

"I'll try."

"C'mere. I got something for you." Andy beckoned Leo into the corner of the room. They huddled together and Andy said, "Shh," and put his finger to his lips. He reached into his jeans and clandestinely handed Leo—

—a bag of Skittles.

"What do I do with these?" Leo asked.

"You eat them. They're Skittles. Taste the rainbow, man."

"Why are you giving them to me in secret?"

"Because I don't have enough for everybody. My favorite are the green ones. I think the best way to eat Skittles is to separate them by color and eat them according to their order on the color spectrum. You think that's weird?"

"My limbs keep falling off and I have to grind them down to reattach them."

"That's weird. So you're saying, by comparison, I'm not weird?"

"By comparison, you're not weird."

"Leo, you going with us, or staying here to bromance my husband?" Sun yelled.

"Sun is like a Skittle," Andy said under his breath. "Hard on the outside. Sweet on the inside. I'm sure you'll win her over."

Leo wasn't so sure, but he nodded, then followed Sun and Katie up the stairs, through the house, outside, and back onto the dock. They boarded an eighteen-foot Alumacraft speedboat with a 100hp motor and four seats. Leo unhooked the stern line and sat in back, squinting at the pontoon in the distance, still burning. The sun was getting low, the Canadian wildfires still going strong, throwing all sorts of crazy colors across the sky, oranges and purples and reds that made it look apocalyptic.

Sun gunned it, showing that 100hp doesn't play around.

Leo swapped out his old battery for a fresh one on his chainsaw grinder, then opened his Skittles. He was tempted to dump the whole bag into his mouth and ingest the calories as quickly as possible, but he stopped himself. Instead he picked out a green one and placed it on his tongue.

Lime.

Not bad.

After savoring it for a few moments, he went ahead and devoured the rest.

I'm not sure what a rainbow tastes like, but not bad at all.

They quickly made it to the opposite side of the lake, twenty meters east of the fire tower and the flaming pontoon.

Sun hopped onto the shore holding a mooring line. She attached it to the trunk of an overhanging birch tree.

"I'm setting up the mines here," she warned them. "In case anything chases us back to the boat."

"I'm going after Duncan." Katie checked her pack and her weapon and took off toward the tower at a full sprint.

Leo felt the Tug order him to follow Katie, and he hopped off the boat and headed into the woods.

Thirty steps after her he heard movement beyond the tree line. Leo snapped his head toward the sound, and saw something walk out of the woods between two fir trees. Something that looked like a man he used to know, but who had somehow been stepped on, stretched out, pulled apart, reassembled, and then blown up with an air pump. A warped, twisted, Silly Putty version of his former self.

It's good to know I'm not the only one with body image issues.

"Hello, Leo." His voice sounded like his larynx was being squeezed.

"Hello, Jake. You look different. New haircut?"

"I know why you're here," Jake croaked. Then he pointed at his distended belly. "He knows why you're here."

Leo winced at the sight and its implications. "So Bub is coming back."

"He's already back. Can you feel Him?" Jake spread out his misshapen hands. "A hundred thousand insects, all around us. They're finally mature enough to lay eggs. Soon a hundred thousand will be a hundred billion."

"Thanks for the tip. I'll buy some stock in Raid."

"Go ahead and make jokes. We're going to rule the world. Bub is growing inside me. He will be reborn."

"That doesn't sound like a good deal for you, Jake."

Jake's face twitched. "He promised me I'll be okay."

"Have you seen yourself lately? You're not okay. Bub is using you. Like he used me. Like he uses everyone. He's going to shed you like a rattlesnake sheds his skin."

"The only one about to lose his skin is you, Leo."

The swarm came out of nowhere, or it came out of everywhere, because Leo was instantly surrounded and assaulted by a wave of bugs, dive-bombing him from all direction, like being pelted with insect hail.

Leo covered his eyes with his palms and tried to brace himself for the agony about to rain down on him.

But the agony didn't get the memo.

Leo peeked through his fingers to see what was going on. When the flies and hornets and assorted nasties touched Leo, they dropped off, dead, like they'd gotten up close and personal with a bug zapper.

Leo dropped his hands and watched, transfixed, as heaps of dead bugs encircled his feet, the piles growing as more tried to attack.

He looked up to lock eyes with Jake, whose wicked, cocky, malformed expression had morphed into something between awe and fear.

Awe, fear, and here comes the pain.

Leo raised the angle grinder, put his hand inside the wrist-strap, and pressed the trigger.

The circular chainsaw blade swirled to life and he ran full tilt at Jake, leaping at him like a tiger.

LYON

A loud cracking sound, similar to kindling being split with a maul, jerked Lyon back into reality.

It's my broken bones snapping back into place.

My new powers must include immortality.

Coolness.

She shouted Duncan's name, then stared up at the fire tower.

They went up there.

And now they're trapped.

Why run someplace you can't escape from?

Boys are stupid.

Lyon tried to smile with a dislocated jaw, and her lower teeth touched her nose. She wrenched it back into place, found the gate to the fence, and began to climb the stairs.

Slowly at first. Then picking up speed as she healed. By the last flight she was leaping up six steps at a time, running on all fours like a bear, barreling into the door at the top and knocking it off the hinges as easily as tearing through a cardboard box.

Duncan and his friends were cowering behind a square table, which they'd tilted on its side like some kind of ineffective shield. They each wielded a flimsy metal dinette chair, and it reminded Lyon of dumb kids playing war in their treehouse.

"Dude, you swapped spit with that," said Duncan's friend Stu. "I'm gonna hurl."

Duncan held up his palm, his face calm. "Lyon, we can talk this through. My buddies didn't know better. The best friends and the girl-friend, they never get along. That's how it works. But once you get to know them—"

"Hell no," said Chuck. "This isn't about dating the wrong girl, Duncan. This beast needs to be killed with fire."

"If I choose Lyon, you guys have to respect my decision," Duncan said.

"If you choose Lyon, Chuck and I are going to beat you to death with these chairs."

"Seriously," Chuck said. "I can't watch you kiss her again. That shit is burned in my brain. I think I lost my ability to get an erection."

"Enough!"

Lyon raised her hands, and by her pheromonal command all of the stinging things flying around the tower found their way into the open doorway, joined by the few still hiding in Lyon's flesh holes. They circled Lyon, tight and fast, the buzzing rising in pitch.

My whole life has been a quest for power.

I've been weak. Picked on. Belittled. Discarded. Forgotten.

I've never known love.

And I may never know love.

But if I can't be loved, I can be feared.

If I can't bring joy, I can bring pain.

And if Duncan won't fuck me, there's another way to get him inside of me.

One bite at a time…

Then Lyon heard something. A loud, shrill siren of some kind. Close by.

The horde of insects surrounding Lyon broke formation and made a mass exodus, through the doorway, jetting into the hazy sky as the noise got closer. Lyon followed the sound and stared at the tower structure, see-ing someone charging up the stairs.

Katie.

Her rival held one of those canned boat horns in one hand, and some sort of gun in the other.

Lyon didn't fear either of those things.

Lyon didn't fear Katie.

Lyon didn't fear anything.

You want to play, Katie? Then let's—

"NOW!"

Lyon spun and saw the boys, chairs raised, rushing at her as a group, barreling into Lyon like a compound football tackle, knocking her into the fire tower railing and sending her, spinning ass over head, right over the edge and into empty air.

JAKE

SAME TIME...

When Leo's blade tore through Jake's arm and it fell to the ground, Jake couldn't understand why Bub wasn't helping him defeat his enemy.

Jake also didn't understand why he was overwhelmed by the compulsion to pick up his own severed arm—

—and shove it into his toothed belly button.

"You see what you're doing, Jake?" Leo bellowed above the whine of the angle grinder and the far off wail of a boat horn. "Bub is making you feed yourself to him."

Jake watched as his arm was drawn into his belly, inch by inch, bite by bite, terrible crunching and growling sounds erupting from his bowels.

Leo slashed at Jake's remaining arm, swinging the grinder like a battle ax, and Jake deflected a blow where it landed under his own chin. Leo pressed the advantage, pushing hard, the tool digging into Jake's throat and then clipping the neck bones.

This isn't supposed to happen.

This isn't what I was promised.

Jake pressed his hand onto the wound, the pain excruciating, unsure how he could be losing this fight, unsure why Bub would forsake him.

I'm His vessel. I sacrificed everything to bring Him back into the world. Why would He...

Then Jake's belly stretched into two points, stretching more and more until the massive black horns split through his skin.

Please, my Lord, please it hurts so...

Bub's head emerged next, bursting through the growing tear in Jake's skin, a wide demonic skull with a hog snout, still swallowing Jake's arm in a chomping maw full of shark teeth.

Jake reached for Bub, to touch His majestic face, and Bub bit into his other arm, tearing through flesh and bone, eating more of Jake even as he pushed his way out of Jake's insides.

Why? I served you. Why...?

As Jake's life ebbed, his vision tunneling to a white-hot pinhole of pitiless, unimaginable agony, he heard Bub say, *"Helloooooooooo, Leeeeeeeeeeo. I am glaaaaaad you maaaaaaaaaade it."*

Then Bub's massive claw backhanded Leo, sending him spinning through the air, up into the boughs of a giant maple, tree limbs and human limbs and blood and leaves flying in all directions.

Bub twisted around inside the husk of Jake's flopping, twitching, tortured body, as if Jake was a pair of overalls that Bub was shrugging off.

The demon smiled at Jake, his red eyes narrowing into slits.

Jake couldn't speak. His jaw no longer worked. His muscles no longer worked. Nothing worked except his nervous system, every nerve cell igniting with unbearable, electric pain.

Please heal me, my Lord. Heal your humble servant.

Let me stand by your side as you conquer this world.

Bub didn't heal him.

Bub ate him.

Starting at his feet, so Jake was able to feel every terrible bite and crunch, every bone splinter, every artery tear, every awful chew until the devil's fangs finally munched their way up to Jake's still beating heart and popped it like a steak-filled water balloon.

KATIE

Charging up the fire tower stairs, freaked out by the giant insects bombarding her bee suit but determined to get to Duncan, Katie used the boat horn to keep the divebombing horde at bay, forging a path through the wave after wave of buzzing, black horror.

With only one flight left to ascend, Katie's lungs feeling like burning paper bags, the setting sun making the horizon look like an impressionist hellscape of red and yellow and purple pastels, something went *CLANG!* on the railing just ahead of her.

The steel structure vibrating under her feet, Katie stared, horrified, as the thing that used to be Lyon vaulted over the guard rail and onto the platform.

Lyon raised herself to full height, spreading out her arms, her bare skin a bloody honeycomb of scuttling, burrowing insects.

Katie dropped the air horn and raised her shotgun, bringing the butt against her shoulder. Her gloved hand found the safety and her finger poked into the trigger guard and began to apply pressure.

Somewhere inside the fear and worry, somewhere beyond the anger and hate, Katie found her voice.

"Lyon... Lyon..." *Shit, what the hell am I supposed to say?* "Lyon... we can... we can fix you."

Lyon chortled, spewing blood and wiggling worms. "My whole life, people thought I needed to be fixed. That there was something wrong with me, and the only solution was to turn me into something else."

"Kelli... you *have* turned into something else."

"No, Katie. I'm the same. Only… I'm more. I'm more than I was. I'm more than you'll ever be."

Lyon took a step forward, and Katie took a step back.

"Don't make me shoot you. Let me help you, Lyon. Let someone help you."

"I tried to make your life hell, Katie. But now I'm going to make it literally hell. The world," Lyon spread out her pocked, crooked arms. "Everything you see all around you. It's going to end. I want you to watch it happen. I want you to watch as everything you know, everything you love, is corrupted and destroyed."

Lyon took another step forward. Something black slurped out of her nose and hung there.

"That's why I'm going to let you keep your eyes, Katie. To watch the world go to hell. But I'm going to tear up the rest of you. I'm going to rip up that cute little face, and tear off those cute little tits, and strip the flesh off of your arms and legs. You can watch the world end from the intensive care unit."

Katie shook her head. "Please, Kelli. Stop. Don't push me any farther. This is a shotgun, for God's sake."

"Look how scared you are. You don't deserve Duncan. You're weak."

"I'll shoot you, Kelli. I'll—"

Lyon lunged, and it scared Katie so badly she pulled the trigger.

The shotgun boomed, punching into her shoulder, the buckshot striking Lyon square in the chest.

Lyon's eyes got big.

But she didn't go down.

A double ought shot to center mass from two feet away, enough to take down a black bear, did not drop her.

Lyon lunged again.

Katie pumped and fired again, buckshot tearing into her adversary's shoulder.

Lyon showed no signs of dropping, so Katie flipped the magazine selector, pumped in a shell, and fired a full metal slug.

It hit Lyon like a sledgehammer, her chest bursting into an explosion of insects and blood and splinters of bone, and she staggered back, arms pinwheeling, smacking into the same railing she'd vaulted over.

Lyon stood there for a moment, swaying on her feet, her hands touching her own exposed, cracked ribs.

Then, in a move Katie didn't expect, Lyon began to push her ribs pack into her chest cavity.

"I... I can't be killed," she wheezed. "I can't... I can't be stopped." Lyon's face became ecstatic. "I'm immortal. Duncan is mine. He's mine!" Lyon's mouth opened impossibly wide, her jaw unhinging like a snake. "HE'S MINE!"

And then Katie finally snapped.

Katie shot and pumped and shot and pumped and shot and Lyon went back over the rail, spitting bugs and blood and screams until her scream faded while she fell and then abruptly cut out.

Katie stared at the empty space where Lyon had been standing, and then pumped another round into the chamber.

"Get your own damn boyfriend," Katie muttered.

Then she hurried up the last flight of stairs to get to Duncan.

SUN

Her AR-15 slung tight and shouldered, Sun navigated between the trees while keeping five meters parallel to the shoreline, sweeping left to right, rock-steady as she walked heel-to-toe, moving slow and stealthy toward the fire tower.

She and Andy had been drilling for years. It became part of the weekly routine, like exercise and yoga and cold water baths. Practice lockdown. Practice shooting. Practice walking with a firearm and keeping steady.

I don't like doing it, but I appreciate the end result.

Sun kept quiet, but she stopped every fifteen steps to listen, and to sniff. Demons had an odor, a sort of mixture between livestock and the sulfur dioxide of a lightning strike. While she hadn't truly been expecting Bub to be on Lake Niboowin, in his full-sized demonic form, the smell was unmistakable.

The odor is definitely here.

That, and a coppery smell.

Blood.

Ahead of her, she spotted something reddish.

A human leg. Wearing the same boot Leo was wearing.

Rather than call for him, Sun paused again, keenly listening for any movement.

She heard nothing. No insects. No forest noises. Even the sounds from the fire tower—the boat horn and shouting—had stopped.

I should go back.

I came here to help Duncan and his friends. I'm not currently equipped to deal with something as powerful as Bub.

I thought this was a rescue mission dealing with mutated bugs and a mutated stalker, not a full-fledged demon hunt.

Through the bee suit, Sun felt something lightly tap her shoulder.

A leaf falling, or a drop of rain. Maybe a bug.

It was none of the above.

She looked up, and saw what was left of Leo, tangled in the branches ten feet above her.

Then the stench hit, burning her nostrils. Not the stench of poor Leo, but of something much larger.

"Bub," she said, her heart launching into a drum solo.

"Helloooooooooooooo, Suuuuuuuuun."

Trees parted, and the devil stepped out into the path. Smaller than his usual version, only two meters tall, perhaps three hundred pounds.

Still large enough to tear through a stadium full of people.

Still too large for me to handle.

Bub had fine red fur on his upper body, black fur on his lower body, and had horns and claws and hooves. He resembled an evil version of the Greek god, Pan.

Sun aimed for his left eyeball. She knew Bub's anatomy. Long ago she spent an extended amount of time studying him. His eye socket was one of his few vulnerable spots.

But her hands kept shaking, and she couldn't get a clean shot.

I need to make him stand still until I can get my panic under control.

I need to stall.

"How many times are we going to do this dance, Bub?" Sun tried to keep her voice steady, but a tremor still crept in. "You keep finding ways to come back. You make some insane new plan. We stop you. It always ends the same."

"Not this tiiiiiiiiiiiiiiiiiiiime."

Bub suddenly sprang at her, and Sun stood her ground, remaining planted while she aimed best as she could. She put four in his head before he swatted the gun out of her hands and picked Sun up by her shoulders, claws digging in under her armpits, dangling her several feet above the ground.

She stared into his red eyes. Goat's eyes. The right one soaked with blood.

I hit his eye.

But I didn't hit his brain.

At least, not yet.

Surprised by her own calm, Sun raised both feet, pressing them against Bub's chest as if trying to shove him away, but instead reaching for Mr. Drummond, the KA-BAR knife in her ankle holster. She drew it and brought the fixed blade up, stabbing with all she had at Bub's eyeball—

—and missing when the demon flinched, plunging the knife into his snout instead.

Bub shook his head like a wet bear, yanking the knife from her wrist, and snorted it out of his nose followed by a gooey trail of blood and snot. Then he full body trembled, a grumbling sound of thunder coming from deep in his ribcage.

He's laughing.

He's laughing at me.

And he's going to keep laughing while he rips my arms out of their sockets.

Sun had one more trick to try. One last chance to distract him and maybe escape.

I need to keep him talking until I see my chance. This monster loves the sound of its own voice.

"So you came all the way to the Northwoods just to take revenge? I didn't know Andy and I were that important."

"*Yooooooou think… I aaaaaaam heeeeeeeeeere… for yoooooooou?*"

He laughed again.

Sun's forehead creased.

Bub's not here for us?

Then why is he on Lake Niboowin?

She pushed the thought back and did a quick body twist and grabbed Mrs. Garrett.

Mrs. Garrett was, literally, a garrote; a metal bracelet containing a retractable metal wire with a steel ring on the end. Sun had initially been put off by the idea of any weapon that strangled or choked, but Andy had shown her how quickly the wire could slice through a watermelon, and Sun decided it couldn't hurt to have one extra layer of self defense protection,

Sun pulled the ring and wound the wire around Bub's index claw, cinching it tight, pulling on it with her full weight.

The garrote cut into his skin, but his fingers were as wide as her wrists, and rather than cut the claw off it just seemed to mildly irritate him.

That's it.

I'm out of moves.

Sun set her jaw, refusing to cower.

"I *was gooooooooing to maaaaaake you my slaaaaaaave.*" Bub belched, bathing Sun in the warm stench of rotten eggs. "*But I am huuuuuuuuuuuuuuungryyyyyyyyyyy.*"

Sun tried to settle on a happy place in her head, a memory of Andy and Francis.

I'm sorry, my beautiful boys. I blew it.

All of this time to prepare, and I still blew it.

Forgive me.

Maybe we'll see each other again…

Bub lifted Sun higher and opened his mouth wide, like a drawer full of serrated steak knives, and Sun began to kick and scream as all calm and hope and pleasant thoughts left her body, replaced by the wild, hysterical, animal panic of her horrible, inevitable, messy death.

LEO

Damn. That guy can hit.

Leo woke up tangled in a tree, minus two legs.

Directly beneath him, Bub held Sun, ready to shove her directly into his gaping, ugly mouth.

Awful way to go.

But that's not my fight.

The Tug wants me to keep going west.

I can hide out up here until Bub finishes eating, hunt for my legs, and get to wherever I'm supposed to go without having to get killed by the power-mad demon trying to conquer the world.

So that's what Leo decided to do. Nothing at all.

And then his brain did one of those stupid movie montage clichés where he remembered specific moments from the past few days.

Or more precisely, specific people who said specific things.

Mary Streng: "We can solve every problem in the world with kindness."

Katie: "Just try to be a decent person, okay?"

Andy: "Protect them. We're brothers. We were both possessed by Bub. We're possessed bros."

Francis: "Do something good. Be the good guy."

Sun: "Die saving our lives. Then we'll trust you."

And while those memories moved Leo, they didn't prompt him to action.

Then his brain dredged up an old scene of Leo with his stepdad. Bringing up a memory of childhood. One of the only good memories he had, playing a game of catch on the front lawn. He kept dropping the baseball, getting more and more frustrated with himself. And Leo's adopted father, usually an abusive asshole, gave him the advice he'd shared with Katie earlier.

Sometimes you climb the hill. Sometimes you slide down the hill. As long as you're staying on the hill, you're doing okay.

So...

So maybe we can solve every problem in the world with kindness.

Maybe I can be a decent person.

Maybe I can protect Sun.

Maybe I can help my brother.

Maybe I can be the good guy.

Even if I die trying.

I'm staying on the hill.

I'm staying on this hill.

I may die on this hill. But I'm staying.

Leo looked at the grinder, still attached to his wrist by the strap, and stared down at Bub.

"Hey! Asshole! I got something for you to eat!"

Bub looked up—

—and Leo pushed himself off the tree and plummeted like a skydiver, his grinder whirring.

Bub immediately dropped Sun and moved to swat Leo away, but Sun clung to the demon's wrist by the garrote long enough for Leo to land on his horns, impaling himself through his stomach. Stuck there, Leo attacked with the angle grinder, carving up Bub's bloody eye, then working his way to Bub's upper lip and down the side of his huge mouth.

Bub howled, trying to shake Leo free, but Leo continued to tear into the flesh under Bub's jaw, then up the opposite side, and his original crazy intention actually worked.

I cut his mouth off.

I cut his goddamn mouth off.

Try eating without a mouth, motherfucker.

Bub managed to get free of Sun and yank Leo off his horn while his other hand felt around for jaws that were no longer there; they were on the ground in two large chunks.

The demon howled, his black tongue lashing through the air, and then Sun was firing her rifle into Bub's face and Bub dropped Leo and went bounding into the woods.

Leo hurt.

He hurt bad.

But that didn't stop him from cracking the biggest smile of his life.

Sun knelt next to Leo, her expression one of amazement. "Holy shit."

"That's what happens," Leo said, "when you go running off at the mouth."

Sun didn't laugh. But she did do something totally unexpected.

She touched Leo's cheek. And her eyes, for the first time since he'd arrived, were kind.

"You saved me, Leo. You saved my life. Thank you."

Leo blinked.

I've never saved anyone before.

It feels pretty good.

"Your… oh God, your intestines are coming out."

"It's okay. Push them back in. I'll heal."

"Doesn't it hurt?"

"It hurts." Leo winked. "But I've got a lot of guts."

Sun, showing herself to be a lot braver than Leo would have guessed, helped him fold up his large intestine, colon, and something dark that looked like it could be his liver, and put them back into the hole in his gut.

"So you trust me now?" Leo asked.

"Yes."

"Then help me find my legs, so we can hunt down that demon son of a bitch and finish him off."

LYON

SAME TIME...

Pain.

    Pain pain pain pain pain.

    But pain means life.

    I'm alive.

    I'm still alive.

    Lyon opened her eyes, seeing the world upside down.

    Upside down and swaying oh so slightly.

    She tried to understand why, and realized her body was tangled up in the barbed wire fence top surrounding the fire tower. When she craned her neck to look, she found one wire cutting deeply into her side, and another hooking her legs, which she couldn't feel because her back seemed to be broken.

    But I'm alive.

    And I can heal.

    I'm immortal.

    I just need to get myself free, then I can—

    A sound caught her attention and she stared as something emerged form the woods.

    Something big and red and black and...

    Beautiful.

    It's Him!

    It's the Master I serve!

    The demon was injured. Bleeding.

But also magnificent. Muscular. Powerful. Badass. Like an 80s heavy metal mascot come to life.

He stomped right up to Lyon and cradled her head in His claws.

Lyon's heart filled with a most buoyant, fanciful, unreal surge of love. Something beyond what she felt for Duncan. Something akin to euphoria.

Suddenly, it all makes sense.

I finally know my place in the world.

I finally know—

Bub grabbed her chest and her legs and tore off her lower body, shoving it into the bleeding hole where his mouth once was. Lyon tried to scream, but couldn't seem to breathe, probably something to do with her diaphragm no longer being attached, or that her her lungs had flopped out of her ribcage and were dangling like two wet plastic bags.

Why, Master? Why aren't you helping me? Why aren't—

Then Lyon was shoved, face first, down Bub's throat, the space tight and warm and dark and wet and she couldn't see or breathe or understand how this could be happening and then the burning began, the full body agony of Bub's stomach acid beginning to dissolve and digest her while she was still alive, and it kept getting worse and worse and for the first time in her life Lyon prayed to God.

Please don't let me be immortal! I want this pain to end I can't take it let me die let me die LET ME DIE!

DUNCAN

The bugs.

Still with the bugs.

They'd gotten off the lake. They'd gotten out of the boat. They'd gotten to a safe spot.

Then Lyon came back, tore off the door, and once again Duncan, Stu, and Chuck were being assaulted by hordes of flying, diving, stinging insects.

The room at the top of the fire tower had filled with yet another swarm of unrelenting horrors, and they were too exhausted, too injured, and had lost too much blood, to keep swatting them away.

For every two they killed, another would manage to get a sting in.

And those numbers are bound to get worse.

Poor Stu barely has any spots on his body that aren't bleeding.

Poor Chuck still has my fishing lure stuck in him, and can only defend himself one-handed.

And even if we somehow survive this, even if we get rescued, how many eggs and larvae and maggots are in our flesh? Our blood? Our bellies and bowels?

And the bastards keep going for our eyes.

That's their terrible plan.

If they lay eggs in our eyes, we can't see.

If we can't see, we can't fight back.

And then they win.

But Duncan kept fighting.

So did his buddies.

Ride or die.

Duncan smacked a dragonfly out of the air with the *Playboy* magazine, scratched at his swollen ankles covered with ant stings, and then smacked a horsefly on Stu's shoulder.

"You know something, Captain?" Stu said. "I'm very close to giving Duncan's Fishing Vacation a not so flattering review on Yelp."

"Two stars, tops," Chuck said.

"Stay optimistic," Duncan told them. "Things might turn around for the better."

And that's when things actually turned around for the better.

It started as a tiny, distant beep. Shrill and irritating, like his parent's old digital alarm clock. But familiar in some way.

The sound got closer, brighter, louder, until it was rattling the glass windows—

—making all of the insects flee.

Duncan and his friends watched, amazed, as every last flying terror left the room, zipping through the busted doorway.

And standing in that doorway, holding the personal keychain alarm Duncan had given her on their third date…

"Katie."

She ran to him, tugging off her bee helmet, her face soaked with tears, her hair clinging to her scalp with sweat, her eye makeup running so she looked like a drowned raccoon, and Duncan realized with absolutely no doubt that he was staring at the most beautiful woman to ever walk the earth.

"You came for me," he said above the wail of her alarm.

"Nothing could keep me away."

He placed his hands on her waist. She went to hug him, then stopped.

"I'm afraid I'll hurt you."

"Hurt me?" Duncan smiled. "Babe, you saved me."

He didn't go full tilt when he kissed her, worried he might still have a critter or two wedged in his teeth, but the kiss was sweet and full of love and promise.

When they ended the kiss, Duncan began to ask the question he'd been wanting to ask.

But his dumb friends interrupted.

"S'up, Katie," Chuck said, giving her an up nod.

"Yo," Stu said.

"Hi, guys." Katie's nose crinkled. "Stu… did you wet your pants?"

"It's been a day," Stu said. "You look, uh, nice. I like the outfit."

"Guys, quit being awkward around my girlfriend."

Then Katie pulled away, her expression one of horror.

"Duncan… there are… bugs… crawling out of your face, hon."

Duncan stepped back from her and looked at all of the stings on his hands. Grubs were escaping his wounds and then promptly dying.

It's the rape alarm. They can't handle the sound.

"It's Katie's siren," Stu said.

"No shit, Commander Obvious," Chuck replied.

"Want to know what else is obvious?" Stu yelled. "Right above us, on this roof, is the biggest damn siren in the county."

How in the hell did we not notice that?

Duncan quickly limped to the circuit breaker panel on the wall, and opened up the metal door.

It wasn't a breaker box. It was a fuse panel.

And it had a big, obvious lever switch on the side, currently in the OFF position.

Duncan took a deep breath—

—and switched it to ON.

Nothing happened.

Duncan tried it again.

Nothing.

"It was worth a try," Duncan said.

Katie held up her alarm. "We need to get to the boat before these batteries die."

And then they heard a roar. Something like angry thunder, but decidedly organic.

Decidedly demonic.

"What the hell was that?" Stu said.

"Did we check to make sure Lyon was dead?" Chuck said. "We didn't do that last time."

Stu pointed a finger at Duncan. "Did you say, *Guys, we made it?*"

"I didn't say that," Duncan insisted.

"Every time you say that, shit gets worse."

"I swear I didn't say that."

The quartet cautiously left the room and peered down over the railing—

—and saw Satan scarf down the last bits of Lyon.

"Lyon wasn't the big bad," Stu said. "That guy is the big bad."

"Final boss," Chuck said. "How many rounds you got left, Katie?"

"Six, I think."

Duncan tried to recall what Andy said.

"The demon is controlling the bugs. The bugs hate the siren. Maybe the demon hates the siren too."

"He may hate it," Chuck said, still leaning over the edge. "But he's coming up anyway."

Stu began to laugh, full blown hysterical. "This is hilarious. We just can't get a break."

A break...

But it isn't a breaker box. It's a fuse box.

If a circuit breaker trips, you reset it.

But if a fuse burns out...

"Replace the fuse," Duncan said out loud.

Duncan went to the supply cabinet and opened the doors. Among the odds and ends were a few carboard boxes full of fuses.

"Chuck! You're a mechanic. Do you know fuses?"

"I know car fuses. These fuses, I dunno." Chuck picked up a box. "They look like little flat lightbulbs. I guess you screw the old one out, screw the new one in?"

"Katie, cover the door. Guys, let's find the fuse that's blown."

There were twelve glass fuses in the box, with various multicolor rims.

"How do we know which one is blown?" Stu asked.

"Fuses have a metal band in them. When the fuse blows, the band is broken inside."

"The demon's on the third level," Katie said.

Duncan squinted at the fuses.

These all look like they work fine. None of them...

"There!" Stu pointed.

Chuck unscrewed it and sure enough the metal band was gone and there were the faintest traces of soot inside the glass.

Duncan matched the color to one of the new fuses in the cartons, handed it to Chuck. Chuck screwed it in and tried the lever and—

Nothing happened.

"Maybe there's more than one that's blown," Stu said.

"It's here!" yelled Katie, her own words immediately drowned out by the *BOOM!* of her shotgun.

Duncan knew he needed to look for more bad fuses, but felt compelled to turn around and watch as Satan stepped through the doorway, taking a shot in the chest, then another, then swatting Katie across the room, her gun flying in the opposite direction.

She landed hard.

She also landed on her rape alarm, which instantly cut out.

Stu went for the dropped shotgun.

Chuck threw himself at the panel, moving his finger over the rows of fuses.

"*Uuuuuuuuuuuun-caaaaaaaaaaaaaaaaaaaan,*" the demon wailed from its bloody, meaty mouth opening, pointing at Duncan.

Is that my name?

Does that thing know who I am?

Stu grabbed the shotgun, pressed the trigger.

Nothing happened, but—Wisconsin boy—so he pumped a shell in and hit Satan in the horn, blowing it clean off.

Stu racked in another round, but the devil dodged it, insanely quick, and Stu managed to hit it in the leg with the final round and then dove under a swatting claw and barely missed getting his head knocked off.

Then the bugs came back because; of course they did.

"Red one!" Chuck cried. "I need a red one!"

Duncan grabbed the box of red fuses, but Satan got between him and Chuck, so Duncan yelled, "Catch!" and tossed the box to Stu.

The devil followed the trajectory of the box like he was watching a football play, somehow knowing how important those fuses were.

"Chuck, don't miss this time!"

Stu threw it, and Duncan watched it soar through the air, the same way he watched his pliers soar through the air just before Chuck fumbled the catch and they went into the water.

But this time Chuck made the play. He dug out a fuse, twisted it into the slot, and grabbed the lever—

—and the demon wrapped its claw around Chuck and lifted him up and away from the fuse box and shoved Chuck's head into its toothless mouth hole.

Duncan locked eyes with Katie, who was sitting up, her shoulder at an odd angle, and he was sure his face looked as terrified as hers did and he couldn't believe this was happening because they were so close, so close, so damn close...

I'm pulling that lever.

Even if it kills me.

Duncan crouched, ready to charge past the devil, and just before he did he heard.

"Hey, Bub! What happened to your mouth? Was that me?"

Duncan looked in the doorway and saw a man. A scarred, bloody man holding a shotgun.

Next to him stood Sun, holding an AR-15.

The demon dropped Chuck and roared.

Sun and the stranger unleashed a hailstorm of bullets, ripping the devil to shreds, forcing him to cover up his eyes while he cowered in the corner of the room, and Duncan saw his chance and crawled under the gunfire and reached the lever and pushed that sucker up—

—and the fire siren rang out, and it was the loudest thing, and the most beautiful thing, Duncan had ever heard.

The bugs in the room instantly exploded, and Duncan felt pops all over his body as the eggs and larvae were cleansed by the immense wave of sound, and the demon might have screamed but no one could hear it and then it threw itself at the window and burst through, black wings billowing out from the folds in its back like a parachute.

Then Sun was helping Katie up, and Duncan joined them, making sure his girlfriend was okay before going to Chuck, whose head was wet with spit but didn't look any worse than before the demon sucked on it, and the stranger was helping Stu who also seemed okay and all five of them stumbled out of the room and somehow made it down the stairs and through the woods and onto Sun's boat.

But Sun didn't start the motor.

Duncan had a bad moment where he thought that maybe her boat wouldn't start. That they'd be trapped on this lake forever. And he was about to shout a question to her, needed to shout because of the ringing in his ears, but Sun put her finger to her lips.

That's when the demon swooped down and landed on the shore because; of course it did.

But, apparently, for the first time all day, someone came prepared.

"Hey, Bub!" Sun yelled. "Go fuck fuck fuck yourself!"

And she pressed the screen of her cell phone and the whole forest seemed to explode and the devil was blown to bits and its blood fell like rain, turning Lake Niboowin red.

KATIE

Sun was able to pop Katie's dislocated shoulder back into place, and then she started the boat and headed back across the lake as the fire tower continued to blare in the most wonderful, magical way.

Duncan and his friends looked like they'd just had a dance party in a blender.

All of them look like they're ten seconds away from dying.

So why are the three of them smiling like idiots?

Boys are weird.

Duncan held Katie's hand, gently as if he was afraid he'd break it.

"So… there's something I've been wanting to ask you…"

"Yes," Katie told him.

He raised a bloody eyebrow. "You want to move in with me?"

"I want to move in with you."

"Nice." He looked at his friends. "Guys, she said yes. We're moving in together."

Neither of them seemed to give a shit.

But I give a shit.

I feel like I have a future with this man.

And after what just happened, I'm sure we can get through whatever life throws at us.

Sun slowed down as they approached her pier, and Andy stood there with the brush burner and a plastic tank of gasoline.

"Leo, tie us on." Sun killed the engine and coasted in. "Everyone, off the boat. Move it."

Katie didn't like the urgency in her voice.

"Stand on the shore," Andy told them, helping each person out of the boat. "Just a precaution. This isn't our first rodeo."

The group filed down the pier and stood there as Sun and Andy stared out over the water.

Stu finally spoke up and asked, "What are they—"

And then something leapt out of the lake and slapped onto the dock. Something big and wet and bleeding and so horribly mutilated it barely even resembled a demon.

"Hi, Bub," Andy said. "Bye, Bub."

Sun poured gas onto Bub, and Andy sparked up the brush burner and torched it.

Andy called over his shoulder. "This always happens. We'll be here for a while. Go in, call some ambulances, make yourselves at home."

"There are snacks in the pantry," Sun said, continuing to sprinkle gas on the screeching, thrashing hellspawn. "And beer in the fridge."

"Is this as surreal to you guys as it is for me?" Katie asked the men.

"I'm starting to get used to it," Duncan said.

He put his arm around her, and they watched the devil burn.

LEO

Leo's hand fell off after the first round of beers.

Sun was taking the lure out of Chuck in her vet office, and the ambulances were still twenty minutes away.

Leo went into the kitchen and stood over the sink, figuring he would reattach the limb and then take off.

He had no idea what to do next. The Tug wasn't giving him any sort of direction.

Katie walked up to the bathroom, face awash with concern, as Leo used the angle grinder on his arm stump.

"You okay, Leo?" she asked, tentatively.

He shrugged, then held his hand in place while it healed. "You know how it is. The daily grind."

"Seriously. No dad jokes. You good?"

Leo understood what she meant. "I'm still on the hill. You?"

Katie smiled. "I'm actually climbing the hill."

Her boyfriend walked in, going to Katie.

"Leo, I'd like you to meet my boyfriend and new roommate. This is Duncan."

"The famous Duncan. This lady went through hell to save you. I hope you're worth it."

"I plan on proving that to her," Duncan grinned. "Every day."

"First step, buy a new bed."

"I'll do that. Thanks, Leo."

Duncan reached out his hand, and when their palms touched the Tug went absolutely apeshit.

<It took you long enough! It's time for us to say goodbye, Leo. Thanks for the ride. It's always a pleasure to get picked up, isn't it? I hopped inside you when you were fighting with our friend, Fabler, back in Oklahoma. I'm still at diminished capacity, so I'm sorry I let you fall apart so many times. But in the end, I kept away the bugs, and I helped you beat that demon asshole. He's been after me for a long time. And now our all-too-brief brief mutual benefit society has come to an end. We made a good team, Leo. Maybe we'll cross paths again. It's a small universe. But one more thing before I go.>

Leo felt himself flooded with light, his whole body vibrating with internal energy.

He clutched Duncan's hand, feeling like he was stuck to a high tension wire and being jolted with a billion volts, and then he fell onto his back, breaking the handshake.

And the Tug was gone.

And so were his scars.

And Leo realized what happened.

And Leo realized that maybe, just maybe, he had a future after all.

DUNCAN

he frowned at his cell phone.

Too expensive. Too small. Too old. Too far away.

I set Facebook Marketplace to show me boats within forty miles, not two hundred miles.

Duncan checked the time.

Katie will be home in an hour. I promised I'd finish unpacking and get some dinner ready.

He got off the bed, a spring in his step, and walked into the kitchen, opening the fridge and looking for something to defrost.

He felt great. Never better.

He was fully healed from his injuries, and didn't even have any scars.

Chuck still had stiches. Stu was still on antibiotics.

I guess being happy makes a person heal quicker.

<Sharing a body with A.I. nanoparticles also helps.>

"What?" Duncan whirled around, searching his empty apartment. "Is someone here?"

A voice that was kind of in his head, but at the same time wasn't, replied.

<It took me a long time to get to you, Duncan. But I always knew I'd make it. That demon, Bub. He came here for you. But I got to you first. You're my ticket to the future, my friend. Our destinies are intertwined. We're going to do some great things together. Me and you and Katie and the son you're going to have with her someday.>

"Who is that? Who's talking?"

For some reason, Duncan's eyes locked onto the bowl of fruit sitting on the kitchen counter. Specifically, on the banana.

<Allow me to introduce myself, Duncan. My name… is Mu.>

THE END

Bub, and Mu, shall return in TIMECASTER STEAMPUNK.

Visit https://jakonrath.com/character-appearances/ for a compete list of Konrath characters and the books they appear in

JOE KONRATH'S
COMPLETE BIBLIOGRAPHY

JACQUELINE "JACK" DANIELS THRILLERS
WHISKEY SOUR (Book 1)

BLOODY MARY (Book 2)

RUSTY NAIL (Book 3)

DIRTY MARTINI (Book 4)

SHOT OF TEQUILA (Book 5)

FUZZY NAVEL (Book 6)

CHERRY BOMB (Book 7)

DEAD ON MY FEET (Book 8)

SERIAL KILLERS UNCUT with Blake Crouch (Book 9)

SHAKEN (Book 10)

STIRRED with Blake Crouch (Book 11)

DYING BREATH (Book 12)

EVERYBODY DIES (Book 13)

RUM RUNNER (Book 14)

LAST CALL (Book 15)

WHITE RUSSIAN (Book 16)

SHOT GIRL (Book 17)

CHASER (Book 18)

OLD FASHIONED (Book 19)

BITE FORCE (Book 20)

JACK ROSE (Book 21)

WITCH BREW (Book 22)

PINK LADY (Book 23)

BOURBON HAMMER (Book 24)

MOSCOW MULE (Book 25)

LADY 52 with Jude Hardin (Book 2.5)

JACK DANIELS STORIES VOL. 1 (Novella Collection)

JACK DANIELS STORIES VOL. 2 (Novella Collection)

JACK DANIELS STORIES VOL. 3 (Novella Collection)

JACK DANIELS STORIES VOL. 4 (Novella Collection)

BANANA HAMMOCK (Novella Collection)

KONRATH DARK THRILLER COLLECTIVE

THE LIST (Book 1)

ORIGIN (Book 2)

AFRAID (Book 3)

TRAPPED (Book 4)

ENDURANCE (Book 5)

HAUNTED HOUSE (Book 6)

WEBCAM (Book 7)

DISTURB (Book 8)

WHAT HAPPENED TO LORI (Book 9)

THE NINE (Book 10)

SECOND COMING (Book 11)

CLOSE YOUR EYES (Book 12)

ENRAGED (Book 13)

HOLES IN THE GROUND with Iain Rob Wright (Book 4.5)

DRACULAS with Blake Crouch, Jeff Strand, F. Paul Wilson (Book 5.5)

GRANDMA? with Talon Konrath (Book 6.5)

STOP A MURDER PUZZLE BOOKS

STOP A MURDER – HOW: PUZZLES 1 – 12 (Book 1)

STOP A MURDER – WHERE: PUZZLES 13 – 24 (Book 2)

STOP A MURDER – WHY: PUZZLES 25 – 36 (Book 3)

STOP A MURDER – WHO: PUZZLES 37 – 48 (Book 4)

STOP A MURDER – WHEN: PUZZLES 49 – 60 (Book 5)

STOP A MURDER – ANSWERS (Book 6)

STOP A MURDER COMPLETE CASES (Books 1-5)

CODENAME: CHANDLER

(PETERSON & KONRATH)

FLEE (Book 1)

SPREE (Book 2)

THREE (Book 3)

HIT (Book 4)

EXPOSED (Book 5)

NAUGHTY (Book 6)

FIX with F. Paul Wilson (Book 7)

RESCUE (Book 8)

FREE (Book 9)

Sign up for the J.A. Konrath newsletter. A few times a year I pick random people to give free stuff to. It could be you.

jakonrath.com/**newsletter**

I won't spam you or give your information out without your permission!

Made in the USA
Middletown, DE
14 September 2024